LORD
MOUSE

MASON THOMAS

Published by

DREAMSPINNER PRESS

5032 Capital Circle SW, Suite 2, PMB# 279, Tallahassee, FL 32305-7886 USA
www.dreamspinnerpress.com

Lord Mouse
© 2015 Mason Thomas.

Cover Art
© 2015 AngstyG.
www.angstyg.com
Cover content is for illustrative purposes only and any person depicted on the cover is a model.

ISBN: 978-1-62798-994-7
Digital ISBN: 978-1-63216-000-3
Library of Congress Control Number: 2015911626
First Edition November 2015

Printed in the United States of America
∞
This paper meets the requirements of
ANSI/NISO Z39.48-1992 (Permanence of Paper).

For Bob, my loving and infinitely patient husband.

Acknowledgments

VERY SPECIAL thanks to Kimberly Gabriel. Without her keen insight and tireless encouragement, this would never have been possible. Thanks also to Jessica Trent and Tye Radcliffe for muscling through the early drafts and taking the time to provide their invaluable feedback.

CHAPTER 1

THE MAN who had taken the chair across from Mouse stared back with skepticism and no small measure of wide-eyed surprise. "So, you're him, then?"

Mouse allowed the corner of his mouth to lift a fraction. He was accustomed to such reactions, of course. Not that it didn't needle him still, but he had learned to accept it. They all came around eventually. Once they saw what he was capable of, they always came around.

He encircled his fingers around the hard leather mug in front of him, considered the contents a moment, then brought it to his lips. He allowed a swig of ale to enter his mouth, but left the mug tilted against his face longer to give the impression that he was taking a much bigger swallow than he had. A stalling tactic. Plus, it sometimes helped to let a client think he was drinking more than he actually was. If it came to negotiating a price, it was best to let the client think he had the upper hand.

He set the mug down again, exhaled, and wiped his chin with his sleeve. "And the nature of this job?" he asked.

The client leaned back and considered him a moment with narrow eyes. The expression revealed everything—Mouse could read the man's thoughts as if they were his own. He was trying to decide if this was a prank of some kind and if he should proceed or just push up from the table and leave the tavern. The man had assumed, as many had before him, that Mouse was merely an intermediary, someone to pass on the message. Not the one he would actually be hiring.

But in all such cases, time was an issue, and it had taken plenty of it to hunt down someone for the job in question. Desperation and hope would keep the man rooted to his seat.

While the client deliberated, chewing the inside of his cheek as he weighed his options, it gave Mouse the opportunity to study him in return. He was a wealthy sot, certainly—though he tried to disguise it with a ratty cloak. But the shiny buttons on his jerkin beneath it didn't come cheap. He had all his teeth and didn't reek like the rest of the lot in this shabby little hole. And his inflection virtually sang of nobility and privilege. No one outside of the aristocracy had that kind of diction.

At least he had the good sense not to have any recognizable livery showing.

The noble dandy's lips tightened. "Perhaps I was misinformed, Master…?" The man lifted a single brow, waiting for Mouse to provide a name.

Mouse didn't fill in the blank for him.

When the silence between them grew unbearable, the dandy pressed on. "I am sorry to have wasted your time. Seems you are not what I require after all. My informant assured me—"

"Not what you expected, eh?" Mouse interjected. He raked back his dark hair with his fingers and leaned in closer. "Not the hulking bruiser you thought you were hiring?"

"I don't—"

"No shiny armor or a conspicuous sword at my belt."

The dandy was showing signs of true unease now. His superior breeding had provided him none of the qualities necessary for this sort of dark business. The slightest challenge had unraveled his resolve. Good.

"I mean no disrespect, good sir," he stammered. "I only meant—"

Good sir? Mouse almost laughed. "Do not let appearances fool you. Whoever sent you to me knows my skills." He paused and leaned in with a wider sly smile. "And knows what I can accomplish if amply motivated. If I was brought up in conversation, it was for good reason, I assure you." This dithering was tediously predictable. Mouse knew he didn't fit the conventional adventuring figure. His size alone was often enough to give potential clients pause. In dim lighting, he could easily be mistaken for a youth. But Mouse wished just once a client would let reputation govern over appearance.

The dandy in the shabby cloak was losing his nerve. He put his hands on the arms of the chair and prepared to push back from the small table. A tiny bead of sweat appeared at his hairline, and his flawless skin—the color of blond wood—grew ruby blotches around his neck.

Timing was everything. Mouse knew when to spring the trap. This scared little rabbit wasn't going anywhere.

"Must be an important job," he said. He pulled a small leather drawstring sack from its hiding place between his legs and let it drop onto the table with a substantial jingle. "Quite the amount of coin here. How much of this were you authorized to spend on hiring me?"

"How—?"

The dandy reached for the purse, but Mouse had his hand over it before the man could reclaim it.

"I give you credit, coming here." Mouse spoke softly but clearly. "Alone. Not your usual quality of establishment, I'd imagine. This place can be dangerous, so in the future I recommend you come armed with more than just this...."

With one hand still on the coin purse, Mouse brought his other hand up and set a dagger in the middle of the table.

The dandy sprang to his feet in surprise, nearly knocking his chair off its legs behind him. Others at nearby tables looked over with raised eyebrows, probably thinking a brawl was about to break out. The bar wench Serafina froze and watched what happened next carefully.

Mouse rolled his eyes. "Sit down!" he hissed.

The man obeyed. With no ensuing action, the other patrons lost interest quickly and went back to their conversations and mugs of ale.

"There are certain tasks," Mouse told him, "that require a more adept hand. Ones that require subtlety and finesse over the clumsy sword swinging of a barbarian. That is presumably why you were sent to me. So, I'll ask again. What's the job?"

The man still seemed uncertain, but Mouse's instinct and experience told him to wait it out. For a moment, the dandy seemed to retreat into himself. He lowered his chin, closed his eyes, and took in a breath. Mouse took the opportunity to let his eyes wander and appreciate the man's form. He was well proportioned. Healthy. Toned. From tennis more likely than swordplay, but muscle was muscle. Mouse didn't typically care how one came about acquiring it. He tried to imagine him without the garments.

The man eventually nodded. "You did come highly recommended." He seemed to be speaking more to himself than to Mouse. "But you'll forgive me, I am finding it difficult to swallow that you—alone—can accomplish the task that I require."

"I work best alone." Mouse leaned back again. "But… if it will put you at ease, I will tell you honestly if it is a task beyond my ability."

Mouse kept his face expressionless. The job was already his if he wanted it, even if the dandy didn't yet know it himself. Now, it was just teasing out the important details and deciding if the task was worth taking on. From the man's demeanor, the job was likely an onerous one, but there was a lot of coin in that purse that could end up in his own.

He waited for the man to begin his yarn.

"I come from Har Dionante. I am a representative of Duke Braddock the Mighty."

Mouse gave a slow nod. He knew of Har Dionante but had never had cause to venture there. It was a heavily fortified city to the south, positioned high on a bluff. The city housed a number of valuable artisans, mainly those working with alabaster. The town was known for it. Its strategic position and surrounding resources made it a historically tempting target for other ambitious lords. But he'd heard nothing of this Braddock, and he almost groaned at his title. Sounded a bit self-aggrandizing. How mighty could he be if Mouse had never heard of him?

"The duke's son, Lord Garron," the man continued, "was sent as an emissary to Har Orentega for some delicate negotiations."

Ah. That was a city Mouse had had the pleasure of visiting once or twice. A story was starting to come together. Har Orentega was also south, even farther south than Har Dionante, and it too was a fortified city. The two cities were notorious rivals, both financially and militarily. Over the centuries there had been numerous scrapes between their two armies. Nothing too serious—just tit-for-tat scrimmages that gave neither any advantage or sway over the other. Lately, though, under the rule of King Harus V, the region seemed to have settled into a sort of delicate armistice. Harus was less tolerant of these regional disputes than his predecessors. The boys were being forced to play nice.

"Lord Garron was to meet with Duke Delgan's court regarding a certain trade dispute." He waved his hand to dismiss it as trivial. "The details of that are not relevant in this, so I'll not waste your time. Garron left for Har Orentega with a small entourage and was expected to be gone no more than ten days. His father had given him clear guidelines of any concessions he could give, but beyond that he was to return if no agreement was made. A messenger was dispatched that Garron had arrived safely and negotiations had begun."

The man took in a long breath.

"But Garron did not return when he was scheduled to. A messenger was sent to Lord Delgan's palace to inquire and was given this." The man reached inside his jerkin over his left breast to retrieve something. His eyes widened in sudden panic as his hand found nothing. He dug around, reaching deeper, unable to find what he was searching for.

Mouse pulled a small parchment scroll from his own jerkin. It was tightly rolled and tied with red ribbon. Fragments of a broken wax seal remained clinging to the paper. "I assume you are looking for this." He held it out for the man to see.

The dandy man's lips tightened. He snatched the scroll from Mouse's hand. "Stop doing that!"

"Force of habit," Mouse said with a shrug. "You might as well hand it back so I can read it. That was the intention, yes?"

The man huffed and tossed it onto the table.

Mouse slid off the ribbon and unfurled the paper.

"Let me know if you need help with any of the words," the man gibed.

Mouse repressed a smile and lifted his eyes. "I'll manage, thank you." The man had some cheek after all. He liked that.

The note was curt, to the point of almost being dismissive and rude considering whom it was sent to. It was a legal document announcing that Lord Garron, the son of Duke Braddock, had been detained for breaking Orentegan law and awaited trial. But the vagueness of the missive was in and of itself noteworthy.

"What crime has he been accused of?" Mouse asked, handing back the parchment.

"We know not. Duke Delgan refuses to respond to our communications or provide audience to the delegates that we have sent. We've appealed to the king… but he seems disinclined to get involved in any legal matters of one of his provinces. Some of our own people inside the city—"

"Spies."

The man shrugged. "If you will. They have learned nothing and cannot get close to him. They don't even know where he is kept. We feel the charges are trumped up to somehow leverage something from Duke Braddock. But we cannot see to what end."

Mouse leaned back in his chair and scratched the stubble on his chin. He was already questioning if he wanted to get involved in this. Political fights could get messy, and the wiser course was sometimes to keep out of them entirely. But that purse sure was heavy….

"So how do I square into this?" He suspected he already knew. But he wanted the man to say it.

"We fear for him, sirrah. We need someone who can get in there, rescue him from whatever dungeon they have him in, and get him out of Har Orentega. Alive and unharmed."

Mouse nodded in thought a moment with pressed lips. A rescue mission, then. He wondered who sent this man to him. Most would know it was a waste of time. With a chuckle, he picked up the leather purse and tossed it back. The man caught it awkwardly over his sternum. "You're going to need a bigger purse, my friend. That, I'm afraid, is not big enough for the job you describe."

Smuggling was one of his specialties, of course. But standard contraband was his forte. Not people. Liberating someone from some unknown internment and then smuggling him out of a walled city was something he had yet to attempt. For good reason. This imprisoned noble from a rival city would be well protected, and should his escape be discovered too soon, the entire city's guard would be assigned to his recapture. This job had the makings of a disaster—especially if the young lord was an entitled fop who wet himself at the first sign of danger. There were too many variables at play in this. Too many unknowns. And Har Orentega courts were notoriously severe with the enforcement of its laws. If he were caught....

The client set the purse back gently in the middle of the table. "This," he said, "is only the first installment. A sign-on bonus, if you will. Agree to take on the job, and you walk out with the entire purse. I am authorized to award you considerably more if the task is completed with the Lord Garron safely within the walls of Har Dionante."

"How much more?"

The man reached down into his boot and pulled out another slip of paper. Damn, thought Mouse, he'd missed one. The paper was handed over.

Mouse tried to maintain a neutral expression when he looked at the amount written there but feared he wasn't entirely successful. His jaw most certainly slackened. "Is this man the heir?" he asked.

"No. He is the second son of three."

Duke Papa must care very deeply for his son indeed. Mouse put the paper facedown on the table and slid it back across without a word.

The dandy picked it up and returned it to his boot. "Should you fail to rescue him," he continued, "you will be allowed to keep the entire contents you have before you but will be awarded nothing further. But we were assured—by people we have great confidence in for such matters—that if anyone can see this done, and done quickly, it is you. I hope their faith in you is not misguided."

Mouse smiled. "It's not." He took a gulp from his mug, a real one this time. Then he lifted the purse and stored it safely away out of sight. "Tell me everything you know."

HE WAITED until the new client was out the door before he rose from his small table and approached the bar counter. Serafina leaned one elbow on the counter, inspecting a coin pinched between her thumb and forefinger. Her face was scrunched as if she smelled something foul. She polished it on her shift, then eyed it again.

Mouse leaned in next to her, his forearms overlapped on the wooden surface, which was polished smooth by generations of patrons with their belly to the bar. At the far end, Ludro was draining a keg into three mugs. Mouse caught his eye and lifted his chin. Ludro returned a quick nod.

"What d'ya make of this, Mouse?" Serafina handed the coin over to him. Mouse took it and turned it around in his fingers.

"Old," he said. "Poorly minted but legitimate. If it is a forgery, it's good enough to pass." He handed it back.

With a shrug, she slipped it into a little cloth purse and tucked it into her bodice. "Quite the handsome dandy you were chatting with tonight. Friend of yours?"

"Client."

She made a noise that said she was either disappointed or didn't really believe him. "Should have given him more attention." She tugged on the sides of her bodice and wiggled her torso to fluff up her tits. "He had coin, that one. A girl can tell such things, you know." Mouse was tempted to comment that the man's disguise as a commoner was about as good as her perfume, but he held his tongue. She straightened as if a thought suddenly occurred to her. "Oh, unless, of course, he swings his sword for your army and not mine." Her eyes narrowed, and the corner of her mouth lifted in a sinister smile.

Mouse's jaw tightened. "Not now, Sera," he replied. Normally he would play along, but tonight he wasn't in the mood. The new client had given him a lot to think about. This changed everything.

Serafina pushed away from the counter with dramatic indignation. "Well, excuse me, *m'lord*." She made a clumsy attempt at a curtsy. Gods help her if she encountered an actual noble. She'd be beheaded on the spot.

Ludro worked his way down the bar counter to join them, thankfully interrupting Mouse's response. Serafina gave the barkeep a warning glare. "Careful, Lu. Someone's ill-tempered tonight."

"Go earn your wage, wench," Lu growled back. "Off with ya."

Serafina laughed and swished back into the crowd, her hips grazing against the shoulders of every seated patron she sauntered past. "I'd be surprised if that toff you were friendly with makes it to his carriage with his purse," Lu said once she was out of earshot.

"Not to worry. He left most of it with me." And Mouse was well aware of the bodyguards lingering outside the tavern. The man had plenty of protection with him.

"Job?"

Mouse nodded. "Going to keep me busy awhile. Get the box for me, would ya?"

"What? Already?"

"Just get it."

Lu bent under the counter, fumbled around a bit, then pulled up a small leather box covered in iron rivets and bound with a buckled strap. He set it down in front of Mouse with a frown. Mouse undid the buckle and lifted the top off the box. Inside was a scrap of parchment—just as there always was.

"How much is it now?"

"Doesn't matter," Mouse answered dourly. He dug out the bag of coin he just received from the new client. He counted out coins from the sack into his palm, then tilted his hand and let them spill into the box. The familiar ring made nearby patrons look up in interest. Mouse returned the lid to the top and secured the buckle. When he looked up again, Lu was staring at him with a dark expression.

"Mouse, you can't keep doing this forever."

"I'll do it as long as I have to."

"As long as you can afford their demands, you mean."

"Drop it, Lu." But Mouse knew he wouldn't. He knew the man well enough to know he was going to hear plenty more.

"Mouse." Ludro reached across the bar and put a callused hand on Mouse's forearm. "Like it or not, I'm the closest thing to a friend you have in this town. So listen to me when I tell you, I know how these things end. These men are going to bleed you dry. The day will come when you don't have the coin to pay them."

Mouse lifted the purse the client had left him. "But today is not that day."

Ludro pulled his hand away and shook his head in frustration. "You're too good to be mugged like this. There's another way...."

Mouse grabbed him by the sleeve before his arm left the bar. "And what would you have me do? You know the law. I will not have him hanged, Lu. Not for my crime."

"Your father is a resourceful man. If you just get word to him, he can—"

Mouse shook his head. "No. He can know nothing of this. I will not bring more ruin upon his life by forcing him into hiding." The man had endured enough shame already. Mouse wasn't about to compound his grief by turning him into a fugitive as well. He released his grip on Lu's sleeve and pushed the box closer to him. "He enjoys a happy, quiet life. I will not destroy that. This is the only way, Lu. Just send the message."

Ludro took the box and held it a moment against his chest but didn't put it away again. "I don't like these people. I don't trust them."

Mouse chuckled in spite of himself. "They're the king's guard. Why would you trust them?"

Lu's head swung about in sudden panic. "Keep your voice down, idiot! You want to get me closed down?"

Mouse held up his palms as an apology. "They've kept their word so far, Lu."

"As far as you know! Your father could be in irons now as we speak, and you'd have no way of knowing."

Mouse's lips tightened. That was true enough. There was no way to ensure his bribe money would continue to keep his father safe, but he wasn't about to admit that. Lu was also right that he couldn't keep paying the amounts they were demanding. The cost of keeping his father from arrest had quadrupled just over the last year. "Look, Lu. Just one more. I need just one more moon. This new job... well, if all goes as planned, I could make enough to buy a king's pardon."

Lu's eyes widened with skepticism. "You're going to bring in a thousand crowns?"

"With enough coin left over to buy you a mead."

Ludro's expression shifted from disbelief to overt concern. He leaned in. "What in the name of the gods does he want you to do for that kind of coin?" His voice had dropped to a whisper. "You have any idea what you're getting yourself into, Mouse?"

Mouse dropped one more coin on the counter and slid it across the bar toward Ludro before tucking the bag away again. Fifty royals. "For your trouble, Lu."

Ludro reluctantly took the coin and slipped it into his belt. "I sure hope you know what you're doing,"

Mouse nodded and pushed himself from the bar. So did he.

CHAPTER 2

MOUSE MADE a gentle roll to the edge of the bed so as not to disturb Taurin sleeping next to him. He grimaced at the creak of the frame. Taurin stirred and adjusted the covers over his shoulder but didn't wake. Mouse smiled at him warmly—with a stirring sense of pride that he had tuckered the man out. He fumbled around the floor among the salad of discarded garments for his own tunic, which he discovered by the shuttered window. How in the name of the gods had it gotten way over there? He pulled the garment over his head and walked about the chamber bare legged.

A splash of water on the face from the basin and rubbed into his eyes dispelled the last of the grogginess from his head, but his body still felt the deep weariness from the road. Ravaging Taurin for a couple of hours didn't help on that score either, he thought wistfully, but smiled again at the memory. That, at least, was energy well spent.

After he'd entered the West Gate of Har Orentega around midmorning, he'd headed directly to Taurin's fine establishment—The Scarlet Unicorn. It had been some while since he'd been through the area, so Mouse wasn't entirely sure what kind of reception he'd receive. But he needn't have feared.

It was near evening, if the angle of light coming through the shutters were any indication, which explained why his stomach had begun to gripe at him. It was later than he'd planned. The nap had felt good after their vigorous calisthenics, but that left few hours to roam the streets before the real fishing work began at the local inns. Of course, he had Taurin's brain to pick at too before he left. That would take time. It was never an easy feat to tease out anything useful from that crafty bastard.

He dropped down in one of the chairs at the round table by the empty hearth, the leather seat cool on his bare ass. He leaned back and pulled up one heel on the seat's edge, then helped himself to the plate of cut figs and the chalice of wine he'd abandoned a few hours ago.

He closed his eyes and allowed the liquid to wash over his tongue a moment before swallowing it down. Taurin always provided the best wine.

In a nearby room, one of Taurin's clients called out with noises that resembled someone being tortured, but Mouse knew better. He'd likely made a very similar commotion a few hours ago. The client certainly was enjoying himself. The girl he was with made coinciding noises, but her vocalizations were less earnest. Her heart didn't seem nearly as invested in the activity. Mouse doubted the man would notice.

When he set the glass on the table, he spied his favorite dagger—his father's dagger—resting there. How careless of him to leave that out in plain view. That was unlike him. He must have been more tired than he thought.

He lifted it by the hilt and inspected it, just as he had a thousand times prior. The strange but unequalled craftsmanship, the red leather bindings that showed no wear or blemish, the unknown rune etched into the metal of the blade itself—all adding up to a mystery he would likely never solve. Without conscious thought, he began the ritual of spinning it through his fingers, an act that always helped him relax.

The relative quiet of the moment felt good. Peaceful. The journey to Har Orentega had been slow going and rough, and the burden of the work in front of him weighed on his shoulders like a stockade. Something about this job felt off. The amount of coin promised seemed rather inflated for the task. Yes, he didn't come cheap, but the figure on the paper even made him blush a little. No question that the duke loved his little lordship, but shelling out that much coin for someone other than the heir seemed… silly. The bad blood between the two provinces could be a motivator certainly. This could easily escalate the conflict—but his instinct told him there were details being omitted. And his instinct was rarely wrong.

A gentle knock on the door shook him from his musing and ruptured the stillness of the moment.

Taurin stirred. "Yes," he called from beneath a pillow. "What is it?"

The door opened, and a young girl shuffled into the room. She was no more than thirteen years of age and dressed plainly in a simple shift and apron. Not one of Taurin's career girls, apparently. She moved into the room with her head bent low, staring at her feet.

Mouse felt suddenly exposed and self-conscious. He glanced down at himself to make sure the front of the tunic covered his three-piece set adequately, and adjusted the fabric a little anyway. The girl struck him as innocent, although surely her time in this place had exposed her to more shocking sights than a man's bare legs. But the laws in Har Orentega were less than friendly to his kind, and Mouse was less than keen in giving anyone leverage that could be used against him.

The girl didn't appear to take in his presence. Her attention was solely on the master of the house.

"Forgive the intrusion, my lord," she said. "But the clients you were expecting have arrived. They have asked for you."

Taurin rolled and sat up in bed in one smooth motion. He clasped his fingers and stretched both arms up over his head. Mouse felt the corners of his mouth lift in a smile at the fine shape of his arms, his shoulders, his torso…. The memory of the last few hours washed over him like a warm bath. Damn. How in the name of all the gods did that man keep such a fine shape owning a brothel?

"Settle them in the blue parlor," he said in a grunt at the end of his stretch. He exhaled and dropped his arms in his lap. "Serve drinks but nothing too high on the shelf. Have…." His mouth scrunched in the corner. "Desna's free, yes? Have her attend to them. But keep Rashiar close. I don't trust them."

"Yes, my lord."

"I'll be down soon. Just keep them busy 'til I get there."

The girl bowed to him as if he were a lord and departed. Mouse caught her steal a glance at him as she closed the door behind her.

Taurin smiled at him from the bed. "Duty calls."

"I should get to work myself."

"Damn." Taurin shook his head. "Sitting there like that makes me want to forget business for a while yet. You still look good, Mouse."

Mouse's smile broadened. "Likewise."

Taurin raked fingers through the tangled curls of his hair. "Just as well, I suppose. I'm going to be sore enough for a while as it is." He was easily ten years older than Mouse, but despite the first signs of gray at the temples, the full head of thick dark hair made him look barely past his youth. Taurin shuffled to the edge of the bed and threw his legs over the side. "It's been a while since I've been fucked like that."

Mouse laughed. "No Orentegan boys around to service you properly?"

"Not like that," Taurin replied with an eye roll. Then his face turned a shade more serious. "Laws here keep many nervous, so pickings are slim. This isn't Har Serina or Har Dionante, where our kind are looked on with more charity. Prudence is a necessary aptitude."

The mention of Har Dionante made Mouse's ears perk up with interest. A strange coincidence that he should mention that particular duchy of all places, the home of his intended target.

But Taurin rolled on, unaware. "Enough drink and a stubborn hard-on will get men to take chances, but you just have to be discreet and choose wisely. When I do get my chance," he added with a wolfish grin, "I usually have to maintain my image as someone in control. Besides, these pent-up blokes sneaking away from their wives all prefer to be the one with their ass in the air anyway."

Mouse gestured toward the door with tilt of his head. "No danger for you?"

"Nah." Taurin stood up from the bed and positioned himself over the chamber pot. The stream hit the side of the pot and rang like a bell. "My girls know what side their bread is buttered. They won't say anything." He shook himself a few times and turned about. "Plus, I'll bed a noblewoman now and then just to keep the rumors at bay." Mouse raised an eyebrow at him and Taurin laughed. "You know how it is. A wet hole's a wet hole. Not that difficult."

Mouse didn't see that way. No matter how beautiful the woman, he never could get himself aroused enough to even get started. He'd tried plenty.

Taurin crossed the room to where Mouse was seated and stood over him, naked. His cock was lifted up a bit in early arousal. Mouse resisted the urge to reach out and take it in his hand. Taurin refilled his own chalice from the bottle and took a long draught. "So, what brings you to this end of the world, you scallywag?"

"Work."

"So, this wasn't a social call? I'm hurt!"

"I came here first, didn't I?" Mouse replied with a smile. "Why do you think I took the job in the first place? Gave me an excuse to stumble this far south."

Taurin tilted his head back and laughed. "That's some horseshit if I ever heard it." He took another drink. "So, what's the job?"

"Missing person."

"Ah. Anyone I'd know?"

"Probably not." He took a swig from his wine to let the thought linger and hang in the air. As much as he enjoyed Taurin's company, he didn't trust him. Not as far as he could toss him. Even now, Mouse knew, Taurin was waiting for a nugget of information that would serve him in return. He was standing over him intentionally, displaying his fine attributes in order to distract and bring Mouse's guard down. Mouse knew to tread carefully. "Right now, I'm just keeping my ear to the wall, seeing if there are any rumors about. Any pillow talk of interest?"

"Nothing about anyone gone missing."

"Anyone of note being kept under lock and key?"

"Ho ho!" Taurin's face lit up with interest. "That sort of missing!" He popped a fig into his mouth, then put his foot on the chair and leaned in with an elbow on his knee. Taurin's big toe was under the hem of the tunic, and Mouse could just feel the tip of it brushing the hair on his sac. "You're looking for a prisoner."

Mouse shrugged noncommittally, ignoring the smell of oils, musk, and sweat emanating from Taurin's skin. "Just covering all possibilities," he replied. "Best to look under the obvious rocks first. The idiot probably found himself in the middle of some tavern brawl and got himself arrested. No one sends word to the family."

Taurin's smirk let Mouse know that he knew he was lying, but he didn't push it. He straightened up again, removing the foot from Mouse's crotch, and set about collecting his garments from the floor. "To afford your services, we're talking someone with coin. Not going to be your typical street thug that got into fisticuffs. So, we're talking about a merchant, I presume. One of some worth. Or perhaps a nobleman."

Mouse didn't respond but watched Taurin like a hawk following the path of a rodent from its perch in a tree as he moved about the room. Taurin dropped the garments onto the bed—and to Mouse's disappointment—began to pull them on, hiding from view his strong physique.

"Well, nothing's come to my ear," he said, lifting his jerkin up by the shoulders in front of him to examine it. "This won't do," he grumbled to himself, and tossed it back on the bed. He opened the wardrobe and pulled out a long surcoat embroidered with gold thread. The fabric was richly designed and clearly expensive. Taurin was doing quite well for himself, it seemed. He slipped his arms into the sleeves and began to button it up from the neck down.

It was Mouse's turn to know that Taurin was lying. He knew something but wasn't about to say it. Self-preservation, most likely. He didn't want what he knew being traced back to his business. Or he wasn't going to give valuable information away for nothing. Whatever the reason, he wasn't divulging what he knew specifically. But that didn't mean there was nothing to learn. Mouse waited him out.

Taurin faced the looking glass standing in the corner. "Ah, much better." He turned to Mouse with his arms extended outward. "Yes?"

"I liked you better without the clothes."

"Of course you did. You're a lech. But I need to impress my guests."

"Then go down there without the clothes. Your equipment impresses the hell out of me!"

Taurin threw him a playful glare as he sat on the bed to pull on his boots. He stopped. A thought seemed to occur to him, then. "Now that I think on it," he said. An obvious ploy that Mouse saw through easily and had even anticipated.

"Yes?" Mouse prodded.

"There *was* talk of a fuss in Duke Delgan's court a few weeks back. Something involving a nobleman from out of town. Could that have something to do with your missing person?" He glanced over at Mouse to read his reaction. Mouse was careful not to let anything show. Taurin was fishing, but his instincts were as keen as his own. He had already guessed exactly who Mouse was here to find.

"No way to know. Who was the nobleman? And what was the fuss about?"

"I really can't say. It was all very hushy-hushy."

"I see." Mouse studied him as he laced up his boots and tied them off. His demeanor had shifted. Few would have noticed, but Mouse knew him well enough to pick up on it. He wore his business face now—the charisma he wielded so effortlessly was more calculated, and the easy genuineness from before had slipped behind a protective veil. Taurin was protecting himself, or maybe his business. If any clients from Delgan's court caught wind or suspected that Taurin was whispering state secrets about, it could cause him problems. But it was clear there were some ugly dealings behind this. And Taurin did not want to be involved.

Mouse dropped his foot back to the floor and leaned in, resting his elbows on his knees. "Any idea who might know more about what happened up there?"

Taurin stood up from the bed, fully dressed. "There," he said and smoothed out his surcoat. "This should serve adequately. But I better go. I've kept them waiting long enough." He moved around the bed toward the door. "Don't feel you have to rush off. You are welcome to stay and enjoy my chambers as long as you require, of course. I'll have Rena draw you a hot bath if you'd like."

"Won't be necessary. I'll be leaving shortly myself."

"Unfortunately, I'll be fully engaged all night. And tomorrow as well, I'm afraid. Can't be helped."

In other words, don't call on me until this business of yours is concluded. "Not to worry," Mouse answered with a warm smile.

Taurin put his hand on the latch and paused. "You know," he began. He cocked his head and cupped his chin in his hand. "There's a man I think you should meet while you're here in Har Orentega. A guard captain by the name of Hawken. I think you two would hit it off famously. Interesting bird, that one. Married, three kids, and loves to have his cock sucked off by a man. Says a woman's mouth just isn't big enough to handle what he's got—which, of course, is ridiculous. I've seen what he keeps in his weapons locker."

"Really?" Mouse replied flatly. "How interesting."

"But whatever you need to hang your hat on to justify it, I suppose." Taurin shrugged. "Why these men just can't admit it's a man they want…. Anyway, apparently Hawken pissed off some of the wrong people of late and has been reassigned. He used to work in the palace, but now he's working the night watch, east wall. You should call on him." Taurin opened the latch and pulled open the door. With one final look back over his shoulder, he gave Mouse a mischievous grin—a genuine one, with bright humor shining in his eyes. "I think your mouth is up for the task."

Mouse returned the grin. "Thanks." They held each other's gaze for a long moment, Taurin's eyes reflecting the warm affection Mouse felt himself for the savvy businessman. "It was good to see you, friend."

"You too," said Taurin.

And he was gone.

CHAPTER 3

MOUSE SLIPPED away from Taurin's personal little empire, quietly and unnoticed. Time for the real legwork to begin. He'd gleaned all he was going to from Taurin, his strongest connection within the Shadow Elite.

Taurin had done well for himself here. Clearly, he had risen higher in the ranks of the Elite than Mouse would have anticipated, but then, he'd always been the ambitious sort. Taurin was driven by wealth, power, and influence, and pick-pocketing or running small cons wasn't going to bring any of those. And if someone with ambitions wasn't lucky enough to be nobleborn, the only option was the Shadow Elite.

The organization was likely made up of merchants, business owners, and guild leaders throughout the kingdom. No one knew for certain. Membership was exclusive and highly confidential. They garnered its power and influence through a blend of bribery, intimidation, and the careful provision of illicit services. Unlike the blunt instrument of street gangs, they functioned more like a sharp butcher's knife, shrewdly carving out the best cuts from the city for themselves. But despite the obscene profits they raked in, they haughtily viewed themselves as the counterbalance of the nobility's power and claimed to work for the betterment of the people.

Which was utter horseshit.

Mouse knew the truth of it—they were nothing more than thugs in fine doublets. For all their vainglorious boasting, the coin never trickled its way into the purses of the lowborn and hungry. And any actual power the Shadow Elite wielded was as tenuous as smoke. Sure, they did evoke some measure of influence and fear, and they could manipulate the operations within the city with their machinations, but they were more under the thumb of the nobility than they would ever admit.

Now it was time for Mouse to look at the underbelly of this city. His first destination—the local thieves' guild.

A long shot, he knew. Cabals in these southern provinces tended to be territorial and suspicious of outsiders. Squeezing coin from unwitting victims was generally more difficult out here, so a newcomer with discernible talent was a direct threat to filling your pocket that day. The locals would be wary of someone encroaching on their established territory. They were going to be less than amiable and loath to cooperate.

But Mouse had to start someplace. And he knew how to make a big splash in a small backwater such as this.

The streets of Har Orentega were in full bustle. A bright and warm day had driven the populace en masse out of doors to take advantage of it. Mouse marched the cobbles at an unhurried pace, following the current of bodies that filled the streets. There was something deeply satisfying about walking through a crowd in a faraway city, alone and anonymous. No one knew him, and there was an exhilarating sensation of liberty with that. He savored the feeling of isolation as he wove his way through the center of the street.

Shopkeepers and food vendors shouted at him as he passed, but he ignored them. He was too busy dissecting the crowd on pure force of habit. Many loitered about the peddlers' wagons or the shops that lined the narrow streets, while others were just out for an afternoon stroll in their finest with the intent of being noticed. But Mouse was more interested in the small minority out for more nefarious purposes.

Finding the thieves' guild headquarters was always a straightforward affair. Regardless of the city. There wouldn't be any advertising placard hanging above the front door or recruiting announcements nailed to the news posts in the square, but Mouse knew what to look for.

It took him little time to locate a pickpocket meandering through the crowd in a spacious plaza with a fountain at its center. He was a gaunt youth dressed as a dock laborer, but Mouse recognized him as a fraud immediately. His movements among the people were too aimless for a laborer during the day and his skin too pale for someone who worked regularly by the river. Plus, the loading and unloading of cargo required far more bulk than this scrawny lad possessed. He canvassed the street for just the right victim. When the moment was right, he would spring the deception that would end with the patsy unaware his purse no longer hung from his belt.

The pickpocket circled the crowd in the same direction water drained, so he favored his right when scanning for potential targets. Mouse easily avoided his gaze, closed in from behind, and appeared at his left shoulder.

The lad started when he finally noticed Mouse hovering there. "Bugger off, mate. Some space if you don't mind." He then sucked in a breath through his teeth when he felt the point of Mouse's dagger poke into his back.

"Some advice, friend. You're sloppy. You pay no attention to your blind side."

"What? I think you're confused, mate—"

Mouse leaned into his ear. "How's business today?" he asked. "So much low-hanging fruit to choose from, eh? So deliciously unaware. Practically inviting you to take their purse."

There was a moment when the lad considered going on with the denial. Mouse watched the calculation pass through his eyes. But instead the lad opted to drop the pretense of innocence.

"Fuck off. This here's my quarter, by rights."

Mouse pushed the point a little more. The lad stiffened and arched his back away from the pressure. "No need to be rude, friend," Mouse replied. "I've no interest in wrestling your territory from you. I'm new in town and just in need of some directions."

"Do I look like a fucking road map?"

"Your guild. Where is it?"

"See, that there is privileged information." The lad, looking over his shoulder, locked his narrow gaze on Mouse and sneered. "Members only."

"Perhaps I'd like to sign up. Think I have the skills?" With his left hand, he lifted a leather pouch and bounced it. It jingled heartily.

The lad's face darkened. His jaw tightened, and his eyes shifted from haughtiness to hatred. "That's a day's work there, mate," he growled. "And me boss's cut."

"Then sing. Or the coin is tossed onto the cobbles, and you can see how much of your hard work you can recoup."

The lad seethed but said nothing.

Mouse extended his hand, ready to flip the pouch over. "There are others who will tell me, you know. And you will still have to face your boss later with a fraction of the day's take."

"Stranger, you are playing at a dangerous game."

"My favorite kind."

"Well, this town isn't that big. I will find you again, I promise. And I will not rest until I see you dead."

Mouse nearly laughed. "Then you will go a very long time without any sleep."

The lad spilled the location. Mouse tossed the bag into the air, forcing the lad to dive for it, then disappeared into the crowd.

HAR ORENTEGA was a fortified town built on a high foothill of the Southern Spine. The manor crested the hilltop like a rusty iron crown, but the town itself swooped down the hillside until it crashed onto the shore of the Dark Maiden, the wide river that bled out from the mountains. The only public gates into the town were on the opposite bank, and two bridges crossed the expanse. The center of each bridge could be drawn up, cutting off all direct access to the town in the event of an invasion or attack. Warehouses and docks lined both busy shores of the river, with the long wooden booms of cranes clawing upward and out over the river like skeletal fingers.

The guild, Mouse learned, was located beneath an old warehouse not far from the river and the merchants' quarter.

The dank headquarters was quiet when he entered. Not surprising for this time a day, but it worked to his benefit. A few skulking wastrels wouldn't cause him the grief that some of the more industrious guild members might if threatened by his presence. Mouse had seen better facilities behind a fishmonger's shop. The ceilings were low—not that it mattered particularly to him—and the ground was haphazardly covered in various wooden planks in a sad imitation of an actual floor. A few lanterns set on makeshift tables cast a grim light about the place. The guild here was more poorly funded than he thought and even more poorly managed. Had he half the mind to, he could wrestle control of it in the better part of a fortnight and turn it into something that could turn a healthy profit. In a well-organized thieves' guild, everybody won.

This was pathetic.

A waifish older man with ripped trousers and no shirt was passed out on some cushions in the corner, and a small group of grunts sat around a table playing at cards. He made for the card game.

"Room for another?" he asked breezily.

One of the brutes looked up, gave him the quick glaze over, and scowled. "Piss off, boy. I'm not your daddy. Tell your whore mum to look elsewhere." He chuckled and looked to his friends to laugh at his joke, who of course obliged him.

Mouse smiled inwardly. The poor light in the room could explain the mistake. But had the brute taken the energy to look at him more directly he would have seen the tightly cropped beard that hugged Mouse's jaw. He cocked his head to the side with an innocent expression of surprise. "Oh, friend, I know there's no chance you sired me. For one, I know who my father is. He's a good deal more comely than you are and, unlike yourself, has the advantage of all his teeth and a thorough cleaning less than a month ago. Second, I'm fairly certain you couldn't find a pussy to stick that tiny dick of yours into with the help of a road map, so there's actually little chance of you siring *anyone*."

The brute slammed his cards down on the table, the impact launching his friend's mug into the air. He attempted to make a dramatic launch to his feet—but too much girth and wine made the effort far clumsier than he intended. His stool toppled behind him with a bang that made the half-naked old man in the corner grumble in protest. "What did you say to me?"

"Gods help me! You're not going to make me repeat all that again, are you? Weren't you listening?"

Mouse could see his hands clenching and unclenching with mounting rage. "I've killed people for less, boy," he growled through his teeth.

"Old women and cripples don't rightly count toward that tally."

It was the final prod the brute needed. He pulled back his arm and thrust his meaty fist at Mouse's face with all the strength he could put behind it. Mouse easily saw it coming as if the man had advertised what his attack would be in the market square a week before. He twisted aside with little effort as the swing sped past him, taking the brute's arm and then the shoulder and torso along with it.

When would people learn that heavy drink did not make you better in a brawl?

Mouse elbowed him in the jaw as his head soared past. He felt something give under the impact. The brute hit the floorboards hard. He lay there a moment, groaning before remembering how mad he was. Then he tried to scramble back to his feet. The ordeal was painful to watch. He looked more like a newborn colt making its first venture into the world of standing.

Mouse stepped back with arms crossed and waited patiently.

Not at all surprising, once erect again, the idiot decided to make another go of it. He lunged at Mouse with a primal shout of rage. Mouse's reaction was swift and precise. He deflected the man's inelegant and haphazard swing with his forearm, guiding the punch safely to the side, while moving himself in closer. He made a sharp sideways kick to the kneecap and felt it shatter beneath the heel of his boot. The leg bent in an impossible angle. The shout from the brute's throat lifted an octave to become a cry of agony.

But Mouse wasn't finished.

He seized the man's hand at his wrist and forced the brute's arm about until his elbow was locked and his body forced forward. The cry elevated to screech, and the brute dropped heavily to his one good knee. Mouse punched with the heel of his hand against the side of the man's face. Once. Twice. Thrice.

Mouse released the arm and the brute collapsed to the boards and was still. His friends stared at the bloody heap in stunned horror as Mouse righted the stool and took his seat on it. Casually, he picked up the cards scattered about the table.

"Mind if we talk while we play?"

THE MEN stared at Mouse with open mouths like three dead fish. They still gripped their cards, but their arms had gone limp and dropped to the table.

"Come now," Mouse said. "Whose turn is it?" He leaned left and whispered conspiratorially to the thug closest to him, "You know, I can see your cards."

The man across from Mouse gathered some of his wits back about him and straightened. "Friend, I don't know who you are, but we ain't got nothin' to say to you." Brave words. But the crack in the man's voice betrayed him. One of the other men stared down at his comrade on the floor, who hadn't moved since Mouse took his seat at the table. "This here is an exclusive organization. It's best you leave. Now."

Mouse smiled back at him. "In time. But first, let's play a simpler game. I'm not really in the mood for cards anyway." He folded up the cards and tossed them in the center of the table, then turned his hand up, revealing a gold coin—a whole crown—he had palmed there. All three opposite him straightened on their stools at the sight of it. It was probably the first time any of them had seen one that close up.

"Shit, is that a real—oof."

The brute in the middle elbowed the one on his left.

"So, here's how the game is played," Mouse said. He gestured to the middle one, who seemed at present the leader of the three. "You. Stick out your hand, palm up. Come, come, I won't bite you." Like magpies, they were all captivated by the shiny coin. The heap on the floor, for the moment, was forgotten. Curiosity got the better of the man; he eased his hand out over the table, and Mouse held the coin between his forefinger and thumb over the man's palm. "I'm going to put this into your hand. Don't close into a fist." Mouse rested the coin in the man's hand, and the man took a slow intake of breath. But he behaved and did as Mouse asked.

"Now. I'm going to hold my hand up here." Mouse lifted it a boot's length above the man's palm. "You cannot close your hand until I start to move my hand, understand? If you close your hand around the coin before I get to it, you get to keep it."

All three laughed. The middle thug shrugged, grinning. "All right, little man. If you want to just throw your coin away like that, I'll take it from you."

"Ah, but if I get the coin out of your hand before you close it...." Mouse paused for emphasis, leaning in. "You have to answer one question."

"Sure. Why not?" He laughed again. "I'll even give you two questions."

"Very well," said Mouse. "Two it is. Oh, try anything or close your hand before I move my hand, and you end up like your friend. Understood?"

The man's hand quivered a little as if suddenly nervous, but then he said, "I don't need to cheat to beat you at this fucking game."

The man narrowed his brow and held his gaze on Mouse's hand, at the same time trying to seem unconcerned. Mouse watched him, smiling. He waited a bit, holding his hand rock steady in the air. Then sprang.

He had the coin back before the fingers barely began to close. The man opened his fist back up and gawked at it, dumbfounded that no coin was in there.

"Hey! How the fuck you do that?"

Mouse displayed the coin, pinched in his fingers once again. "Two questions, was it? First one, then. And lie to me, I'll know it, so don't try. What are your names?"

"Excuse me?"

"Your names. What are they?"

The thug glanced to his two comrades as if looking for help in remembering. "Why do you want to know my name?"

"I like to know who I'm speaking with," Mouse replied with a grin. "Call me old-fashioned." In truth, Mouse wanted to be able to track any of them down again should he have need of them or have follow-up questions. Not that there was much of a chance that these morons would yield anything useful. Also, guild members as a rule tended to be wary of strangers asking questions. It was helpful to drop the name of another member once in a while during a chat to minimize suspicion.

The thug considered for a while, clearly worried that he was giving away something valuable. "Berrun," he said. "Name's Berrun."

Mouse nodded as if the information was vitally important. "And your friends?"

"Peddux, and that's Ludlow."

Peddux was the smallest of the three. He was likely a pickpocket or a lookout of some kind. Took part in nothing too dangerous, anyway. He had a persistent eye twitch that was clearly a reaction to anxiety. Ludlow seemed to be the brooding type. He was hunched into himself, his brow deeply furrowed, and he massaged the heel of his palm absently with his thumb.

"Excellent." He allowed his smile to broaden. "See? Now we're all friends. So, Berrun, my second question. Who here is the highest ranking in the organization?"

They all turned their gaze to the unconscious mound on the floor. "Well, he is," said Peddux. "Er... was, anyway."

Berrun bent forward and rested his sizable bulk on his elbows. "That'd be me now, I reckon," he said with a sneer.

Mouse leaned back and crossed his arms. He kept his face neutral, looking like he was carefully considering him, but he was mostly attempting to avoid the man's toxic breath. Mouse noted the scars on the man's knuckles. He was a bruiser, nothing more. Not a new recruit, but not high in the ranks either, and not privy to any strategy planning. He was muscle brought in to lean on nonpayers and those that didn't follow the guild rules.

None of these grunts would know anything. He suspected that coming here, but that really wasn't the point of his visit anyway. And if he asked questions pertaining to the job, word of why he was in town would drift through the guild like egg farts at a tea party. He wasn't ready to tip his hand to the entire duchy just yet. These three were just blunt tools in the workshop. He needed to speak to the craftsman that used them.

"Next question, then," he said.

"Hey!" Ludlow perked up. "That was two questions. That's all you get."

"So it was," Mouse replied, waving a finger at the man. "Ah, would have gotten away with it if it weren't for you."

Ludlow looked to his comrades with a single eyebrow raised and a satisfied smirk, very proud of his clever catch.

Mouse held up the coin. "Another go, then?"

"Sure," Berrun said. He adjusted himself on the stool and held out his hand. His brow tightened into a determined scowl.

"Same terms? Two questions?"

"One question this time," Berrun answered. He was going to play tougher this time around.

"Hmm." Mouse pursed his lips, assuming a conflicted expression. "But I have two questions left for you. So...." He lifted his shoulders in a shrug. "Let's make this interesting." He flicked his hand and now held two crowns in his fingers instead of one.

"Sorcery!" said Peddux.

Berrun backhanded him in the face. "Don't be an imbecile. Just a tavern trick." While Peddux rubbed his cheek looking stunned, Berrun returned his hand to the center of the table. "Seen it a hundred times."

Mouse doubted Berrun could count to one hundred without help, but he wasn't going to quibble.

"Go on, then," Berrun said to Mouse.

Mouse placed both coins in Berrun's palm. "I retrieve only one coin," he said. "I get one question, and you keep the other coin. If I get both, two questions."

"Deal." Berrun seemed confident now.

Mouse positioned his hand again. "Ready?"

Berrun brought his face forward, and his eyes narrowed. He focused on Mouse's hand with the intensity of a hawk following its prey. A vein popped to the surface of his forehead so prominently that Mouse was concerned he might burst something in his head.

But the result was the same. Mouse had both coins back in his hand before Berrun closed his fingers halfway.

Berrun pounded his fist on the table, upsetting the mugs and spilling sour ale over the cards.

"Sorcery, I tell you," Peddux said again, still rubbing his cheek. He flinched when Berrun threw an angry glare his way, but this time Berrun didn't strike.

"Well, then," Mouse said in a satisfied tone, holding up the two coins. "Next question. Who's your guild leader?"

Uneasy silence dropped onto the table like a stone brick. The three exchanged nervous glances, no one wanting to be the first to open his mouth. Mouse had caught them off guard with the question, and they recovered slowly. Guild leadership was not information typically shared outside the organization.

"Come now. We had a deal, remember?" He erased the easy smile from his face and dropped his voice into a sort of growl to remind them he meant business. "Answer the question."

"Man named Keeler," Ludlow answered finally in a voice barely above a whisper. He ignored the hard stare he got from his two comrades.

"Ah. And what is your opinion of your commander? Does he run the guild the way you would want or expect?" Not really vital information, but Mouse wasn't going to let the question go to waste. He liked to know who he was dealing with, though, but he knew he was really pushing his luck this time. Speaking ill of a guild leader was dangerous territory for any member. But even if they refused to answer, it would tell him plenty. Singing the praises of your leader was easy, so if they hesitated, he already knew the answer. They all squirmed on their stools now, avoiding each other's eyes.

"Need I remind you that you agreed to the terms," Mouse prodded.

"Hard to say," Berrun spoke up bravely. "He's new to the position." He shrugged then, noncommittally. "We were all surprised when he came out on top. Waiting to see what happens."

A coup, then. This Keeler had managed to swing control of the outfit. And he wasn't the second-in-command apparently either—the typical successor to a guild. Mouse got the sense he wasn't even among the officers. A whole new administration was in place, which would explain the current pathetic state of the guild, but was that the cause of the coup? Or the result of it?

Mouse lifted from the stool. "Send him a message for me. I want to talk to him. No lieutenants. No other officers. Only Keeler himself. He either finds me, or I'll find him."

He turned to leave.

"But…. How will he find you? What's your name?"

"That's his problem. Thanks for your help."

Mouse tossed one of the crowns on the table. He could still hear the brawl when he was out on the street as the three of them fought for the coin.

Mouse shook his head as he hoofed back uphill toward the market district. What a shithole. Of course, he hadn't expected to squeeze out much juice from that rotting fruit—but he accomplished what he needed to do. Somebody knew something, and his visit would catch the necessary attention of those higher in the ranks. He just needed to draw them out.

CHAPTER 4

MOUSE WANDERED the market district during the remaining hours of the day.

He played the role of the earnest shopper with coin to spend. He perused the stalls and loitered through shops with keen interest, fingering textiles with groans of pleasure or turning the stoneware about in his hands, all the while keeping his ear to the conversations that buzzed around him. Gossip was always richest and most current in the markets—because for all intents and purposes, the people who were there were not really there to shop. It was, first and foremost, a social gathering. And at such events, people talked. If one wanted to learn the latest news, one struck up a conversation with the cobbler or leaned on the counter of the butcher and made some small talk while he trimmed the fat from your cut. Bored with their work, shop owners were always looking to pass the time with some informative banter. In the time it took to purchase your lamp oil and have it poured into your leather flagon, the latest news about town could be exchanged in efficient bite-sized portions.

But although there were plenty of morsels chucked about that afternoon, none of them seemed related to his mission. There was prattle about some intrigue at the court, but the details were fuzzy at best. No one actually knew anything, so speculation was rampant, and most of the rumors and claims were outrageous enough to be dismissed out of hand. And although town folk seemed to be aware something scandalous had occurred, none of the rumors even mentioned a foreign noble.

The lack of talk was telling in and of itself. If a foreign noble had been arrested, it would be heady news indeed. People would be buzzing with speculation, wondering if this meant the start of another war. Everyone knew that putting a foreign nobleman behind bars tended to piss someone off. And military tussles had been sparked by far lesser offenses.

But none of the gossip around the market square even hinted at an arrest, or of a high-level prisoner being kept in some dark hold somewhere.

So, young Lord Garron's imprisonment was not being made a public affair. In fact, the arrest had been conducted in utter secrecy. Interesting. This meant Duke Delgan was keen on this not becoming a political issue. The arrest wasn't to score any points or stir up trouble.

Did that mean the arrest had legitimacy?

Mouse doubted it. Standard practice among nobles was to turn a blind eye to bad behavior and just send the miscreant packing.

Some around town knew details of the arrest—obviously. Taurin deduced straight off whom he was seeking out. The members of Duke Delgan's court that frequented Taurin's little haven must talk in their sleep. Which meant it was safe to assume that all of the Shadow Elite here in Har Orentega were informed.

Well, Mouse reminded himself, his task wasn't to figure out why he had been arrested. Just to get him out. He just needed to find out where he was being held.

Evening crept in, and the crowd thinned. Shops packed up their wares and pulled their shutters closed, so Mouse ambled off. He crossed over the bridge and lingered around the East Gate for a time. He made some small talk with some of the guards stationed there, playing the tourist. Bored, they were friendly enough and answered all his questions.

Mouse took his cue from the lamplighters as they began their nightly ritual of shimmying up lantern poles that it was time to find his room. He skirted the shadier parts of town that he would normally inhabit on such a job—"low town" as it was cleverly named—and hiked back uphill. He roamed the neighborhood where the more respectable merchants laid down their heads. He walked past a number of quiet little inns—he had no use for quaint and sleepy—and eventually found the inn he was looking for. A sizable one with a full and lively tavern.

The Blue Stag.

The innkeeper took his coin, but not before he gave Mouse's garb a suspicious twice over.

"Is there a problem?" Mouse prodded.

The innkeeper smiled thinly through his well-manicured beard. "Not at all, gentle sir," he answered in a haughty tone. "But this is a fine and peaceful establishment. I hope you've no plans on using that dagger I see in your belt during your stay."

Mouse returned the smile. "As long as no one gives me cause to, it shouldn't be a problem. Here's hoping your patrons are as *fine and peaceful* as your inn."

The innkeeper's smile faltered. "One night only?"

"To be determined. My key, if you would be so kind."

The innkeeper lost all pretense of maintaining the smile. For several moments he stood unmoving, mulling over what he should do. Mouse could see the internal debate in the man's eyes—whether or not to return the coin he had just pocketed. It was late, and the odds of renting the room now were slim, and Mouse had paid the premium without question. After a long awkward stall, greed championed over his apprehension. He extended his hand, and Mouse gingerly lifted the skeleton key from the man's sweaty palm. "Much obliged to you. I'll be taking a moment or two to check out my accommodations and see that all is in order. When I return I'll expect a freshly prepared plate. And a tankard of something worth drinking. Have the table prepared." Mouse fought to keep his grin from widening. The poor man was seriously confused now. Mouse, dressed like a scoundrel, spoke with the unquestioning self-assurance of a nobleman.

"Of course… sir."

As Mouse marched up the stairs, he stole a glance at the tavern below. The innkeeper had hurried over to a big man leaning on the bar. The innkeeper spoke quickly to him, and the man looked up over his shoulder at Mouse on the stairwell. An off-duty city guard that spent time in the tavern playing the heavy for free drink and maybe a coin or two. Someone Mouse was sure to become acquainted with later over his meal.

THE NIGHT'S dinner was a succulent meat pie, which Mouse approved of enthusiastically. And the mead the inn served was of equally high quality. He tucked into both with gusto at a small table by the fire that awaited him after he returned from his surprisingly spacious and rather posh accommodations. He would have to be careful. He could easily grow used to this treatment. Usually his budget didn't afford him such luxuries.

He sensed some of the other patrons eyeing him with trepidation, but for the most part the room carried on much as it had before he took his seat. He ate and drank without making eye contact with anyone, making loud approving noises as he chewed, and kept lifting his tankard to the innkeeper across the room.

The room was full. Conversations around him were loud and lively. No matter how much coin you had in your pocket, you talked louder with a belly full of mead.

A shadow crossed over him while he sopped up the juices on his plate with a hunk of bread. Something very large blocked out the lamplight.

"Have a seat, friend," Mouse said without looking up. "Wondered how long it would take for you to mosey over."

The large man didn't say a word, so Mouse placed a shiny gold coin on the table in front of the seat across from him. "Come now. Let me buy you a mead."

Of course, the coin far exceeded the price of an entire barrel of the stuff. The man, still without uttering a word, pulled out the chair and dropped heavily upon it. Mouse offered a cheery smile back at him and waved at the wench, signaling for her to bring one for his new friend.

"What brings you here, mate?" the man said, crossing his forearms on the table and leaning in.

"Business," Mouse answered. "You?"

"Loric, the keeper here, is a *personal* friend of mine." The emphasis he put on "personal" was intended to sound vaguely threatening, but the man had had enough drink in him to dispel the intended effect.

"Is that so? Seems a charming fellow."

"He wants no trouble."

"Then we are of like minds."

Frustrated that his intimidation tactics weren't having the desired impact, he settled for something more straightforward. "We've no need of your type here."

"My type?" Mouse raised an eyebrow. "Whatever do you mean? What type am I?" He leaned in too so their noses were a hand's width apart. "Am I your type?" he whispered, and added a salacious wink to prevent any chance of being misunderstood.

Startled, the man jerked back as if Mouse had punched him. The chair tipped onto its two back legs and with any more force he would have tumbled backward. He flushed in embarrassment and anger. "I know a scoundrel when I see one."

Mouse let the corner of his mouth lift. "I'm certain you do."

The wench arrived with the tankard and set it front of the man, then gave Mouse a curious look as she moved on. Mouse lifted his tankard to the man. "To your health, Hawken."

The man lifted his tankard with a scowl and was about to drink, but stopped short. "Hey. How do you know my name?"

"Your reputation precedes you."

He put the tankard down again. Hard. Mead splashed onto the table. "What's your game, little man?"

Mouse pushed the plate aside and leaned in on his elbows. "Take the coin that's in front of you. It's yours. Put it in your purse, and just talk to me for a bit. No harm in that, is there?"

Hawken's eyes lowered and stared at the coin. It was more than Loric was paying him, surely. More than he would make in a month as captain of the night watch.

"It's your night off. Live a little."

His eyes shifted upward to meet Mouse's unwavering gaze, and his mouth tightened, but he slid the coin off the table into his palm and tucked it away at his belt.

"There now," Mouse cooed. "Easy as that."

Hawken seemed to relax a bit, but he still held on to his scowl. He leaned back in his chair with his hand cupping the tankard. He'd taken the coin and was willing to play along, but he clearly was unsettled. The furrow in his brow implied he was still wary where this conversation was going. "You didn't answer my question."

"A friend suggested I call on you." When Hawken tensed and made to straighten again, Mouse added quickly, "A discreet friend."

When the meaning of what Mouse alluded to seeped through the mead-filled brain, Hawken paled slightly. Worry flashed across his features. His shoulders tightened toward his ears. "I don't know what you're talking about."

Mouse knew to proceed carefully. A man with a dark secret to protect could be easily spooked. Hawken had much to lose if his secret compulsion was exposed. His position in the guard certainly, and likely his family as well. But Orentegan morality law was strict on the matter. If caught, he would be thrown in irons. At the minimum.

But it was those dark impulses that kept him at the table, kept him talking. Mouse had piqued his interest enough for him to face the danger. Perhaps the risk was even part of the appeal.

"Oh, cut the shit. You know."

"What do you want?"

Mouse chuckled and narrowed his eyes. "I think you can guess."

Hawken stared, his mouth tightly pressed. Mouse could see in his eyes him weighing the risk against his desire.

"I think we can help each other out, friend. I understand the great pressure you're under. I will gladly provide you with the relief you require. And then some. I just have a small favor to ask in return."

"A favor?" Hawken's expression darkened. "I've no coin to—"

"No, no. Nothing so base, I assure you." Mouse took a drink from the tankard, and as he set it down again, he made a show of wiping his lower lip with his forefinger and thumb. "If what you see doesn't appeal to you, then take the coin, and our business is concluded. I will bid you a fair evening."

Hawken didn't move. In fact, he'd turned so rigid Mouse wondered if he'd turned to stone instead. But from the corner of his eye, he could see the pinky of the man's left hand quivering.

"But as I understand it," Mouse continued, "sometimes it gets rather late, so you decide to take one of the empty rooms here instead of heading home to your adoring wife. Yes? Well, take Loric up on the offer tonight as well. Only…." Mouse paused and gave the man a wry smile. "Tonight there'll be a slight change."

Mouse took Hawken's silence as permission to proceed.

"Between your legs on the chair you'll find my room key. Use it. I'll be awake and waiting for you. And just so as to not arouse any suspicion, I need you to threaten me. Loud and public. Make it look good."

Hawken's hand moved down beneath the tabletop. Mouse could tell the instant his fingers discovered the location of the key, and grinned as the man tried to work out how it got there. Then Hawken sprang to his feet. The chair capsized behind him with a dramatic crash. In one fluid move, with speed that surprised even Mouse, he moved around the table, grabbed Mouse by the jerkin, and lifted him bodily from the chair. He pulled his face in close—so close Mouse wondered if Hawken would kiss him instead.

"Listen, little man," he barked. The room around them had fallen suddenly silent as everyone turned to watch the spectacle. "I've heard enough of your lies tonight. You get one night here and that's all. Then I don't want to see your face again. Understood?" With a mighty shove, he flung Mouse back down into his chair. "Any trouble and I'll gut you."

Without looking back, Hawken crossed the tavern and took his seat at the bar. A good performance. Mouse did his best to look shaken by the incident as everyone around him pretended they weren't watching the scene and picked up their conversations again. Satisfied, he straightened out his jerkin, drained the last of his mead from the tankard, and sauntered back to his room.

THE FIRST time, Mouse had him cooing like child. After the second time, Hawken was eating out of his hand. For a chance at a third go, Mouse was pretty sure the guard captain would do just about anything.

Panting and covered in a slick sheen of sweat, Hawken slumped back against the bed frame. "Gods!" he grunted. "You are strong for your size." His hand moved to his cheek as if just noticing something. It came away with a shiny wet pearl on the tip of his finger. He held up his finger to show Mouse and made a low sound that might have been a chuckle. "And that's a first."

"That's nothing," Mouse replied with a laugh. "You actually hit the bed frame behind you."

Hawken glanced over his shoulder at the wet spot and opened up with a laugh himself.

"Well, now," said Mouse, sitting back on his heels. "I was beginning to think you weren't capable of that."

Hawken looked up at him with his head askew. "Of what?"

"Laughing."

The transformation in a few short hours had been striking. The tense and brooding man that arrived at his door was now relaxed and lively—if a bit winded at present. He was very nearly giddy, as if he had drank in too much too quickly. Being in a big comfortable bed helped. It was probably Hawken's first time fully naked and in an actual bed with a man which, having previously only experienced backrooms and alleys, tended to change one's perspective on the event. Hawken's horizons had been now irreversibly opened to new and unforeseen territory. Anything was possible now. At this rate of progress, the tables would be turned about, and Mouse would be fucking the goon by morning.

Hawken grimaced sheepishly. "I have been accused from time to time of being too serious."

"You don't say."

Hawken put his foot on Mouse's chest and playfully pushed him backward. "I suppose," he said, a hint of sobriety seeping back into his tone, "I hadn't had much cause to laugh. Before now."

"Well, you should make a point of doing it more. It becomes you."

Hawken smiled back at the compliment.

Mouse propped himself up with his arms behind him, thankful for the respite. For him, the night wasn't exactly recreational. In point of fact, it was a lot of fucking work. As was typical of bedding men like Hawken, it was Mouse who ended up doing most of the heavy lifting. Men new to this variant approach to coitus tended to drop into their typical one-sided role. Stick it in something, move around a bit, then leave. At some point during the second romp, though, Hawken figured out there was more to it than just thrusting the hips with his eyes closed, and lo and behold, he did his own part to experiment.

A bit.

Mouse—not one to be passive—also reminded him, albeit gently, that he didn't need to be in complete control now. A novel idea.

Despite Hawken's awkwardness and narrow view of what could happen between them, it wasn't a horrible experience. The man was remarkably fit. But then, one does not become captain of the guard by sitting around eating biscuits and salted pork all day. His legs and ass alone could keep Mouse entertained for some time. And he was actually more hygienic than he expected. He'd had a thorough scrub down within days, not weeks. Not always the case on such jobs, so a pleasant and unexpected windfall.

All in all, he'd encountered worse.

He reached over to the small bedside table and grabbed his pewter mug of wine and a bunch of grapes from a tray, and in one fluid motion tossed his leg over the big man's midsection. Straddling his waist, he took a long swig from the mug then dangled the bunch over Hawken's mouth, who plucked off a few with his teeth while growling like a sad imitation of rabid dog.

While he chewed, his face lost some of its joy as a thought occurred to him. "Will I see you again?" he asked.

Experience lit a warning in his mind. He had seen that particular look in the eye enough times before, heard that distinctive tone in the voice.

There was a danger here, and he would need to navigate this delicately. When used to quick alley encounters, time in a bed for the first time had a new intimacy that could be exhilarating and intoxicating. And what was once a pragmatic satisfying of base urges could become an emotional connection never considered possible. That could lead to all kinds of unpredictable behaviors. Mouse knew to tread carefully.

"We are hardly finished with tonight, my dear," Mouse replied. He took another gulp of wine, then leaned in to put the mug back on the tray. Their bellies touched. When Mouse moved to push himself back up, Hawken put one strong hand at the back of Mouse's neck and pulled his face toward his own. Their lips pressed, and Mouse opened up his mouth to allow Hawken's hungry tongue to penetrate. Hawken pressed harder. The kiss was something beyond passionate and closer to something resembling desperation.

Mouse allowed it for a time, then gently pulled away, making certain he had a smile on his face.

"I'm sorry," Hawken said, suddenly sheepish. "I've never done that before."

"What? Kissed? That's what two people do when they're in bed together."

"I mean, kissed… you know…."

"A man," Mouse filled in for him.

"Yeah. I never wanted to before."

Mouse leaned forward and kissed him this time but softer. He needed to keep this moving—keep him talking before ideas about round three entered his head. Or the opposite happened. Hawken was at risk of becoming serious now, sinking into a maelstrom of new emotions.

He peeled himself off Hawken's lap and crossed the room to his pack that was sitting on a chair. All the while he felt Hawken's eyes on him. He dug through the pack until he found his pipe and small leather pouch of smokeweed. He packed the pipe, lit it with a candle flame, then puffed until the end glowed red.

Hawken scooted back until his shoulders were higher up against the headboard. "You never really answered my question."

"What question was that?" Mouse puffed out a tiny cloud as he returned his pouch, acting casual. He knew very well what the question was.

"Will I see you again? After tonight?"

"I'm in town for only a few days. I have some business to attend to, and once it's concluded, I have to leave. But until then...." He gave Hawken a generous smile with the pipe still clenched in his teeth. "I am your toy to do with what you will."

The big man's expression was relief with a little disappointment mixed in behind it. He was already hoping for a long-term affair. Of course, Mouse would ensure he never saw the man again come morning. No good would come of prolonging this further.

Mouse intentionally kept his distance while he puffed away at his pipe to keep things from slipping again into becoming physical. He played an act of looking for something in his pack and let a silence linger between them a bit. And as he'd hoped, Hawken wanted to keep up the connection he was feeling, so he filled in the distance with conversation.

"What nature of business?"

"Missing person," Mouse replied matter-of-factly and pretended to give up whatever he looking for. "Which, since you bring it up...." He moved over to the bed again, climbed up and sat on his heels next to Hawken, "Reminds me you now owe me a favor."

Hawken's expression was a mix of suspicion and curiosity. "All right, then. I suppose you held up your end of the bargain."

"I held my end up twice if you'll recall. Or more accurately, you held it up for me."

Hawken let his head fall back to bark out a laugh. "True enough. What's this favor?"

"I need a little information. I was informed you might be able to help me out."

Hawken raised an eyebrow. "Is that so?"

Mouse grinned wolfishly. "Might be something special in it for you." He threw his leg over Hawken's waist again and straddled him. "A very distinctive reward."

That got his attention. Hawken returned an eager boyish grin. "Oh really? How's that?"

To make his point, Mouse shifted his hips side to side, grinding his bare ass against Hawken's groin. "If I get this wrapped up quick, I can spend more time here. I have yet more wisdom to impart to my new and rather skilled apprentice."

"I'm listening," he replied, his grin broadening.

"I'm looking for a nobleman that's disappeared here."

"A nobleman, huh?"

"Rumor around town says he was arrested for some reason, but I checked with all the jailhouses and found no sign of him anywhere."

Hawken pursed his lips. "This wouldn't happen to be more than just any nobleman, would it? Someone big, like the son of a provincial duke, perhaps?"

"It's possible. My client had coin to spend. But all I have to go on is a name."

"Garron?"

"Yes, that's the name. You know of him?"

Hawken's expression turned murky. "You're not going to find him in any jailhouse. Where they have him exactly, to be honest, I'm not sure. He was arrested at Lord Delgan's manor by the chancellor himself. He is likely being kept in there."

"The chancellor?" Mouse feigned that this wasn't information he already knew. "That would mean a crime against the state."

"That is what I assumed at first as well."

Mouse studied him a moment, trying to read him. Something behind his eyes told him this wasn't mere hearsay. He took a calculated risk. "You were there when it happened."

"Yes," Hawken replied in a tight voice. "I was assigned to Duke Delgan's court at the time."

His reassignment could have had something directly to do with this business—something Mouse hadn't anticipated. Taurin had selected his contact well. "So, what happened?"

"The chancellor described it as 'corruption of the duke's nephew.' I don't know what that means, but the charge against that Lord Garron was bogus."

"How do you know?"

"I was assigned to the apartments of Lady Calpha, Delgan's sister. Rax, the nephew, was never in any direct contact with Lord Garron, so whatever 'corruption' took place, it wasn't Lord Garron who did the corrupting. I said as much to Chancellor Elasiar. He didn't appreciate my contribution."

"Is that what got you reassigned?"

"Maybe in part." Hawken smirked with a mischievous glint in his eyes. "But I would wager it was me shoving a mouthy prig down a privy hole that probably had more to do with it."

Mouse couldn't help but reflect Hawken's grin. "Worth it?"

Hawken shrugged. "Maybe. Except for the lower pay grade. But I'll get back in the manor eventually. I already hear grumbling that things aren't run properly. They'll be asking me back to straighten the ship right again in no time."

Mouse didn't get the sense that this was idle bragging or some misguided delusion. He believed the man was probably good at what he did. "So no ideas where they are keeping this corrupter of Orentegan youth?"

"Are you here to negotiate his release of something?"

"Not exactly."

Hawken's eyes widened with sudden understanding. "Oh. Well, you won't be able to get to him if that's what you're thinking. Delgan will have him heavily guarded. My guess, he's not in the dungeon. Delgan may be shrewd, but he holds the aristocracy above all. I doubt he'd stoop to throwing a noble in a rat-filled hole."

"Where is he, then?"

"For my coin, I'd wager he's locked away tight in one of the manor's four towers. Which one, I couldn't say." Hawken propped himself up on his elbows and leaned in close. "That's all I know. So… enough talk. I'm ready for my reward."

Mouse thought about pressing the matter but acquiesced. There was probably little more he knew, if anything. Mouse had enough to go on now anyway. So, one more wrestling match between them, then slip out while Hawken was asleep and find a place for him to catch some himself. Too bad it wouldn't be here, he thought—but such was the life of a man in his profession. He grinned impishly down at the big lug. "And well deserved it is," he said. "Hope you've caught your breath. No quarter for you this time, Captain."

CHAPTER 5

MOUSE WANDERED a few streets over from the Blue Stag and rented another room—one greatly inferior to the one he left behind but comfortable enough. Two strides in, he unloaded his gear, stripped, and collapsed on the small lumpy bed. He slept deeply until late morning. Then he washed from the basin, dressed again, and was back out on the streets.

A ceiling of low clouds had rolled in sometime during the night, making for a cooler day. Fewer idlers and gadabouts were out to congest the streets and plazas, and shopkeepers kept their tables of wares off the curb for fear of rain. Mouse could now traverse the network of byways with ease; he preferred to avoid the major arteries whenever possible. He pointed himself toward low town. He would swing through the market square, this time more for a quiet meal and some processing time than for digging up any information.

Except he realized almost immediately that he was being followed.

He went about his business, acting casual and forcing his pursuer through clusters of people or large open areas that would make it hard for the clumsy oaf to stay inconspicuous. Mouse had no intention of losing him, which would be an easy enough affair. The idiot's skill at tailing someone was laughable. But for his own petty entertainment, he wanted to make the poor bastard work for it. He would find out who it was soon enough. In fact, he counted on it.

Mouse arrived at the market square soon after with his frustrated pursuer in tow. Strolling among the haphazard cluster of booths, he allowed a portion of his concentration to ponder the next stage of his mission. Hawken had given him a rough idea where Lord Garron was being held. That was all he really needed. He could work out the details once inside Duke Delgan's manor house—the sprawling, fortified structure that rested atop the crest of the hill. The city region of high town surrounded it like a dingy cowl. A high wall surrounded the entire manor, and as far as he could discern, it only had one gate. Breaching that would be tricky business, but he already had a plan taking shape in the back of his mind.

Locating the young lord would be easy enough, certainly—getting him out again would be another matter. The logistics of the task began to weigh on him more and more. Compared to his typical work, like smuggling contraband or relieving an unsuspecting countess of her jewels, this job was fraught with too many potential hiccups. The size of Delgan's keep alone was daunting. Plus, Mouse had no idea yet of the duke's manpower inside, or how much of it was dedicated to protecting the prisoner. Was the young lord starved and beaten to the point that he would be too weak or too injured to transport out? Or so fat and entitled he couldn't wipe his own ass without a team of advisors and servants to guide him through the process? Either way, the escape attempt could fail before it began.

The word on Lord Garron's crime seemed to be some sordid insinuation that he preyed on young lads—a high crime here in Har Orentega. But Hawken's pillow testimony implied the charges raised against him were trumped up. They chose something that would be particularly heinous in the public view, which meant should word of his arrest and imprisonment leak, they wanted no one second-guessing the wisdom of the seizure. And there was also the issue of Lord Garron's sentence. What did they intend to do with him? A lengthy internment was unlikely. Was he already scheduled to meet his fate at the gallows? Time was now pressing in on his mission. If Mouse didn't locate him quickly, it might be too late for the poor lad.

And one other vital question remained. Why was he arrested in the first place?

The question nagged at him like pinching smallclothes on a hot day—irksome and unrelenting. Two days of digging, and he was no closer to an answer. The more he learned, the more politics or leverage seemed unlikely motives. So... what, then? Was this some kind of revenge plot?

He pulled up a stool at a soup vendor's counter and when he caught the cook's eye, gestured toward one of her steaming cauldrons. A bowl of hot stew and an iron kettle of tea arrived in front of him moments later.

He spooned the first taste into his mouth.

Some small, more logical corner of his mind chastised him. He was doing it again, of course—wasting mental energy on elements that had no bearing on the job at hand. The "why" was irrelevant. The details of his mission had been clearly defined. Rescue him. Get him out of this city and home to his duchy and his family. He wasn't being paid to find out what game Duke Delgan was playing at.

But he was always a sucker for a mystery. For his own good night's rest, he knew he would need to untangle this little knot. He knew himself well enough to know that he would be unable to just let it be. Delgan was up to something sinister, and Mouse needed to unravel what it was. If only for his own satisfaction.

The oaf that had been pursuing him so ineptly finally took a seat on the stool next to him.

"Wondered how long it would take for you to get here," Mouse said without even looking up from his bowl.

"Expecting me, were you?"

"Might as well put a cowbell around your neck. Wouldn't make you any more obvious." From the corner of his vision, he saw the man tighten up. He had already guessed who he was and what this was about before the man opened his mouth to tell him. "Your guild is shit, Keeler. You are aware of that, right?"

The man started at the use of his name, though he tried to disguise it. It had been a guess on Mouse's part—though he was pretty sure the idiot would come looking for him himself. Not having worked his way up the ranks like most guild leaders, he was likely unaccustomed to delegating out work. He was a hands-on man, used to working the streets on his own. He was overconfident of his own abilities and did not trust others to do a job properly. Plus, Mouse knew, curiosity would get the better of him. He would want to see for himself who this mysterious intruder was that wreaked havoc in their guild headquarters.

Mouse knew all this because it was exactly how he would act himself if he took over a guild.

Keeler was silent a moment while he readjusted his strategy. He quickly seemed to realize that his initial tactic of intimidation wasn't going to work with Mouse. "We're in transition," he replied. "Change in leadership."

"So I understand. Question remains which direction the organization is 'transitioning' toward. I have half the mind to usurp you and take over myself just on principle."

"You're an arrogant little bastard."

"It's hardly arrogance, I assure you. No idle boast." He took another slurp of stew. "You received my message, and you had your demonstration of what I'm capable of. I assume that's why you've decided to come."

"You nearly killed my lieutenant."

Mouse nearly choked on his stew suppressing a guffaw. That was an *officer* in this shit organization? "Consider it an object lesson on courtesy. And never underestimating who you're dealing with. It was his ill manners to blame for his current condition. And the ale. I merely pointed that out to him in a way he'll remember."

The man nodded in thought for a moment, clearly annoyed at Mouse's audacity at not being intimidated or affected by his presence. "I'm speaking to you now as a professional courtesy. Guild member to guild member. I could have just as easily stabbed you in the back, you know."

"Try that tactic next time and see what happens." Mouse pushed aside his empty bowl and turned on his stool to face the man directly for the first time. He was what he expected—a brutish man, unkempt and excruciatingly obvious. Any guild member worth his salt, especially the one at the helm, knew how to blend in and not draw attention to himself when necessary. Every citizen on the street would take a single look and know Keeler for a thug. He had no finesse. No style.

"I appreciate you coming here to save me the trouble of hunting you down. So, now that you're here, a few questions, then."

Keeler stared at him agog. "I did not come here to answer your questions. I came here to tell you I want you out of my city. You have one day to be out of Har Orentega."

"I need to know what the guild knows about the arrest of a certain Lord Garron of Har Dionante. Not the official bullshit word you'd give the guard either. I need to know what you really know."

Keeler put his palms on the counter and started to push himself up. "We're done here. One d—"

Mouse moved his hand to the man's shoulder. The long thin dirk palmed in his hand was little more than a needle. He pushed into the man's neck with just enough pressure to divot the skin without breaking it. "Sit down, friend. We aren't nearly done yet."

The man lowered his wide ass back onto the stool.

"Make one move," Mouse added softly into his ear. "And I'll puncture your neck with a barely perceivable hole…." He applied a little pressure to emphasize his point. A tiny drop of blood appeared beneath the tip of the dirk. "It will puncture your windpipe. And as you fall to the ground and gurgle and choke, I will tell everyone you're choking on a chicken bone and slip away quietly when they are trying to save you."

"I'll kill you for this," he growled.

"Better than you have tried. Now, what do you know about Lord Garron?"

"I don't know nothing."

Mouse was starting to lose patience. "Stop," he growled in his ear, pushing a little harder, "wasting my time."

"All right. *All right!* We knew the arrest was going to happen. Days before."

"You knew ahead of time? How?" This was an interesting development. And unexpected.

"We have a plant in the manor's kitchens to keep an eye on the rich peacocks that come and go in the city. Many of them are the personal guests of Duke Delgan, and we like to keep tabs on what they're doing with their money."

Mouse was genuinely surprised. "Well, how about that? An effective plan with actual merit."

"Like I said, under new leadership. We are attempting to move things in the right direction here."

"If you're not careful, I might start to think of you as a legitimate professional. What did you learn?"

"Days before the lord's arrest, a visitor came to talk to the duke, and over dinner, the plan to have him taken was laid out. Our mole overheard a good portion of it."

"So one, it was a trumped-up charge dreamed up ahead of time. And two"—and the more important, in Mouse's view—"the order came from *outside* of Har Orentega."

"Yes and yes," the guild leader responded.

Mouse took a moment to chew on that. So, someone outside of the town wanted this wealthy aristocrat out of the way. And this mysterious puppeteer had strings in Duke Delgan's hands and was making him dance along with his scheme. Was Delgan getting something in return for this, or did the visitor have some power over the duke?

"Any idea who this stranger was that called upon the illustrious Duke Delgan?"

"None whatsoever. His name was never used."

"Convenient. So why the hush-hush, then? Why is the guild sitting on this information and not using it?"

Keeler winced and shifted on his stool awkwardly. "A representative from the manor showed up at our *secret* guild house, bold as balls. Said Duke Delgan knew of our mole and what she heard. Said if the guild kept quiet she could remain doing guild business as long as she didn't interfere in the dukedom's affairs or get in Delgan's way. If word got out of the plan to arrest the young lord, he'd know where the leak came from, and he'd have her arrested and executed for treason. The choice for us was obvious. For the betterment of the guild, we kept quiet."

Mouse pursed his lips and nodded. Given those options, he would have made the same decision, at least until he was able to get a new mole secured in the manor and a new base of operations established. He wondered if Keeler even thought to do either of those things.

It explained why his poking around had made people like Taurin a bit jumpy. The Shadow Elite were always closely aligned with guild activity, and Mouse's inquiry could cause business to turn south if the guild was reined in. A lot of coin could be at stake. The duke had very effectively kept the information about Garron contained. Mouse was getting the sense that this Delgan was a savvy one.

"So where is the lord being held?"

"In one of the towers, I'm told."

Good. That corroborated Hawken's opinion. "Which one?" he asked. "There's four."

"The tall one—ow!" Keeler flinched when Mouse applied a little more pressure with the dirk. He wasn't in the mood for any of Keeler's cheek. "I don't know," he added quickly. "I do know it's heavily guarded. You'll never get in there, if that's your plan."

"My plan is none of your concern."

He pulled the dirk from the man's neck and slipped it back into his boot. The man put his hand to the spot, then checked his fingers for blood. "You have nothing to worry about from me," Mouse told him. "I have no intention of upsetting the operations for the guild here in Har Orentega. Or endangering your plant in the manor. But if anything were to change, I'll send word that she should disappear from the manor."

"What is your angle in all this?"

"Never mind. But I'll not get in the way of guild business if that's what you're worried about." He threw some coin on the counter to cover the cost of his bowl of stew and stood up. "You'll not see me again."

As he walked away from the vendor's stand, he heard the guild leader mutter, "Fine by me."

CHAPTER 6

THE FOUR-TEAM carriage pulled through the first open portcullis into the arched entry of the gatehouse, the sole entry into the walled complex around Duke Delgan's expansive keep. Though quaintly referred to in the city as the manor house, the structure beyond the gate was by all accounts a fortress. Though not particularly majestic or architecturally inventive, the manor house was, with its dark volcanic stone and soaring towers, an imposing structure nonetheless.

The grand team of horses stamped to an impatient halt at the second closed gate while bored guards in fine Orentegan livery drifted out of their chambers to address the new arrival. The guardsmen lumbered into position around the carriage at a languid shuffle, like the dead roused from their graves. Some were still pulling on their helms as they stumbled from the gatehouse, looking annoyed that their naps or card games had been interrupted. They kept close to the walls and eventually posed themselves at attention, their ceremonial lances planted on the ground next to them. A well-practiced routine that had lost its intended pomp.

As soon as the carriage rolled to a halt, one of the four hulking bodyguards that accompanied it on foot marched up to the carriage door, opened it wide, and positioned a stepping stool beneath the opening. The other hired men joined him in a snappy choreographed display. They flanked the carriage door with stiff backs, wide stances, and hands clasped behind their backs.

Very official, Mouse thought, as he viewed the proceedings from inside the carriage. They had only practiced it a few times but still managed to pull it off swimmingly. Coin was a terrific motivator.

To pull this off, Mouse had had to return to the Scarlet Unicorn and rely heavily on Taurin's generosity and fine taste. Only, Taurin wasn't as of yet entirely aware of how generous he had been. Or how generous some of his current patrons were either, who hopefully wouldn't be missing this fine carriage and its team of horses anytime soon. Taurin had made it exceedingly clear how unavailable he would be, so Mouse didn't want to trouble him with such trivialities. So, he absconded quietly with a few borrowed items.

Mouse wouldn't have need of these items for long. He hoped to have them all returned to the Scarlet Unicorn before anyone took notice of their absence.

Mouse grinned at the young man sitting across from him, a sharp-witted young stable hand named Jastar. When Mouse first discovered him, he was filthy and unkempt, but Mouse sensed the potential underneath the layers of grime. And he was right. The lad had cleaned up remarkably well and was exactly what he needed. "Ready?"

Jastar squirmed in his new finery but nodded. It hadn't taken much to convince the lad to join in, but now he seemed less certain.

Mouse stepped down from the carriage, scrubbed clean, freshly shaven, and resplendent in his newly acquired regalia. He was enshrouded in a heavy surcoat of ocean blue, embellished with gold thread piping and swirling brocades at the sleeves and hem. On his head was a matching plumed hat so ridiculous it made Mouse laugh just to look at it. It was a style thankfully now out of fashion, which explained why it was buried deep in one of Taurin's trunks, but it was ostentatious enough to suit his current guise. The boots, hose, and ruffled chemise were all borrowed from Taurin's wardrobe as well. The garish jewelry on his fingers and draping over his breast came from the same patron who so generously supplied the carriage, who was likely still passed out from too much physical activity with one of Taurin's girls and the strong mulled wine.

Mouse couldn't wait to doff the lot of it. Especially the hose. He despised wearing hose.

The young attendant followed him out of the carriage, handed Mouse a cane, and draped a small cape across his shoulders.

The captain of the gatehouse approached and made a perfunctory bow. "Good day, m'lord," he greeted flatly. He opened his mouth to launch further into his standard speech but stopped short when something caught his eye. His gaze was pulled to the bodyguard standing at Mouse's right hand, and his eyes widened in sudden recognition.

"Ah," Mouse said with a bright smile. "I see you remember my recently acquired footman."

The guard stared at Hawken in unabashed shock. "Yes," he replied, then remembered himself. "I mean, yes, m'lord."

Hawken allowed himself a satisfied smirk in return. He said nothing, embracing his role as a rich merchant's bodyguard. He'd been quick to agree to this scheme, even before he learned how much coin Mouse was adding to his purse.

The gatehouse captain did his best to recover, but even as he spoke to Mouse, he repeatedly shifted his gaze toward Hawken, who continued to grin down on him. "Your… your business here at the manor, m'lord?" the guard asked.

Mouse assumed an expression of surprise and mild irritation. "Were you not informed of my pending arrival?"

"I am afraid not, m'lord. You are?"

Mouse's narrow gaze swung to Hawken, who made a slight eye roll and shrugged. "Appears your assessment of the place was depressingly accurate," Mouse said to him in a low voice but plenty loud enough for the guardsman to hear. "Small wonder you were quick to take my offer." He returned his gaze to the flummoxed guard and managed to squeeze out a condescending smile. "Yazura Tenda." He waited for the guard to respond, and when the guard just stared, he added, "From Arendia. The capital? You bumpkins down here have heard of the capital, yes? It's the big city to the north, where our glorious king resides."

The footman to Mouse's left, a bruiser by the name of Reginus Fenn, snickered deep his throat. Hawken had dredged him up from the docks somewhere. Mouse presumed they knew each other from some dubious connection, but he didn't ask. The man was enormous, larger than Hawken, even, and had a mane of wild, rust-colored hair that Mouse insisted he comb out and pull back into a tail behind him.

"I'm familiar with it," the guard replied, his jaw line tightening with annoyance. "You have papers, I presume?"

Mouse sighed as if this was all too much for him bear. He nodded to Jastar. The lad reached into the carriage, fumbled with the insides of a wooden box, and pulled out a bone scroll case. He handed it to Mouse, who slid out a scroll sealed with wax, and then passed the scroll over to the guardsman.

Mouse hoped the ink had had enough time to dry. The forged papers were scribed just an hour before. The seal press had indeed come from Arendia. Mouse had stolen it from a well-connected family last time he'd been to the capital city. The family had certainly realized it had been stolen by now and updated the seal, but there was little chance this grunt was going to expend the energy to cross-reference the image imbedded in the wax with his records.

The guard broke the seal and studied the document a moment. No surprise he could read—he wouldn't have been assigned to this particular post otherwise—but his skills were not likely strong enough to spot a well-made forgery. After a thorough scan, he handed the parchment back to Mouse. "My apologies, Lord Tenda. Your visit was not relayed to us. We will open the gate for you immediately and someone will direct you to the manor. Is His Lordship, the duke, expecting you?"

"Well, I certainly hope so. Announce me nonetheless." Mouse didn't wait for a response. He spun on his heel and climbed back into his borrowed carriage. Hawken and the attendant climbed in after him.

The inner gate cranked open with a steady grinding and scraping. Once the portcullis was fully raised, the team was brought into motion again. Mouse reclined back in his seat and smiled.

Jastar breathed out heavily, puffing out his cheeks. "I can't believe they fell for it."

"Of course they fell for it," Mouse replied.

The lad shook his head. "Amazing. You actually got us into Delgan's manor. I thought for certain the guards would see right through it and arrest us all on the spot."

Mouse chuckled at his youthful astonishment. This was the easy part.

"You're enjoying yourself," Hawken said with a tightened brow.

Mouse couldn't deny it. He caught himself grinning wider. "As are you, I imagine."

Hawken shrugged wryly, but Mouse could still detect the gleeful glint in his eye. He'd created a convert, it seemed.

"Ah, be careful, my friend," Mouse told him. "The taste of adventuring is the most potent of wines. Too large of a draught, and you might find yourself lost in it."

"Then I shall curse you henceforth for my crapulence, Mouse. It was you who first handed me the cup."

CHAPTER 7

THE CARRIAGE was led to a side entrance of the manor where guards delicately delivered "Lord Tenda" from the carriage and escorted him inside. A midrank guardsman and a man Mouse assumed was the chancellor awaited them in a receiving area just inside the door.

The man, clothed in official-looking robes, glided forward, long hands clasped at his waistline as if protecting his groin. He stopped a pace or two in front of Mouse and pushed his shoulders back. He was gaunt to the point of frail, sallow to the point of sickly, and everything about the man said prickly and ill-humored.

"Good day to you, Master Tenda. I am Lord Elasiar, Chancellor to Duke Delgan and custodian of the seal of Har Orentega."

The greeting was civil but held little warmth. The man was understandably suspicious, but he had no reason to turn them away just yet. He studied Mouse with narrow birdlike eyes, his lips pursed behind the closely trimmed beard. With a brow slightly raised, he waited for Mouse to acknowledge his station.

Mouse did his best to look unimpressed. He returned a weak smile and spoke to him as if he were the stable boy. "Has the duke been informed of my arrival yet, Chancellor?"

A noticeable pause. "A messenger has been dispatched, yes," Elasiar replied. Which meant they were still trying to figure out what was going on. "If you would indulge us, sir, and present your papers again…."

Mouse made a dramatic show of rolling his eyes. "If you insist," he huffed, "but this grows tiresome." He snapped his fingers. The attendant reached into the haversack slung on his shoulder and again removed the bone case with scroll. He handed it to Hawken, who pulled out the scroll and passed it on to Elasiar.

The chancellor froze momentarily when he looked up and noticed for the first time who was handing over the parchment. Hawken returned a knowing smile but said nothing. Elasiar recovered quickly. He unfurled the scroll and read through the credentials with a critical eye. Brow tight, he scanned it thoroughly before handing the scroll back to the Hawken.

He seemed disappointed he couldn't find anything amiss. "Seems, Master Tenda," he said, "you have taken one of our own in your employ."

"Indeed!" Mouse beamed with excitement. "You know Hawken? Quite the find, I'd say. I discovered him stationed on the wall of all places. A diamond tossed in the shit, if you will. Ridiculous! What blind idiot thought to waste him there? I spotted him training some of the wall grunts and recognized his talent immediately. Small wonder it took little convincing to have him take my offer."

Elasiar's lips tightened a fraction, though he clearly was fighting to keep his face neutral. Mouse resisted a wider smile. He'd guessed correctly that it was Elasiar who had reassigned Hawken. Mouse thrilled at any opportunity to abuse one of the elite. The chancellor would be unaccustomed to being so openly criticized but was savvy enough not to offend someone of a higher station than himself by taking umbrage. Instead of responding directly, he went back to the matter at hand.

"It appears, sir, that your arrival in our city was not properly relayed to us."

"So I've been led to believe," Mouse replied with an air of well-measured hauteur. "Honestly, to be treated such after so long a journey. I've a mind to just turn about and head out again. I'm sure some other far-flung village around here will appreciate my proposition. Har Dionante perhaps...."

Elasiar forced a smile. Mouse could read the dialogue moving through his mind from the reddening color on his cheeks. Fucking big-city types marching in here thinking they can tell us how to function.

"Allow me to direct you to a chamber where you can wait comfortably until I've heard from Duke Delgan himself. I'm certain we can get to the bottom of this unfortunate misunderstanding."

"I certainly hope so. This ordeal has been quite taxing, I assure you." He turned his head to Hawken, who shook his head in dismay. Then he gestured toward the entryway. "Lead on, Chancellor."

His party, consisting of Hawken, the attendant, and the other three footmen, was escorted down a series of corridors to a small but elegant chamber, complete with wash basin and basket of fruit. Mouse nodded in approval. He'd learned to gauge his perceived influence by the accommodations they settled him into. Had this been a barracks or some nondescript meeting room, he'd have been nervous and might have looked for an excuse to slip out hastily. But the chamber was of decent quality.

Not a high-end apartment meant for visiting nobles but good enough. The accommodations suggested some uncertainty on Elasiar's part, so the manor staff wasn't uncorking the good wine just yet.

He had to move things along quickly. He checked the latch on the door. Unlocked. That was a good sign.

He pulled the door open a fraction to get a glimpse of the corridor. As far as he could tell, no guard had been posted outside. At least none directly outside the door. But that didn't mean a guard wasn't stationed close by, or the room itself wasn't being spied on through a peephole. He put a hand to the shoulder of one of the footmen and leaned into his ear. "Do a quick loop around the halls in this area and report back anything you see. If anyone questions you, ask them where the privy is. If pressured or followed, don't take any chances. Just head back. If you're escorted back, sneeze when you reach the door." The footman nodded once and slipped out.

Mouse turned to Jastar. "Ready?"

The lad made a small bob of his head.

"Get started, then," Mouse told him. Jastar nodded again and started to disrobe. Mouse did the same, tossing the ridiculous hat onto a chair and unfastening the buttons of his surcoat from the neck down. Hawken looked on with pressed lips, clearly dubious.

"Are you certain this is going to work?"

"Without question." Jastar was specifically chosen because he was very nearly Mouse's size. To them, Mouse was just an arrogant fop in a big hat. "They won't be expecting the change, so they won't see it." As long as the lad could continue the role in a convincing manner, of course, but he kept that to himself. He turned his gaze toward the attendant with a smirk. "You can act snide and superior, right?"

Jastar grinned.

"Just keep the tone elevated like I taught you," Mouse added. "No street talk."

Jastar unlaced and removed the jerkin, then pulled the tunic off over his head exposing his near-hairless and well-proportioned torso. Mouse turned his gaze away. Elsewhere, he might have taken the opportunity to appreciate the lad's form, but not here. He would not allow his base urges to undermine his focus. Hawken, on the other hand, could not pull his hungry leer away—he looked like a wolf eyeing a chicken. Mouse made two quick snaps of his fingers to draw Hawken's attention from the show. Hawken started as if awoken from a dream and, looking at Mouse, winced.

"Time for that later, friend," Mouse told him quietly as he began to disrobe as well.

Hawken nodded sheepishly.

One by one, Mouse stripped off each item of his lavish garb and tossed it off to Jastar, who stood nearly bare in his smallclothes, waiting. *What a compromising predicament it would be should a guard or the chancellor himself return now*, thought Mouse. Two nearly naked men standing about in the chamber. How would he spin a yarn to explain that, he wondered. The other footman scooped up Jastar's garments from the floor and handed them to Mouse an item at a time.

In short order, the lad was fully dressed in the blue surcoat with gold buttons and the monstrous hat that looked like a giant bird landed on his head, and Mouse in an attendant's jerkin and hose.

"How do I look?" Jastar asked.

Mouse bobbed his head in satisfaction. "Every bit the entitled noble shit."

Hawken looked more unsure. "What if Duke Delgan actually grants the audience with him?"

"He won't. We will be politely told to bugger off today and come back tomorrow when his schedule is cleared."

"How can you be so certain?" Hawken glanced at the lad with clear concern. "What if they investigate who this Lord Tenda is?"

"They will find he is wealthy beyond measure and very well connected in the king's court."

Hawken raised an eyebrow. "You've run this scam before?"

Mouse chuckled as he guided Jastar by the shoulders to the center of the chamber. He sculpted the lad like a clay doll. Lifted his chin, pushed in his lower back, positioned one hand on his hip while the other gripped the cane. "When you walk," Mouse told him, "remember to think someone has wired your shoulder blades together."

When Mouse glanced over, Hawken still had a brow knitted with concern.

"If they notice you missing…." the big man began.

Mouse reached up and grabbed Hawken's shoulders. "We've gone over this. A stiff neck like the Elasiar pays not a speck of attention to ground beetles like attendants or footmen. They're invisible to him. Furniture. The puffed-up sot will make his appearance just long enough to send us packing until tomorrow, then be on his way. They will assign a few guards who will see us out. Guards that have no idea how many of us came in."

Hawken shook his head. "I certainly hope you're right."

"It will work. Trust me. Just make sure you're ready and available for tomorrow."

"Tomorrow?"

"An official visitor will call at your residence." Hawken went a little ashen. Mouse smiled. "Not what you're thinking. If you were hired by someone as powerful as Tenda, you *must* be more valuable than they realized. The chancellor will offer you a position back here in the manor. Effective immediately, most likely, and I would wager at an increased wage."

"You have it all figured out, don't you?" His tone was sharp, but there was a glint in Hawken's eye when he said it.

"I have indeed," Mouse replied coolly. "When they arrive, just make a convincing show that you are packing to relocate to the capital. I, they will have learned, have already left for Arendia spitting with indignation."

The door to the chamber opened, and the young footman slipped in. He moved directly toward Jastar now dressed as Tenda and was about to start a whispered conference with him but stopped short, realizing suddenly it was not Mouse. He looked around, embarrassed until he saw Mouse waving at him.

Mouse glanced up at Hawken. "Still any doubts?"

The footman grimaced and made his way over.

"The corridors are clear," the footman told him. "No one stopped or questioned me. But the chancellor is making his way back. I returned as soon as I spotted him coming down the corridor."

Mouse nodded. "Good."

"There is more," the footman added as he looked over his shoulder to see if the chamber door was opening yet. "I happened on two lords talking about an area of the manor they referred to as 'restricted.'"

Mouse's back straightened. "Go on."

"I didn't learn what part of the manor it was. Neither seemed to know why it was closed off, but only those with certain approval are apparently free to go there. Both spoiled dandies were miffed about their exclusion from the list and expressed hope they would be allowed to return soon. That was when one said he heard it rumored that it was only a matter of day or two before they were."

Mouse tightened his lips as he clapped him on the shoulder. "Well done," he said just as door to the chamber swung open. "Well done, indeed."

If this rumor was true, that meant Mouse had less time than he'd hoped.

Guards preceded the chancellor and took position flanking the doorway. Elasiar glided into the room with a stiff-backed gait, like a man who assumed everyone was rapt by his very presence. His gaze centered on Jastar alone. All others in the room did not warrant his attention. "Lord Tenda." He greeted him with a polite bow that carried no warmth. "I pray we did not keep you waiting too long."

Jastar scowled and shifted his shoulders back a fraction. "I'm certain it was just these dreadful accommodations that made it seem so."

Mouse nearly broke a smile. He'd chosen his doppelganger well, it seemed.

"Forgive us. It was what we had available at such short notice." The chancellor approached and wore his political face—the one that broadcast he really, really cared. "I'm afraid I'm going to have to test your patience further. It appears His Grace is unable to pull himself away from some important state business. Which means he will be unable to meet with you today. But if we could impose on you further, we will gladly find room in our docket tomorrow."

Jastar rolled his eyes. "Was hoping to be back on the road tomorrow." He stomped the end of his cane on the floor like a petulant child that didn't get the pony he demanded. "I've had just about all I can take of this uncultured backwater. Can you promise at the least it'll be in the morning?"

Mouse winced. That sounded too deferential. Too meek. A fop like Tenda would never *ask* Elasiar for anything. Mouse had coached him with the proper words to say and the diction in which to say them, but in the moment, there was always the need to extemporize. Though the lad had taken his notes well, there was a danger of him improvising too much, going too far. Mouse watched Elasiar's face for signs of alarm but only saw irritation.

"I'm certain we can make it work at your convenience," Elasiar replied.

Mouse slowly exhaled.

"If you were concerned about what was convenient, I'd be speaking to the duke at present. But very well." Jastar threw up his hand. "Tomorrow it is. I'll be here early. Make certain the gate is prepared for me this time."

Mouse wondered if he should take this protégé under his wing when he left the city. The lad had promise.

"Of course," said the chancellor. "I have taken the liberty of seeing your carriage prepared." Which meant the chancellor had already had it thoroughly searched. "It awaits you in the yard. These men will direct you. I take my leave, and I look forward to receiving you tomorrow."

Jastar waved him off.

Elasiar bowed and turned to leave but stopped unexpectedly to face Hawken. "Sir Hawken, I was hoping perhaps I may have a word with you tomorrow as well. While His Grace and Master Tenda are meeting perhaps?"

"Of course, Lord Chancellor." Hawken lowered one knee in a respectful bow. "I am at your service."

Elasiar's mouth lifted at the corners into something that resembled an authentic smile. "Excellent. I look forward to it." And without another word, he spun about and departed.

Hawken looked to Mouse with an arched brow. "Are you ever wrong?"

Mouse shrugged. "People are predictable. Mostly."

This time tomorrow, Hawken would be better placed in the manor than he had been before. Mouse wondered if he'd ever see him again. He was surprised to realize he liked the man—and felt he could indeed be better utilized elsewhere than this backwater shithole of a duchy. He'd be happier, certainly. But if all went according to plan, Mouse would have freed the imprisoned Lord Garron and be long gone before Hawken took up his position in the manor again.

"You'll do me the kindness as to follow me, Master Tenda," said the guard at the door.

Jastar still looked annoyed. He flapped his hand toward him as if swatting at a fly. "Lead on, then."

Out in the courtyard, it was a simple matter for Mouse to slip away unnoticed. The open area was a bustle of activity, so when Jastar began his performance of making a fuss about how his team was not being handled properly, it drew enough attention for Mouse to dip into the shadows of an alcove by the stables. No one would be counting footman or attendants at this point.

He stripped off his attendant's jerkin—easily identifying him as someone that didn't belong—and tucked it behind some crates. Now, it was time to wait. Wait for the carriage to exit the gates. Wait for an opportunity to get back into the manor.

CHAPTER 8

THIS WAS indeed his favorite part. The carriage was gone, safely beyond the gates with the portcullis once again closed, and he was alone with only the sum of his strategy and skill. And his dagger and small kit of thieving tools, of course.

Now, the adventure was afoot.

There is an undeniable thrill that one experiences when he finds himself alone in the enemy camp. It's exhilarating and intoxicating in equal measure. The senses become amplified, the blood is roused, and the fingers are set to tingle. There's a glorious tightness of the gut—like the one felt just before the first punch of a brawl or when dice are in hand before the cast. The unknown awaits, and the tension is delicious.

The exuberance of the moment, however, was somewhat diluted. He had chosen to lie in wait next to a particularly potent crate of onions.

For the residents of the keep, the brief excitement of Tenda's visit had ended—if it could rightly be called that. It was more a welcome interruption of the mundane. Manor life returned to what Mouse reckoned was the norm. An industrious but relative quiet hung over the grounds. The drudges of the keep went about their manual labors, while guards, stable hands, maidservants, and the like milled about the open courtyard like busy ants on a hill. Some traveled in pairs, engaged in quiet conversation, while others ambled about alone and consumed in their own thoughts. A group of hired masons toiling with an overburdened wheelbarrow of bricks provided Mouse the cover he was looking for. He slipped from his smelly hiding place and strolled along behind the lot as if he belonged.

He kept pace but was careful not to stray too close and pull their attention. The group was deep in a heated flap over the previous night's dice match, so there was little danger of being noticed. Any who happened to glance in his direction saw only an apprentice tagging behind his betters. The benefits of a youthful look and a small stature.

He made a casual but careful survey of the grounds while he strolled along. The inner ward surrounding the main structure of the keep was a wide-open field between the gates and the primary entrance, but to either flank was a mishmash of outbuildings. The masons led him toward the northern wall, past the guards' dormitories. A few off-duty grunts loitered about sharing a wineskin, grumbling about their shift. Their path then took them past a smithy, easily identified from the black smoke billowing from the chimney and the telltale repetitive clang of a hammer coming from inside.

One of the bricks in the wheelbarrow slipped off the top of the stack, but none of the masons noticed. Without slowing his stride, Mouse swept his arm down to grab it. Shortly, the masons angled toward the shadowy northern face of the keep, and Mouse spotted their destination: a building with a partially collapsed wall. As they veered toward it, Mouse called out to them.

"Ho there, masters."

The argument came to a sudden halt as they stopped and turned around in unison.

They eyed him with suspicion as he approached. Laborers were always wary of unsolicited attention. It typically meant more work on their docket.

Mouse held up the brick for them to see. "Dropped this back there." He extended his arm to them.

"Ah," said the eldest among them, a sturdy man of about fifty years. He looked noticeably relieved. "Thank you, friend." He took the brick from Mouse and set it back onto the stack.

"Thought it felt a bit light," joked the hulking man who'd wrestled with the wheelbarrow the entire journey.

Mouse chuckled freely. "What an unfortunate irony it'd been if your job ended up one short."

They all laughed.

"What was all that excitement about earlier?" Mouse asked them, leaning in conspiratorially and thumbing back at the gate.

"That carriage?" scoffed the older mason, waving him off. "Just another fucking bloated peacock in an oversized codpiece. No end to them lately."

Mouse couldn't help but smile at that. He shook his head in a woeful expression. "Ah. Thought it might have something to do with that prisoner the duke has hidden away up in the tower." It was worth the gamble to prod a bit. Laborers like masons had a different brand of access inside keeps such as this, and they were most often overlooked and ignored. That meant they observed things others didn't.

But he was met with blank stares. One of them shaded his eyes and looked up at the closest tower. "There's some prison'r up in there?"

Mouse shrugged. "So says the rumor mongers." He offered a warm tip of his head. "I'll trouble you no further. Good day to you, masters."

He abandoned them and slipped in among the cluster of low wooden storage sheds while they trudged on, picking up the threads of their argument where they'd left off.

As he'd hoped, the area was quiet and sparse of people.

He weaved among some of the buildings, heading farther along the keep's northern side toward the back corner of the keep. He came across an arched opening. More tunnel than passage, it extended through the thick stone wall of the keep. But two paces inside, an iron gate barred the way. Mouse made a quick scan for witnesses and slipped inside the passage. With his thief tools, it took but a moment to spring the mechanism within the lock—so simple in fact that Mouse wondered why they bothered to lock it at all. He closed the gate behind him and emerged onto a perfectly manicured path surrounded by artfully trimmed shrubbery, statuary, and a little stone bench.

He was at the narrow end of a garden courtyard.

He stooped and slunk into the foliage. Dressed as he was, he would not be permitted here. This isolated haven was for the aristocracy—for those with the right blood or with the proper size purse. He remained still for a time, listening. He heard the sound of water, and as he crept a bit, he spied a round fountain at the center of a clearing with more paths leading off in other directions. With its gently meandering pathways and secluded corners, this was a garden designed for privacy. Only the black stone walls surrounding the courtyard spoiled the illusion that the garden was miles from the city. And the prospect of solitude was shattered as well when one considered that three walls of the manor were lined with windows and balconies. Any activities that took place in the garden could very well have an audience.

Mouse remained in the leafy cover and skulked along close to the wall, circling the garden. He listened for others who might be enjoying the garden with him as he cat-pawed over the soft loam. He caught a tiny titter of laughter.

Gently, he lifted a bough out of the way to have a look.

Not far from him, a young couple was seated on a stone bench. Knees touching, they stared at each other with grotesque expressions of longing. The young man cupped her hand in both of his as if it were something precious and fragile. The lad leaned in and whispered something that made the girl giggle again. She put her fingers to her mouth and looked away, blushing. Mouse rolled his eyes and fought the urge to throw a rock at them.

Behind them, watching the spectacle with the scrutiny of a warden, was the girl's nurse. The woman leaned her back against the wall with her arms crossed tightly over her excessive bosom in a tight knot. From her expression, she was clearly waiting for the lad to make the wrong move and give her the excuse to break up the visit and drag the girl inside.

The nurse had chosen to perform her skulking surveillance immediately beside the only door Mouse had seen so far. Presumably, the only door out of the garden.

There was no sneaking past her—that was clear. He had to find another way in. He made a quick inventory of the balconies of the second floor. Sure enough, a door was ajar.

There was always one. A manor of this size was simply too big to secure properly all the time—especially when those within felt safe and simply grew careless.

Mouse inched his way closer and positioned himself under the balcony. His movements would be in direct line of sight from both the lovers and the nurse. Any movement or sound would draw their attention with ease.

He considered waiting, but the two of them could be at this for hours. And he wouldn't be able to stomach it for another five minutes before he lost control and dumped cold water on the sticky couple. No choice but to act.

He studied the wall, paying close attention to the massive bricks of the keep's foundation and how they were connected, noticing which corners stood out more than others. His ascent would have to be quick. He planned his approach—footholds, handholds—and mapped it out in his head. Then checking on the activity and attention of the other three, he launched at the wall.

He made all his grips as planned, and his footing was secure, and he scaled the wall like a squirrel scales the trunk of a tree. He made it to the bottom of balcony with ease. Within two heartbeats, perhaps three, he was pulling himself over the balustrade. By the time the three were aware of the sound and movement and then located the source, Mouse was leaning his elbows on the balustrade and smiling down at them.

The young lad's eyes turned cross when he focused on Mouse. "Ho there! Some privacy if you don't mind." From birth, the elites were trained to believe that what they wanted actually mattered.

"Ah," said Mouse with a carefree smile. "My apologizes, my lord. I was unaware this was a private event."

He slipped inside the open door. He was inside the manor.

Now the real work could begin.

THE SMALL two-room apartment was probably for some lesser noble. Not currently in residence, apparently. The bedside washbasins were empty, no supply of wood was stacked by the fireplace, no tray of sweet pastries on the table, and a layer of dust covered the surfaces. The bed coverings had been disturbed, though. Chambers like this were often the clandestine meeting place for lovers since there was little chance of discovery when the rightful occupant was not around.

A thorough search ferreted out enough to piece together a new outfit. Strolling around in a tunic and hose was fine for the ward, but inside the manor he needed proper attire. He found some green woven trousers and a fine leather jerkin that fit him surprisingly well. With his own tunic and boots, the look was satisfactory. He would blend in nicely. Nothing flashy or too specific but discreet enough not to draw any notice.

Mouse was always astounded with what he could get away with when he'd infiltrated a place. After leaving the chamber, he strode the corridors as if he'd been there all his life. He needed to get a sense of the layout, which meant a systematic survey of the passageways and the various wings. He'd learned some time ago that if you act like you belong, no one will challenge you. You're a guest of the duke, residents tell themselves, or a member of the extended family in for a visit. Or perhaps part of an entourage. No one wants to be the foolish snoop that embarrasses himself or insults someone important by asking if they, in fact, belong. That sort of thing is always best left for others.

He swept the wing of apartments and living quarters first. He picked a few locked doors to gauge their quality and gain a feel for the mechanisms inside. Every locksmith designed his own device, each with its own particular qualities and nuances. The one who installed the locks around the manor was no different. Mouse had it figured out quickly and could have a door opened faster than someone could with the proper key.

He scavenged for any useful items he might need. Then he went about storing little caches around the manor. Anything that might have any use at all, he tucked it away in some storeroom or unused chamber, and he kept a catalog of all of it locked away in his head.

Once he was satisfied he had enough supplies squirreled away, he made a pass through the belly of the keep. He swept through the servant work areas and the kitchens. It was Mouse's firm opinion that the state of these areas was the true test of a nobleman's worth and distinction. How someone treated those beneath him spoke a great deal about his character. In general, filth and squalor was ubiquitous in the work zones of every keep and castle in the kingdom. But the conditions here were appalling and some of the worst that he'd seen. Duke Delgan did not much care for those who labored for him, it seemed.

Mouse marched into the kitchens and demanded with authority a tray of the night's meal from the cook on duty, a grim woman who clearly did too much taste-testing of the meals she prepared. Promptly, a tray was thrust into his hands without a word. He slunk off and found a quiet place to eat and plan.

Then he tackled the more dicey areas of the manor. He carried his tray around as he explored. As a rule, no one ever challenged you if you carried a tray. With a tray in front of him, he could likely stroll right into Duke Delgan's own bed chamber and not be called out.

He wound his way up to the third level. The first tower was easy enough to locate. He followed the winding open stairwell to the top— which turned out to be a guard station and lookout. Currently empty. Chairs and a table in the center of the room with a cup of dice, cards, and flagons with stale mead swimming in the bottom was all that was there. It was possible that the guards stationed here only occupied this lookout at night. But it was more likely that they knew their captain wasn't going to haul his ass up all those stairs to check up on them, so they weren't going to either. They probably had slunk off to pinch a drink somewhere, shag a maidservant, or sleep off a hangover.

Tray still in hand, he pressed into another corner of the manor and found the stairs that led up to the second tower. A rope hung down the center from the top of the open stairwell. The bell tower. Not much chance of a prisoner held up there. There were no guards or any signs of recent activity, but he checked it out just to be thorough. As he suspected, it was empty. Someone had assembled a small pallet bed in one corner, but this was not where the prisoner was being held.

When he entered the area leading to the third tower, he sensed something different in the air almost immediately. The corridors possessed a cold vacancy. No one lingered here. The few he encountered moved with determination and purpose and eyed him with a hint of suspicion as he walked by. He felt the prickle of danger on his skin. It had the hush and heft of a restricted zone, an area of authority. He rounded a corner and spied four guards down the far end of the corridor, two flanking an open doorway, and two standing against the opposite wall.

This was it.

CHAPTER 9

THIS WAS why Mouse didn't take on rescue missions. When hired to liberate pretty little baubles from their unsuspecting owners, they never had this much protection.

Keeler had warned him, but four guards still seemed especially excessive. And there were more guards farther up the tower, certainly. A lot of manpower dedicated to one prisoner. Was the man dangerous? Mouse doubted that. Someone would have mentioned that particular detail by now. Had he attempted an escape already? Or did Delgan anticipate an attempt?

Mouse ran a catalog of ideas through his head. Getting past the guards undetected would be a trick—even for him. He could find a way past one or two, but four seemed overly ambitious. It took only one to raise an alarm. He toyed with the notion of one of his many ruses that might gain him entry but rejected them all. He preferred not to risk any suspicion just yet. Slaying them all wasn't an option either. Even if he managed to keep it quiet, four bodies would be difficult to hide, and their absence would be noticed before he even had the prisoner out of the tower. No, too great a gamble. He needed another way.

With the manor's layout conjured up in his mind, he skulked down a side corridor and chose a door that he hoped would serve his needs. It was locked, but a quick fiddle of the insides with his tools gained him his access. He ducked inside.

The chamber was a small office, just large enough for the desk that occupied one whole wall. Heaping piles of parchment, scroll cases, and ledgers cluttered the surface of the desk and a fair portion of the floor as well. This was the workspace of some journeyman scribe. He lifted one of the loose sheets of parchment from the top of a pile and scanned through it. Legal, by the look of it. Since this wing was deemed off-limits to most, the lowly scribe was likely reassigned to another part of the manor, so there was little danger of Mouse being discovered here. He headed straight to the solitary window. He flung back the shutters, leaned out on the sill, and looked up.

He'd guessed correctly. The window provided him both a clear view of the tower and also access to the roof if he climbed up. From the roof, he could scuttle over to the base of the tower.

It was a square construction, like the others, and made with the same black stone as the rest of the manor. It had arrow slots at the various corners, which would be the locations of the staircase landings inside. There were two sets of shuttered windows—halfway up the tower and near the top. The guardroom was likely the lower set of windows.

Mouse knew the protocol. Guardsmen assigned to an important prisoner would not sleep back in the barracks with their brethren. They would be sequestered there at the tower for more efficient shift rotation and to provide a quick response should something happen. That chamber would not be empty.

Mouse would find his quarry inside the upper set of windows.

But of course, it was the tallest of all four towers.

Mouse leaned his elbows on the sill and studied the construction of the tower with a pursed mouth. The stone blocks were large and roughly hewn, similar to the stones he had shimmied up earlier. He spotted a few areas that looked troublesome, but from his angle they seemed infrequent and could probably be avoided. Halfway up, the walls were reinforced with iron bands to take some of the stress from the weight up above it. The bands were interspersed regularly up the sides.

He bit the inside of his cheek. It could be done, he told himself. It would be tricky. One might even say foolhardy. But considering all his options, which were few, and the risk associated with each of them, he saw no other way around it. To get inside the tower, he would have to scale it.

Fuck.

Not his favorite of activities. Scaling was an art form. Mouse had enough experience to know that every stone wall had its own personality and its own surprises. It was always a dangerous and uncertain business. He could plan for days, but the one thing he didn't account for could mean his downfall. Literally. A fall from the second floor of a jeweler's residence might mean a broken leg, but a fall from a tower this high meant certain death.

The stonework would offer plenty of handholds, certainly—masons never assembled the stones with absolute precision. But what concerned

Mouse was the age of the tower. Over time, weather could undermine the masonry, making it weak and unstable. Old brickwork could break off under his weight, or the mortar could fracture, causing stones to loosen and shift unexpectedly. From the window, he could spot some areas of degradation. He could avoid those easily enough, but it was the areas he couldn't see that troubled him. He would be climbing the wall in the dark of night, after all. Wind could be a factor as well. Unpredictable gusts were not unusual at such altitudes, and considering the keep was built atop the crest of a hill, this tower reached very high indeed.

It would be a long climb. A great deal of strain on his hands and no room for error.

One last time he brainstormed for a way around this course, but nothing came to him. It was his best, if not only, chance of getting to Lord Garron undetected and quickly.

His revised plan required new preparations and new supplies. He set off to pilfer what he needed, slipping out of the little office to plunge back into the lower floors again. With a tray in hand, of course. This time, he looped through deeper regions of the manor, foraging through the now quiet workshops and dens. He even skulked out to the inner ward again, back to where the masons were repairing the wall, and through the smithy's workshop, which despite the cooling of the evening was still oppressive from the heat radiating from the furnace. In under an hour, he slunk back to the third floor, small linen sack slung over his shoulder filled with supplies. He shut himself back in the same quiet room that looked out at the tower and went to work.

He stripped out of his garments, stored them and his boots in a trunk under the desk, and pulled on some leather riding trousers he'd unearthed. Tailored for a lad, they were snug around the ass and thighs, but he cut a slit down each leg to loosen them and free up his movement. He strapped iron spikes and the sheath for his dagger to his legs with some leather lacings he had found, and to his waist, the small sack of chalk powder he'd lifted from the masons. He bound wider strips of leather around his hands and feet until just the ends of his fingers and toes were exposed. Lastly, he threw a coil of rope over his head to rest on his shoulder and against his side.

He left his tunic off and would remain bare chested. He could handle the cold—he just wanted nothing on that would snag as he climbed or could be seen flapping in the wind. The last thing he needed was to look like a flag hanging from the side of the tower.

It was edging on toward evening when he was finished and satisfied. The sun, swollen and red like a blister in the sky, was descending toward the distant tree line to the west. He climbed out the window and sat on the narrow sill with his legs dangling. From this perch, he waited and watched twilight descend on the city. Once the sun had fully set, he would begin the climb.

Darkness gathered first from the deepest and narrowest streets and rose up slowly like a tide of shadow. Little by little, the buildings were consumed, swallowed up by the dark, as the sky surrendered too and gradually deepened into indigo. Then one by one, lanterns flickered to life—on the manor grounds beneath him and out around the city. It seemed peaceful from here. Quiet and undisturbed. Though he knew all too well what nature of wickedness came with the nighttime. Thievery. Malice. Bedlam. Murder. He knew because much of the time it was him down there in the gutter, ushering in the chaos himself.

But for now, from this high vantage point, he could imagine it was a tranquil city without all the festering ills that invariably lived in its underbelly. A city at peace. A city lumbering off to its bed. Such thoughts were an indulgence, he knew, but it was nice for a change to pretend that the world was not the polluted cistern he knew it to be. It was nice for a change not to be down there wallowing in it waist-deep. He could feign the ignorance so many others possessed, and for the moment, he could ignore the truth of what he was.

But his fantasies of a serene and uncomplicated life darkened along with the western sky, for his heart knew where this night would lead him. Before it was over, he would once again sink deep into the catacombs of the human experience. He would be the shepherd of chaos and death. To complete this job, to rescue this young nobleman, he would have no choice. The night would be filled with bloodshed.

MOUSE MADE one final inventory of his supplies before he hoisted himself up onto the roof and jogged at a crouch to the base of the tower. It loomed over him, encased now in shadow, blocking out most of the blue-black sky.

He shivered and told himself it was the wind. Which was stronger than he liked. And as the night deepened, it would grow stronger still.

From near the top of the tower, a light suddenly spilled from a window. The young nobleman was not ready for bed yet, apparently. He'd be awake when Mouse reached to the top. Good. Lord Garron was about to have a busy night.

Mouse reached up, found his first handhold and a place for his toes, and pulled himself up.

For obvious reasons, night climbs were the worst. It was a lot of groping and fumbling, feeling about in the dark for a suitable ridge or protrusion to grab or put his weight onto. Tonight was no exception.

Belly to the cold rough stone, he worked his way up, inch by painful inch. For a time, the stones were uneven enough for him to find purchase with his fingertips and his toes, but higher up it seemed a better mason was in charge. Mouse found fewer suitable protuberances. With one hand gripping a stone lip, he reached out with the other, blindly searching with his palm until he found something sticking out enough for him to tighten his fingers onto. Then trusting the stone would hold, he pulled himself up a little farther. Each time was more harrowing than the last and set his heart racing.

He reached the first of the horizontal iron bands around the tower's girth. It was thick and smooth, giving his fingers something comfortable to grip for a change. He felt around for a place that he might pass the rope through, but there was no space large enough. The band was flush against the stone. The next one, perhaps.

He pulled himself higher to stand on the iron band for a bit. It gave him a moment to catch his breath and relieve his muscles, which were already tightening and starting to ache. A gust of wind tugged at him mischievously, toying with him. His body tensed, both from the sharp, cold air against his skin, slick with sweat, and from an unexpected splintering of his nerve.

Fuck. This was a bad idea.

He took a moment to loosen the drawstring of the sack at his waist, and he reapplied the chalk to his hands and his toes—tricky to do when standing on a ledge the width of a knuckle. Then onward he crept. He stretched and reached, curling his fingers around the thin grips he could find in the dark; then he pulled his body up by small degrees, inch by inch. A sudden stronger gust brought him to standstill. He shifted his weight, pressed his body to cold stone, and waited for the wind to subside. Another one like that at the wrong time could easily pluck him from the wall. He had to make a change. When the wind died back, he shuffled horizontally, then maneuvered around a corner—another perilous move, but he was now on a side that was better shielded from the wind.

But his new path took him directly through a zone of crumbling masonry. Almost immediately a fragment broke off in his hand as soon as it held his weight. He jolted as he caught himself, his heart leaping into his throat. The shards fell from his hand, and it took what seemed an eternity before he heard it clatter on the roof below. He pushed his cheek to the cold wall, closed his eyes, and forced his breathing under control again.

Fuck.

No choice but to slow his pace further. It was that or head back down—and retreating wasn't an option he was willing to entertain. He'd committed to this and was too far up to turn back now. But more time spent clinging to the wall meant more strain on his hands, arms, and feet. He tried to ignore the cramping in his left hand as he tugged down on his next grip a few times to insure its strength. Then he lugged himself upward again.

His shoulders now burned from the strain. And he was pretty certain that he had cut open the ball of his foot on a sharp edge. It stung when his weight was on it. There was nothing he could do about it now, so he pushed it out of his mind and pressed on. More shards broke loose in his hands, but now he was ready for them. Only it was getting harder to find safe grips. He was reaching farther and farther away from his position.

Then a welcome discovery. He found an area where the mortar between the bricks had fractured and loosened. He removed one of the iron spikes tied to his thigh and with a bit of prodding and jabbing was able to create a gap big enough to wedge the spike on in. Testing it with a downward tug, it held firm. He climbed up and stood on it with one foot for a few minutes, enjoying the relative security of the wider surface. His muscles enjoyed the respite as well. He added a second spike for a handgrip, and took time again to apply more chalk.

After agonizingly slow progress, he reached another of the iron bands and again took some time to gather his strength. And his nerve. In the dark it was hard to gauge, but he believed he'd made it past the worst of it. The masonry seemed stronger above him. A quick glance down told him he was about halfway up the side. Maybe a little more. Around the corner was one of the lower windows. He could hear sudden explosions of raucous laughter. The men were enjoying their time off duty—which hopefully meant plenty of drink.

He wondered whether he could get through that window unseen by the guards. Possible, he thought, but he had no idea if the window led right into their barracks or into the stairwell. And there might be a guard posted outside the cell door as well. Too many unknowns. It was too risky, he decided. He was better off proceeding as planned.

He heard a bell tower far below in the city mark the time. He'd been climbing for more than one hour now. This was taking too long.

Creeping ever closer to the lit window above him—groping, stretching, reaching, and pulling—his arms and shoulders truly burned now. The pads on his fingertips were worn raw, and the arches of his feet were on the verge of cramping. He couldn't take much more of this. Some part of his body was bound to give out.

His fingers discovered another hole between the bricks, and he quickly inserted another spike, wedging it in tight. He was about to test its hold when something crashed against the side of his head. It threw him off-balance. One foot slipped from the narrow lip, and before he could catch himself, his full weight was hanging from the iron spike. He hung suspended for several heart-pounding moments, dangling by one hand. The spike shifted but held firm. He dragged his feet down the wall, looking to gain purchase on anything. His toes caught an edge. It was sharp, but he managed to lift himself enough to grab hold of another stone with his free hand.

He leaned his body against the cold stone while his heart rammed against his sternum. What the fuck was that? Had someone thrown something at him? He looked up, then down. Nothing in sight. Then it happened again, but this time from the opposite direction, and it was preceded by a high squawk. It hit the top of his head with some force, and he felt a sharp scratch on his scalp. Whatever hit him wasn't hard like a rock.

Looking over his shoulder, Mouse caught a glimpse of dark wings reflecting the light from the window. A fucking bird. A sizable one too, judging from the wingspan. He watched as it swooped around in a wide arc for another attack. He must have strayed too close to a nest. The ridiculousness of it almost made him laugh out loud.

"Get away from me, fucker!" he called out.

It squawked back indignantly.

"Don't make me kill you." He pulled the dagger from the sheath and waited for the next pass. He slashed upward as the bird closed in. Despite Mouse's speed, the bird avoided the blade easily and struck him again against the head. Both the impact and his sudden movement upset his balance. His body twisted dangerously, and the spike he'd inserted in the wall shifted again. An attack wasn't going to work. The bird was flying too fast, and it was too dark for him to track it properly.

It made another taunting cry somewhere behind him.

He had no desire to leave the relative security of the spike, but he knew the bird would not relent until Mouse was off the wall. One way or another. It would continue to bombard him, and with his limbs and fingers sinking further into exhaustion, each strike threatened more and more to knock him loose. He pushed upward again. He had to get to that upper window. He was standing on the spike when the bird swooped in close yet again. He ducked his head just in time, and the bird swooshed past without contact.

"Ha! Missed me, fucker!"

The window was close. Only a few more feet....

He scrambled to get higher. The window was getting closer. He could make it as long as there were places to grip. The bird made a shorter circle this time and wasn't going to fall for the same trick again. It made a hate-filled shriek as it dove in. Mouse dropped his head again, but the bird had compensated its flight path and made contact. Hard. Even though he was prepared for it, the blow weakened his already precarious grip on the wall.

Then he was hit again.

It was too soon for the same bird. It could only mean a second angry parent had thrown itself into the fray. "Fuck!" he called out again. The toes of his left foot found a lip to step up onto. He reached up with his right arm, searching with his palm like a blind man scavenging for a dropped coin. Nothing. He could find no purchase for his hand. The window's sill was a mere foot out of reach, but there was no place for him to grab and pull himself up.

The birds made a coordinated assault. One whacked him against his shoulder while the other clouted him again on his head. Even harder this time. Its claw sliced a finger-long gash across his brow, just missing his eye.

His right foot peeled off the edge. As his leg dropped, a sharp protrusion in the rock sliced a gash in his chin. Panicked, he tightened his remaining fingertips and simultaneously flailed his foot and right hand against the wall in search for the edge. But he couldn't find it. His grip was weakening. One by one, the fingers of his left hand popped off the edge. His throat constricted with the sudden realization. He was going down.

After everything he'd been through in his life, after all the times he should have been dead but somehow managed to find a way to survive, it was a fucking bird that accomplished what no one else could. A bird was going to bring about his demise. A fucking gods-cursed bird. The absurdity of it all almost made him want to laugh.

Almost.

Then something had hold of his wrist.

He looked up to a dark silhouette leaning out of the window. "I've got you."

CHAPTER 10

MOUSE WAS hoisted up through the window with little effort, lifted as though he were a child. His rescuer didn't grunt or seem to strain.

The hand around his wrist released him once he was fully through the window and into the chamber. Mouse propped up his torso with hands on his knees and dropped his head, afraid he might pass out. Blackness encircled the boundary of his vision. His heart hadn't yet learned that he wasn't going to plummet to his death. It felt like it might break through his chest.

"Well, this... is a strange... turnabout," he forced out between gasps. "I'm supposed... to be rescuing... you."

He lifted his head and took his first look at the young lord—and any words he planned to say failed him.

Garron had backed away and stood by his bed. He was dressed simply: brown leather trousers cuffed at the knees and an untucked sleeveless tunic, which exposed his powerful arms. The size of his biceps and shoulders certainly explained the ease with which Mouse had been lifted up. He had a full head of thick hair, the color of pitch. It was cropped short, a style currently unfashionable in the capital, but Mouse preferred it to the flowing locks all the foppish lords were now wearing. His face was rugged but striking. He had a thick brow and square jaw, covered now in days of unmanaged growth. His fair skin was flawless and iridescent in the soft candlelight—not a blemish anywhere.

But what captivated Mouse most of all was the man's eyes.

They were a brilliant emerald. Bright, nearly luminescent, and they cut into Mouse with shocking intensity.

"I heard someone," Garron said. He was still wide-eyed and confused. "Someone calling out. I thought at first it was coming from outside the door." As if Mouse needed help with his meaning, he turned and pointed at the solitary door. "From one of the guards."

"Well, you have my thanks all the same. A moment later, and I'd be a stain on Delgan's roof."

"You're bleeding." Garron gestured to his own forehead.

Mouse put a hand to his brow. When he pulled his hand away, it was stained with a crimson smear. Fucking bird. "It's nothing," he said.

"Who are you? Why are you here?"

"Not obvious?" Mouse asked with a tilt of his head.

Garron stared back him.

"All right, then. We'll take this one step at time. People call me Mouse."

"Mouse?"

"Mouse."

"What kind of name is that?"

"It's my name. Moving on to point number two." He took his first sweep of the room. It was a small chamber, but not uncomfortable as far as prisons went. He had a full bed, not some cot or pallet on the floor, and a writing desk and a table with a couple of chairs—as if he were receiving visitors. And the single door. "I've been hired with the singular purpose of getting you out of here."

He moved over to the door, crouched down onto all fours, and put the side of his head to the floor. The gap beneath the door was just large enough to allow torchlight from the other side to shine through. The corridor beyond was well lit, but the light was obstructed along the right side of the gap. As he suspected, a guard was posted out there. He was seated on the floor and leaning against the door, likely asleep, but Mouse wasn't going to take chances.

He returned to Garron and stood in front to him. Garron was a clear head taller than him. Mouse looked up at him and spoke in a low voice. "Your family is concerned about you. They'd like you to come home now."

"My family." Garron repeated tonelessly. His voice had the deep resonance of a drum. He seemed to have recovered from the shock of finding a stranger hanging outside his window and now stood with the straight-backed self-assurance of the aristocracy. He stared down at Mouse for a moment with a questioning look. Mouse stubbornly held his gaze.

Garron's head tilted in curiosity. "You are an uncommon sort. It is not often I encounter someone bold enough to look at me so directly. Even in here."

"We are not at court. Boot licking and servility are luxuries we can ill afford at the moment. I'll make sure to bow properly and avert my eyes once we are out of here. But for now, I'm here to rescue you, not dress you or wipe your bum."

Garron's face darkened at Mouse's crudeness. "Bold *and* cheeky. Impertinence is something you're accused of frequently, I'd wager."

"The least of my crimes, I assure you."

Garron broke off the gaze with pressed lips and moved to the window again. He leaned out over the sill. "You climbed up all that way? How'd you manage that?"

"Not all that well, as you observed yourself."

Garron shook his head in wonder. "And this is what you do? Rescue people?"

From his tone, Mouse couldn't tell if that was just a general question or a judgment on his ability. "Not exactly. But I can promise that I am the most qualified man around for the task." The man was asking a lot of questions. Mouse felt the need to move this along a bit faster. "So, how do you feel about rappelling? I brought rope." He lifted the rope off his shoulder and presented the coil to him. "Coming down with me?"

Garron looked at the rope as if it were a snake, then out the window again.

"Look," Mouse prodded. "The sooner I can get you out of here, the longer it's going to take for them to discover you're gone. And that way is going to be the fastest."

When Garron looked back at Mouse, he was a more than a little pale. "Well," he said, "if that is your plan, I fear you've wasted your time. It's not likely to happen."

"It'll be an easy climb with the rope. You're fit enough, certainly, and I—" The look on Garron's face stopped him short. "Oh, never mind. Stop gawking at me like a startled rabbit. It's clear enough you can't handle heights."

Garron looked wounded. "I...."

Mouse waved him off. "Forget it. I know few who'd have the balls for it, really. I was just being overly optimistic that this might actually be easy. Besides, if you fell to your death, I wouldn't get paid."

Garron frowned. His gaze was narrow, and he gave Mouse a long, measured stare before he spoke again. "So, what, then?"

"We do it the messy way."

"Which means?"

Mouse chose to not hear the question as he looped his way around the space, making a quick survey. It was comfortable enough, not typically what one would think of as a prison cell. No rats, no shackles and so forth. The floor was covered in thick rugs, and heavy blankets were on the bed. Downright cozy. So despite his accused crime, he was being treated with a certain level of respect worthy of his station. Interesting. Considering the accusations against him, the duke could have thrown Garron into the darkest dungeon. Instead he was being treated reasonably well. But regardless of how posh the surroundings, it was still a prison. It had a heavy door locked from the outside. Nothing he could pick.

Garron shadowed Mouse as he moved around the chamber, but at a distance. "What cause do I have to trust you?"

Mouse stopped and looked at him curiously. "How long have you been here?"

Garron folded his arms. "I've started to lose count. Three weeks, I'd wager."

A long time. "And they've told you nothing of what they are going to do with you?"

"No. They accused me of...." He stopped and adjusted what he was going to say. "Of something I didn't do, then threw me in here. Nothing since."

"No trial? No one's arrived to discuss the crime or your sentence?"

Garron shook his head.

Mouse pursed his lips and made a slow nod of understanding. "They don't know what to do with you," he said. "And that will make them nervous."

Lord Delgan had followed whatever instructions he'd received from outside, but now, for whatever reason, they hadn't followed through to the next stage. So what was their plan? Three weeks was enough time for any payment to exchange hands—if that's what was happening. Was the duke waiting for more instructions? Was he feeling squeamish about ending Garron's life? Perhaps he was having second thoughts.

Or did the original plan develop a snag and they were reassessing?

Keeping the young lord here indefinitely wasn't an option. Eventually they would have to act before the situation became untenable. Word of his internment would eventually leak out. "You've been lucky so far," he said, "but you are running out of time. At this point, they are obviously not going to pursue those charges. They would have done so by now. And they are not going to just let you walk out of here either. This will end only one way."

Garron's suspicions seemed to dissolve. His face grew more ashen, and his shoulders fell a bit. "You believe they intend to kill me, then."

Mouse shrugged. "May not have been their initial intent, but…." He let the thought hang in the air a moment. "From what I've managed to dig up, this wasn't Delgan's idea. The strings are being pulled from outside the city. Any notion why someone would want you out of the way?"

Garron's lips tightened. "I can think of one or two," he replied softly but said nothing more. Mouse didn't press it. Garron didn't look like the type to have enemies, but one never could tell.

He stepped closer and looked up into Garron's emerald eyes. "I am going to get you out of here. I won't promise it'll be easy. You should be prepared for a rough go of it."

"What does that mean?"

"It means getting out of this room is the easier part. Getting you safely out of the keep and out of the city will be far more difficult. But," he added with a finger in the air, cutting off Garron's response, "I'm very good at what I do, and I have never failed a job." He chose not to expound on the fact that he'd never attempted to smuggle a living person out of a heavily guarded palace before either. "I'm going to need you to trust me tonight. And do precisely as I ask. Without question or hesitation. Agreed?"

Garron weighed the conditions a moment, then nodded. "As best I am able," he replied. He squared his shoulders in an attempt to appear ready for what was to come, but his eyes betrayed his uncertainty.

Mouse nodded too. "Seems there's only one guard outside. That normal?" He started to unwind the leather binding that surrounded his hand.

"This time of night, yes. Sometimes during the day there are two, but it has been less often lately."

Just as he suspected. Garron was a good little prisoner who didn't cause a fuss. The guards were growing complacent. "I need you to get that guard to open the door."

"How do I do that?"

"Think of a reason. You've been here for weeks and caused no trouble. They'll trust your word."

Garron looked reticent at first but then nodded and strode toward the door. "Guard?" He waited a moment, then knocked and called again. "Guard?"

"What? What d'ya want?" came a muffled voice from the other side. There was a sudden shuffle of moment. He sounded groggy. As Mouse had predicted, he'd been asleep.

Garron looked to Mouse, who nodded in encouragement. "My chamber pot was never emptied today."

"Ah, fuck! You're telling me this now? It can wait 'til fucking morning."

"It's full," Garron called back.

"Fuck!" came the reply. "That's the chambermaid's duty!" There was a pause. Mouse wondered if he'd left to go fetch a chambermaid. But then, "Dammit. All right. Hold on a minute."

Sounds came from the opposite side of the door: thumps, the clank and click of a lock being released, then a scraping sound as the bar was removed from across the door. Mouse positioned himself behind the swing of the door while Garron stepped back so he would be the first thing the guard saw.

The door swung into the room. A standard in jail cells so the prisoner couldn't rush the door.

"Hope you be appreciating this, Your Lordship," the guard grumbled. "Not something I—wha—?"

Mouse shouldered the door closed and before the guard could react, he slipped his thin dirk cleanly into the man's throat. Warmth splattered onto his hand. The guard shuffled sideways and made sickly gurgling sounds as his hands flung to his neck, blood spilling from between his fingers. His eyes rolled back, and he collapsed in a heap. After a few final spasms, he bled out onto the floor and went still.

Garron stumbled away from the corpse and had to steady himself with a hand to the wall. "Gods!" His breath came in quick bursts "What have you done?"

"Keep your voice down," Mouse hissed. He grabbed the guard's legs and dragged the body away from where most of the blood pooled. He rolled the body over. Some blood had splashed on the man's armor, but dark brown leather would mostly wipe clean. "Help me remove his uniform." Mouse knelt on one knee next to the body and began to release the fasteners down the front.

"How could you just kill someone like that?" Garron looked like he was about to be sick.

"He was a guard," Mouse snapped at him. "Employed by the man who imprisoned you." He tugged off the helm and tossed it on the bed—and realized too late his mistake. Garron stared directly at the dead man's face. His young face. Mouse should have left the helm on for now and kept him as a nameless and faceless grunt.

"He didn't deserve that," Garron replied.

"Pull yourself together. What did you think was going to happen?"

Garron shook his head with a tight jaw. His complexion had lost all color. "Not this...."

The pampered fop wasn't going to be any help, Mouse realized. He untied the thongs laced at the shoulder and slipped off the sleeves, then wrestled the thick padded jerkin off the body. "Well, I'm fairly certain that asking politely to be let out isn't going to work. But if you insist on it, we can give it a go and see what happens." He carried the vest to the washbasin to clean the blood splatter covering the front. The water turned instantly into a swirling maelstrom of red.

A hand grabbed him underneath his arm and spun him about.

Garron glared down at him, his eyes narrow and his jaw set. "Not again," he growled through his teeth.

Mouse yanked his arm back but failed to break Garron's powerful grip. Damn, the man was strong. Stronger than he'd thought.

Garron pulled Mouse closer to his face. Mouse felt the hot puffs of his breath against his cheeks. "No more killing."

"If you think you will get out of here—"

"I will not have any deaths on my head. Understood? I would rather meet my fate here."

Mouse stared back defiantly. "You do realize they will be attempting to kill us, right?"

"No matter. They are innocents—"

"Hardly!" Mouse spat back.

"Accept my terms, or leave the way you came! I will not tolerate such... such wanton disregard for life."

Mouse yanked his arm again, this time with more force and a twist to break the hold. His arm came free, and he stepped back and took a defensive stance. If Garron went to grab for him again, he would be ready. He *should* just leave, he thought. Keep the coin he had and leave this coddled idealistic dandy to his fate. All he needed to do was report back he couldn't spring him, or it was too late.

But that would mean admitting a failure. His first notch in the opposite column. Something he'd never had to do. And it meant giving up on his chance for a king's pardon, his sole hope of removing the threat that ever loomed over his father's head.

"Careful, Your *Lordship*," he spat the title with clear disdain. "I am sorely tempted to take you up on that offer. I am your last and only chance. You are a quandary Duke Delgan will not want to suffer with for much longer."

Garron looked down at the dead man at their feet. A wave of sadness washed over his face. "I don't care."

Seven hells! Mouse knew he was going to regret this.

"If you expect *me* to passively submit.... If my life is in danger—"

"Then defend yourself!" He locked his eyes into Mouse's. The fury behind those emerald orbs almost made Mouse step back farther. "But no more of... of this. Nothing so cold-blooded." With a rigid jaw and tight fists, Garron's body shook. His voice took on a deep intensity that punctuated his resolve. "Swear it to me now. If you comprehend the meaning of honor, swear it."

Despite himself, that stung, and anger surged up in him. He was honorable, dammit—in his way.

"Swear it!" Garron growled again.

Mouse sighed. "Very well. I swear it. But this severely cuts our chances of success, you realize."

"If it means never witnessing something as atrocious as this again, so be it. What kind of man are you?"

"One who gets things done. It's a rough world outside your gilded chambers, Your Lordship."

Garron held Mouse's hard stare for several heartbeats. Then the fire in his eyes faded, revealing something deeper beneath. Sadness? Resignation? His shoulders lost their tension and dropped a fraction as he turned away from Mouse and the body on the floor. "Save your sanctimonious rhetoric, scoundrel," he replied softly. "I am well versed on the brutality of this world."

CHAPTER 11

GARRON GRABBED a mug of something off the table, studied its contents a moment, then drained it. His face had turned hard and unreadable. "So, what now?" he asked, looking at nothing in particular.

Mouse tossed the jerkin over to him. It landed by his feet. "Start by putting on his guard uniform."

"What?" Garron scooped up the vest, wadded it into a ball, and threw it back at Mouse. "Forget it!"

"Don't be a prude, Lordship." Mouse walked the jerkin over to him this time. He extended his hand with it hanging from his fingertips. "I cleaned off most of the blood. And it's not going to fit me."

Garron made a face as he took the garment. He slipped it on over his tunic and started to buckle it up over his chest.

"Wait," Mouse said. "You'll need a tunic with sleeves." With a tilt of his head, he indicated the dead man. "Have one?"

Garron nodded and went over to a small chest at the foot of the bed and pulled out a clean white tunic. "I was saving this," he said, more to himself than to Mouse, "for my eventual release."

Mouse stole a glimpse at Garron's torso as he stripped off the old tunic. As Mouse suspected, the man's chest was as perfectly proportioned as his arms. He had a swath of short hair that followed the inner contour of his breasts with a dark line that ran down the length of his abdomen to disappear below the waistline of his trousers.

"What are you going to have me do?" Garron asked as he buckled down the front of the jerkin.

Mouse brought over the sleeves and gestured for Garron to slip his arm through. "We'll get to that," he said, as he laced the thong through the grommets at the shoulder of the jerkin. "But you're going to have to pocket that accent of yours. It's too formal. Practice slurring your words, blending them together. Say something."

Garron turned to glare down over his shoulder at him. "I think you're a murderous, cold-hearted villain."

"Your diction is still too proper. Articulate less. Round out the vowels. Like this, 'I think you're a privileged, self-righteous prat that is damn lucky I've arrived in time.'"

Garron scowled and looked the other way. Mouse had to fight down a smirk. Clearly, His Lordship was not used to being spoken to with such brazen insolence. *Well, get used to it*, Mouse thought. *I'm not being paid to handle you with white gloves.*

"Try this," he said. "Repeat it just like I say it. 'His Lordship's claimin' he nev'r got no sup t'night.' Make the lordship bit sound like an insult."

Garron repeated it.

"Better." Mouse said the phrase again and made Garron repeat it twice more. "All right, you're getting it. When do the guards change?"

"I don't know. I'm always on this side of the door when it happens."

Fair enough. "My guess is not 'til morning." With both sleeves reattached, Mouse retrieved the guard's boots and handed them off to Garron one at a time.

"This'll never work," Garron said. "They'll recognize me."

"They believe you're still secured on this side of the door. They won't see you at all."

"Then they'll at least recognize that I'm not one of *them*."

Mouse sighed. "You are giving them too much credit. Look. People don't notice changes they don't expect to see. You're the right size—I'd do it if I was, but I'm not. You'll have the helm on which covers a good part of your face. And you'll be likely waking them up on top of it."

"It's late. Won't they get suspicious? I would have said something earlier."

"If they're all asleep, they will have no idea what time it is. It could be just after dusk for all they know."

"That's a lot of 'ifs' this plan is balanced on."

Mouse smiled. "That makes it exciting! Just make sure they send for a wench to bring you a meal."

"I don't see how she's going to help us."

"Don't worry about that right now."

Garron's eyes narrowed in sudden seriousness. "You swore me an oath. You're to honor that? No harm is to come to that maidservant."

"Gods! Don't be daft!" Mouse went to the door, listened first, then opened it up. Outside was a narrow corridor lit by a solitary wall sconce opposite the door. Mouse slunk out with his weight on the front of his feet and followed the short distance to where the corridor turned, and peered around. A stairwell descended fifteen or so steps to a landing at the corner of the tower and then continued down along the outside wall.

He tiptoed back. "Halfway down the tower… three, maybe four turns down, there'll be a chamber. Usually used for storage, but also additional guard support if needed. Do you remember seeing it when you were brought up?" Garron nodded. "Should have two, maybe three guards at the most."

"How can you know that?"

"This isn't the only tower in the world, Lordship! They all function pretty much the same. Haven't you ever explored the towers of your own family's manor?"

"What if this goes wrong?"

"Then you won't find me waiting here for you when they drag you back up in shackles." It was a jest, but Garron clearly did not find the humor in it. "Stop fretting. Just do as we practiced and it'll work. See to it they fetch that wench. Ready, Lordship?"

"Stop… stop calling me that."

Mouse narrowed his eyes at him. "That *is* your title, is it not?"

"You make it sound like…." He sighed. "I would just prefer you not use it."

"How would you prefer I address you, then?"

Garron shook his head, a look of frustration on his face. "Just… just Garron. Call me Garron."

"As you wish," Mouse replied with a shrug. "Now, we've wasted enough time. Get your ass down there and make it convincing."

MOUSE STOOD at the first landing, straining to listen. He could just hear them but couldn't make out the words. In truth, he was far less confident than he let on. Garron's highborn inflection was too deeply inset to be masked entirely, and if any of the guards had more sense than a cabbage, he'd be found out. Which meant Mouse would have to act. And act fast.

On the balls of his feet, he stole down to just past the next landing. The conversation drifted up to him, resonating off the walls. He could make out the individual words. Garron sounded gruff, which was good.

At least he thought it was Garron. Gods help him if he overplayed it somehow and set them off. He kept an ear for fast-moving feet on stone just in case and held his fingers on the hilt of his blade.

The discussion was brief, followed by the clap of boots on the stairs. Mouse tensed, waiting. Then Garron rounded the corner from the landing below. He climbed the stairs at a hurried pace and pulled off his helm.

The wry grin on the lord's face told Mouse the answer he sought, but when they were both back in the chamber and the door was closed, he asked anyway. "Well?"

"Appears they're going to summon a maidservant for me."

Mouse did his best to mask his relief. "Not a surprise," he answered coolly, returning to the chamber. "People are daft, as a rule."

Garron's satisfied smile faded some. "That's a grim view of the world."

"Well, you said it yourself. I'm cold-hearted."

"Perhaps," he said with a challenging glare, "my performance was just that convincing."

"Doubtful," Mouse responded glibly. "More likely they had too much drink, and they wouldn't have noticed if you sang it to them in four-stanza verse."

That killed what remained of the smile, which satisfied Mouse.

Garron dropped the helm on the table. "I don't understand how this ruse is going to get us out of here?"

"Patience, Lor—" He caught himself and smiled impishly. "Garron." He picked up the helm and pushed it against Garron's chest until he put his hands on it again. "I hate spoiling surprises." He actually didn't want Garron overthinking his plan and cultivating any doubts about it. The less he knew in advance, the better. "Now, back out there and reprise your winning performance as a guardsman of the manor one more time." He put a hand to Garron's back and guided him back toward the door, unable to ignore how solid it felt beneath the layer of leather. "Lock the door. When the wench arrives, admit her."

Once Garron was out of the chamber again, Mouse set to work quickly. He dragged the body of the guard to the opposite side of the room and threw a blanket over it. Then he slid one of the rugs over the large bloodstain on the floor. He finished just as he heard Garron fumbling with the keys to unlock the door again. Mouse dashed behind the door as it swung open.

"Your Lordship?" came a quiet voice. "I have the meal you requested. Lordship?"

Mouse waited until she was fully into the room. He moved fast before she could process was happening. In one swift movement he had her from behind, one hand around her waist pulling her against him, the other over her mouth. The tray she was carrying flew from her grasp and clattered to the floor, making a mess of gruel everywhere. She flailed in her panic, but Mouse held her firm.

"Quiet now, poppet," he whispered into her ear. "No harm's to come to you, so easy now."

She struggled harder, wiggling and kicking, but she was a slight thing and no match for Mouse's strength. Soon, her energy flagged, and the fight in her weakened.

Garron came in from the corridor and eased the door closed behind him. As he pulled off the helm again, the wench clearly recognized him. She froze a moment as the realization of what was happening must have dawned on her—then she resumed her struggle, but with less fervor.

"He speaks truly," Garron told her. "We will not harm you." Unconsciously, his eyes shifted around the room looking for the body. "You have my word as a nobleman."

Mouse pursed his lips at him. *And what is that worth,* he wondered. It was a nice touch—the girl noticeably calmed against him—but gods help them if he went around making that promise to everyone.

"I'm going to pull my hand away now, dove," Mouse told her. "No screaming. Understood?"

She nodded.

Mouse released his hand from her mouth. The girl didn't make a peep.

Ah, refreshing. Someone who understood how this works and didn't do something heroic or stupid.

"See?" Mouse said. He kept his arm around her waist but relieved the pressure. "We've no desire to see you ill-treated."

Mouse felt her shoulders and back relax a degree. "What... what do you want from me?"

"A pittance, dove. I just need you to do me the smallest of favors. I'm going to need you to slip out of that shift for me." Her eyes widened and her body stiffened. "Ah now, don't you let that mind go places," he added quickly. "Our friend here spoke true. Neither of us is going to abuse you. You're pretty and all, only not my type. It's your shift I want, not your dignity."

She nodded and her body loosened again. "All right. If that is your promise."

"It is. Now, I can tell you're a clever thing, so I needn't explain to you what's happening here. Yes?"

Again, she nodded.

"Excellent. I don't want you to face any trouble on our account. It wouldn't do to have them think you did anything to help us. So a second thing I need you to do is let us tie you up for a bit. Now, I know what you're thinking. But it won't be long, I promise. You'll be discovered up here in no time."

She thought about it a moment, her eyes shifting from Mouse to Garron and back again. She quivered a little but nodded her consent.

Mouse smiled at her. "See, Lord Garron? And you said the pretty ones were unreasonable."

Her cheeks reddened, and a small smile lifted one side of her mouth. Mouse could see it in her eyes: She was starting to buy into this as some sort of adventure. Fear had segued into exhilaration. This would be a story she could relay to her friends in the kitchens: how she was abducted by savage killers and she was lucky to get out of it unscathed.

She was a model of cooperation. Her shift was off almost immediately, and she stood there between them in feminine smallclothes. She covered some of her more exposed places, but it was more out of habit than any real modesty or embarrassment. She stole glances at Mouse's bare chest, which told Mouse that she was quietly hoping the two might actually make a little time to ravage her anyway. Mouse guided her to the bed and had her sit on the edge. "It won't hurt, will it?" she asked.

He winked at her. "Not the slightest." He tied her hands behind her back—nothing too tight or uncomfortable. He held a glass of water to her lips.

"So you don't get thirsty, dove," he told her and tapped a finger to her nose.

She giggled at him and took a sip. Then he removed her bonnet and brought a strip of cloth up over her eyes. She tensed with sudden anxiety. "Must you?"

"I'm sorry, but yes," he cooed. "It'll be quite fine. Just lie there and go to sleep until you're found."

He guided her down onto the bed. "Comfortable?"

"Quite," she answered.

"Wonderful," he said, and stroked her hair. "Now make sure you tell them what horrible and dangerous brutes we are, and how you feared for your life."

She giggled.

Mouse looked over to Garron and rolled his eyes. Garron, who watched him with arms crossed, stared back with a tight brow.

Mouse put a finger to his lips as he stood up. He tied the rope he had brought along with him to the leg of the bed, flung open the shutters of a different window, and tossed the loose end out the opening. The rope uncoiled as if fell to the dark depths below.

Garron looked alarmed and scurried over to Mouse's side. "I thought—"

Mouse shoved his palm over his mouth. "But they won't know that, will they?" he mouthed with an arched brow. He pulled the girl's shift over his head, wiggled his arms into the sleeves, and tugged at the sides until it hung properly. It was a bit short on him but otherwise fit rather well.

Garron was at his side again. "That is not going to work," he whispered furiously. "And if you're caught dressed that way—"

"Oh, gods help me!" Mouse shook his head. "Lord Delgan's morality laws are the least of my concerns at this point. And besides—" He pulled the bonnet onto his head. "—I make a very convincing wench."

From the look on Garron's face, Mouse could tell he agreed. "It's unseemly."

"Hardly. Remind me later to share with you a story or two about what true indignity looks like."

He moved to stand by the window with the rope. "Okay, Your Lordship," he said in his full voice. "Ready? Now, like I told you, lower yourself down slowly." He banged the shutter a few times. "Careful now. That's it."

Garron watched Mouse's performance with folded arms. He closed his eyes and shook his head.

"But it's so high!" Mouse replied in his best noble accent. Then he changed back to his own voice. "It's all right, your Lordship, I have you. You'll be safely down in no time. That's right. Slowly now."

Garron scowled at him, which made Mouse almost laugh out loud. He shooed the young lord out the door, grabbed the tray from the floor—

always have a tray on hand—then followed him out. Once out of the chamber, Mouse closed the door as gently as he could and locked it with an audible click. Garron cringed next to him.

"Relax. She believes we went out the window," he whispered. "She won't even notice that."

"I still don't see the point of the rope...."

"They'll be operating on a faulty assumption. Which means they will hopefully be looking for us where we are not." He started down the stairs. "Come on. We have to make good use of the time we have. We are not even close to being out of this."

CHAPTER 12

MOUSE HOPED they had until morning before the alarm was raised. Realistically, they had a few hours. At best.

The girl's long absence would be noticed by some old hag in the kitchen that kept her staff on a short lead. It was only a matter of time before someone would be sent off to investigate.

So, first order of business—get Lord Green Eyes as far from the fucking tower as possible before that happened.

They tiptoed down the stairs as fast as they dared. At the guardroom door, Mouse peered around the corner. Two guards, both sprawled out on wooden pallets, dead to the world and snoring happily. An empty flagon of wine was on the floor between them. Mouse looked at Garron and gestured with his head that it was safe to proceed. Normally, Mouse would have crept into the room and made extra certain they would not be coming for them later, but he kept to the agreement he made to Garron, and he let them be.

He was, if nothing else, a man of his word.

Or at least tried to be.

Downward they went, Mouse leading the way. They passed one locked door, which Mouse forced himself to ignore. He hadn't foreseen a chamber being there. Not knowing what was behind the door needled at him like an itch. They turned another corner, and the inner wall was gone. The stairwell opened up—it still hugged the outer wall but was open to the center. The drop to the base of the tower was at least fifteen paces.

Garron subconsciously moved to the wall side of the stairs away from the edge, steadying himself with a hand to the stone. The man's squeamishness around heights was no small matter. How was he ever to get him over the outer wall that surrounded the keep when just an open stairwell made him dizzy?

He'd have to work that out later. Right now, the priority was getting somewhere out of sight for when the manor discovered his absence.

"Stay here," he whispered. "Count to one hundred after I'm gone—"

"Where are you going?"

"Relax. I'll be waiting for you around the corner of the next corridor. There are guards just outside." He pointed at the opening at the bottom of the stairs. The guards had left the doorway into the tower open after the serving wench had been sent up, which was a strong indication of their complacency. From Garron and Mouse's angle on the stairs, they could make out one of the guard's legs in the hall. "It'll look suspicious if we walk out together."

Sudden unease widened Garron's eyes.

Just the notion of Mouse leaving him unattended put Garron near panic. Now free from his confinement, Garron was gripped by the concern of possible recapture. Mouse had inspired some measure of confidence, it seemed.

He resisted a sigh of impatience. That wouldn't do, he told himself. He needed the man calm and compliant, and acting snappish or frustrated would be counterproductive. He would have to find a way to exercise more patience. This was the sort of thing Mouse did regularly, he reminded himself. It was all quite new to the nobleman.

He stepped closer and kept his voice calm. "Follow me out after you've counted to one hundred. Just walk out with intention, like you belong here. Like you've done it every day for weeks. They have no reason to suspect anything. If they say something, just play along."

Garron nodded, still looking uncertain.

"Just remember to talk like one of us lowlifes."

Garron's expression darkened. "Do I really sound like that much of a prig?"

"No more than every other high born in the world, Lordsh—oops, sorry!" In truth, Lord Green Eyes was very nearly tolerable. Over the years, he had suffered far worse arrogance and entitlement from various nobles, but he wasn't about to let him off the hook yet. "One hundred," he reminded him with a pointed look. He adjusted the bonnet on his head, smoothed the shift on his front, then skipped down the stairs brandishing his tray in front of him.

He stepped out into the corridor. Either side of the doorway was flanked with a guard. Two more faced him along the opposite wall. Thankfully, the lighting was poor. Only a single sconce bore a lit torch, and it was nearing its end of pitch. The guards all looked up and turned to him as he crossed the threshold. One instinctively lowered his hand down to the hilt of his short sword.

Mouse kept his head low in a demure and respectful manner and offered a gentle curtsy.

"Up there awhile, you were," one commented.

Mouse shrugged and made a high-pitched titter into his shoulder but said nothing. He scurried away down the corridor.

"Little trollop," Mouse heard one of them grumble. "Looks like she's serving up more than gruel to that Dionantian prig."

"I'll take a bowl of what's she's offering."

"Ho there, we're all hungry too. When do we get our share?"

They all laughed.

Mouse rounded the corner out of sight of the guards and waited. It was late—the corridors were quiet and would likely stay that way. As he counted down in his head, he pulled out his dagger. He didn't expect trouble, but it always paid to be prepared. The guards made quiet banter among themselves, then....

"Hey. Where're you off to?" one of the guards exclaimed.

Mouse stiffened and leaned around the corner. Garron was out of the tower and strolling down the corridor. He moved straight-backed and rigid, and his gate was paced too fast. He looked guilty of something, like someone not wanting to be noticed but wanting to get somewhere else quickly. He slowed but didn't stop. "Urgent message for the chancellor," he called back over his shoulder. "From His Lordship!"

Mouse laughed inwardly. Garron spoke with the same intonation that he himself would have said it. The prat was learning after all.

"What kind of message?" one of the guards called after him.

"For his ears only, you dullard!" Garron snapped.

Mouse was impressed. Garron understood that none of those standing guard would know why the prisoner was even here. Though there'd be rumors, they would assume it was something political. Garron rounded the corner, joining Mouse. He exhaled heavily and slumped against the wall.

Mouse smiled at him. "Appears you're learning a few new skills." He clapped the lord on the shoulder. "Congratulations. First step accomplished. You are officially out of your tower."

Garron scowled inwardly. "But for how long."

"Permanently. At least as long as I have anything to say about it."

"That supposed to be comforting?"

"Come on." Mouse started down the corridor.

Garron followed at his heels. "Where to?"

"Somewhere they don't expect you to go?" In other words, he wasn't sure yet.

MOUSE ESTIMATED it was after midnight, but he would keep his ear open for a crier or a bell to give him a better indication. In a few hours at most, the manor would come awake and residents would filter out into the corridors like water filling the gutters after a spring shower. Earlier risers—the cooks, stable hands, maidservants, and valets preparing their master's and lady's garments for the day—they were the eyes that potentially could remember them after Garron's absence was noticed and someone sounded the alarm.

Mouse knew it wouldn't take much deductive power to work out their method of escape once the tied-up wench and the dead guard were discovered in the tower. The rope out the window would stall them at best, but a short debriefing with the guardsman at the base of the tower would unearth the truth of how they escaped. When that happened, it made their current disguises useless. Best to ditch the outfits now. First stop—the storeroom where he'd stashed the other clothes.

He led Garron down the corridor to the small office he'd infiltrated earlier. They ducked inside, and Mouse locked the door with his tools.

"Handy skill," commented Garron.

"You have no idea," Mouse replied.

Garron pulled off the helm and tucked it under his arm. He took in the chamber with a curious expression while Mouse rummaged in the corner to retrieve the clothes he had stashed there earlier. "So do you have an actual plan?" Garron asked.

Mouse deposited the clothes and boots on the small desk. "You sabotaged the one I had in mind—thanks equally to both your high morals and fear of high places. A good plan, mind you. I'm being forced to improvise."

"So... that's a no."

Mouse gave him an exasperated look. "This is not my first day at the tourney. I have more than a few tricks—" He stopped.

He heard something—a sound he was all too familiar with. Damn.

He grabbed Garron by the front of the jerkin with both hands. "I apologize for what is about to happen."

"What—"

"Play along!" Mouse pulled Garron toward him pressed his lips firmly against his.

Garron's entire body stiffened. He made a startled grunt in this throat and on instinct tried to pull back, but Mouse held him firm. The helm dropped to the floor.

They heard the lock release, and the creak of the hinges as the door was pushed open.

Garron must have understood, for he stopped struggling. Mouse threw his hands around Garron's neck, who in turn slipped his arms around Mouse's waist and pressed back against Mouse's kiss with greater force. Gods, he had soft lips....

Behind Garron, someone made a sudden gasp. "Oh!"

Garron pulled his face from Mouse and shot an angry look over his shoulder. "What the fuck are you doing? Can't you see I'm a little busy here?"

Mouse ducked his head into Garron's chest so the intruder could only see the bonnet on his head and not his face. He made a convincing giggle.

"Ho, ho!" came the reply. A man's voice. "Sorry 'bout that, mate! I'll come back later. Don't let the night captain catch you, though. Or the cook! They'll have your balls after the wench's done with them."

"Just bugger off!" Garron's lips returned to Mouse's with relish, and they continued their performance. Garron's mouth opened, but Mouse fought the urge to give in further and thrust his tongue past the opening. The bristles on Garron's face burned with sweet friction on the skin around his mouth. He could picture himself doing this for a long time—in fact, felt himself respond and start to swell. The man knew how to kiss, that was certain. And Garron's body felt solid and warm against him. Moments later he heard the door close and the latch click. But the kiss continued. It was Mouse who broke contact.

"I believe he's gone," he said, a little breathless. A feeling of relief washed over him. If it had gone on much further, Mouse might have lost control and crossed over the line.

Garron released his tight hold on him and stepped back, his cheeks betraying his embarrassment. "Oh. Sorry. I was just making certain." He used the knuckle of his forefinger to wipe the corners of his mouth.

Mouse was caught at a loss for words, which was new for him. He turned his body away so Garron wouldn't see how the front of the shift protruded conspicuously. "We better move on quickly," he managed to choke out.

"Sure," Garron replied. "Of course." He was trying to sound nonchalant, but Mouse could sense the tension in his voice. An awkwardness had materialized, like some invisible curtain that separated them.

For Mouse, the play-acting had somehow slipped into something real. The sensation of that kiss lingered and filled his head like an intoxication. Dammit all! Had Garron sensed that? Did he sense how much Mouse actually enjoyed that? Had he felt Mouse's stupid fucking cock pressing up against his leg?

His back to Garron, he pulled the shift off over his head. He fought the urge to see what Garron was doing. A part of him fantasized that Garron was watching him undress, but he didn't dare turn to look. His cock was surging even bigger at the mere thought.

Fuck! Get a grip on yourself!

Gods, when did he start losing control? The man was a nobleborn— an entitled prig that shat gold and pissed fine wine. And here Mouse was snogging him like a drunkard in the back of a tavern. He loathed the nobility. He despised the injustice of their power and influence, their pomposity and superiority, their shameless self-interest while good people toiled beneath them with no hope of a better life. In his privileged life, Garron had never known strife or hardship. Like all his kind, he surely treated the common folk no different than the others: like shit stuck to his heel. So what in the seven hells was his cock thinking?

He pulled on the blue breeches. They helped to mask the effect at his groin, but he tied them tighter to be sure. Then he quickly donned the rest of the garments and tugged on the boots. He shoved the shift, bonnet, and tray behind the crates.

Garron was leaning against the wall, arms folded across his chest and staring downward at his own feet.

"Ready?" Mouse asked. He was surprised to hear a measure of anger in his tone.

"I suppose. But where are we going?"

"First and foremost, I want to get you out of that guard uniform—" He closed his eyes and cringed at how that sounded. "And into something they won't be looking for," he added hastily.

"You have something in mind?"

"Always. Don't forget your helm."

Garron scooped it up from the floor as Mouse opened the door to peer outside in the corridor. All clear. He was just about to slip out when the loud clanging of a bell rang out into the night and throughout the manor, followed by more bells. Someone had raised the alarm. Garron's absence had been discovered.

Fuck. Fuck. Fuck.

CHAPTER 13

MOUSE KNEW they had to act fast.

He was nothing if not flexible. In his vocation, it was often necessary to shift tactics. He worried about Garron, though. Lord Green Eyes would be unaccustomed to this sort of pressure and could come unnerved. Something neither of them could afford.

"Does *that* mean what I think it means?" Garron asked.

"Come on."

"But—"

Mouse grabbed him by the front of his jerkin and pulled him into action. Time here was vital. They had ten… maybe fifteen minutes. Already people around the manor were scurrying to report in—many being brought out of a sound sleep—in order to find out what the alarm was about. But it would take a little time for the news to break and the details to spread.

Time he needed to use to his advantage.

Finding a new way out of the manor had become a secondary priority. Right now, they had to keep a step ahead of the search. He'd figure out the escape later.

He jogged down the corridor, Garron on his heels. A sleepy older man still in his nightshirt rounded the corner in a huff and seeing Garron, grabbed him roughly by the arm as he tried to pass. "What's this about, boy? We under attack?"

Garron's eyes widened in alarm for a moment. He shifted his gaze toward Mouse, looking for aid. "Uh… I know not, m'lord," he managed to blurt out. He winced, realizing he hadn't adjusted his diction and sounded too high born for a guardsman. He adjusted, adding, "Only just reportin' to the night captain, now."

The man released him with an irritated grunt. "Well, find out and get back to me," he grumbled. He didn't seem to notice the discrepancy in Garron's voice. "Better be a fucking invasion, waking me up like this from a dead sleep. I'll be in my chambers." Without looking back, he shuffled back down the corridor from where he came.

Garron turned to Mouse with an arched brow, a surprised expression that said, "Could it really have been that easy?"

Mouse shrugged, then signed for him to follow.

No one else challenged them. Everyone spilling into the corridors was scrambling to get somewhere in response to the alarm—in that, Garron and Mouse fit it perfectly well. Mouse led him down a stairwell, through a main artery of the manor, then off into a darkened wing. He located the door he wanted at the far end of a corridor, and with quick work with his tools, he unlocked a storeroom. They slipped in and shut the door behind them.

Garron leaned his back against the door, gulping in heavy breaths.

"All right. We're going to have to do this quick," he said digging out a leather pack from the inside of an empty crate.

Garron could not hide his surprise. "Where did that come from?"

"I'm a good planner." From the corner, he pulled out a bucket of water. "Take off the jerkin and tunic and…." He made a quick scan of the room. He lifted the empty crate and positioned it in front of a lone barrel against the wall. He considered the height with his head tilted and nodded in satisfaction. "And sit there," he added, pointing to the crate.

Garron eyed him suspiciously. "What for?"

Mouse pulled out his dagger—his father's dagger. It was the sharpest one he had. Garron's eyes widened a fraction when he saw it. "Relax. That beard of yours hasn't been cut in three weeks. They'll be combing the shadows for a shaggy escaped prisoner. Not a neatly trimmed aristocrat."

Garron still looked wary but started to unclasp the front of his jerkin. "If you stashed away a looking glass somewhere, I can shave myself."

"We don't have that kind of time. I will shave you much faster than you'll be able to do it yourself. Besides this blade is sharper than anything you've ever used."

A group of heavy footfalls clapped on the stone floor of the hallway and seemed to stop just outside the door. Booted. Clearly guardsmen. Mouse held up his hand, but Garron instinctively knew to freeze in place. Both stared at the latch of the door, waiting for it to move. Mouse repositioned the dagger in his hand. He could hear the muffled voices of the men outside though he couldn't make out any of the words.

Then the footsteps resumed and faded.

Garron looked pale as he exhaled slowly. Mouse gave him a knowing look with a single raised eyebrow to emphasize his point. Time was short. Guardsmen could start sweeping chambers and storerooms at any time.

"Let's get to this," he said.

"Have you ever shaved someone before?" Garron asked in a voice that was nearly a whisper.

"Many times." It was exactly three, but Mouse wasn't about to confess that. He set the bucket within reach and climbed up on the barrel with his legs spread apart.

Garron hesitated as if still uncertain, but with a barely perceivable nod he stripped off the garments, once again exposing his perfectly formed torso. The man's tone was fair like white marble, and his shape seemed to have been sculpted by a gifted artist.

"Sit." Mouse pointed at the crate with the blade. "And lean your head back against the barrel."

"You sure about this?"

"Trust me."

Garron complied, lowering onto the crate and tilting his head back. His shoulders were tight and his hands clenched. "I still think it would be easier if I shaved myself," he grumbled.

Mouse guided Garron's head back a little further to lift the chin. His hair was soft. Mouse resisted the urge to run his fingers through it. "Well, then I would be denied the joy of putting a knife to a nobleman's throat, now wouldn't I?"

Feeling the weight of Garron's head against his lap, another fear suddenly occurred to him. Gods, what if his fucking prick decided to act up again? It apparently had a mind of its own lately. All he needed was for it to start poking Garron in the back of the head.

He shoved those thoughts back and focused on the task at hand. He began on the jawline, dipping the blade in the water and making short strokes upward on the face. He didn't run the edge directly against the skin, but instead kept Garron's beard short and neatly cropped. Cleanly shaven might draw attention. A day or two's worth of stubble would raise fewer suspicions. But the neck would have to be clean. A good shave always had a clean neck.

"Lift your chin more."

"You have a steady hand," Garron said through his teeth, as Mouse made slow deliberate scrapes up his throat.

"So I've been told." Mouse dipped the dagger back into the bucket and spun it about in the water.

"Glad you're here to rescue me and not kill me."

"Well, we'll just see how much gold Duke Delgan is willing spend to get you back."

It was a joke, obviously. Mouse would never switch sides when he was hired for a job. It was bad for business. If word got out that he was not trustworthy and his allegiance could be easily swayed with a few more coins, the jobs would quickly dry up.

But Garron didn't know that.

As Mouse moved to bring the dagger back to Garron's neck, Garron shoved the arm away and sprang to his feet. He backed away and looked down at Mouse with sudden fire in his eyes.

Mouse put his hands on his knees and let his chin drop. He knew better than to say something like that. Even in jest. He needed Garron to trust him fully if he was going to get him out of here alive. "I'm sorry," he said. "That was a stupid thing to say."

Garron glared back at him with tight lips, looking a little foolish with one half of his beard long, and the other neatly cut.

Mouse looked up and held Garron's hard gaze. "I know you don't view me as having much honor, and you have no cause to believe me. But I would never betray you."

Garron didn't reply, his expression hard.

Mouse took in a long breath; then he held up the dagger for Garron to see. "This dagger belonged to my father. It is all I possess of my family, from my life before. It is the only thing that has any meaning to me. On this blade, I swear to you. I will remain loyal to you and my mission until the end. If you will it, the knife shall be put in your keeping until you are safe from here." Mouse extended the dagger to Garron.

Garron took the blade from Mouse's hand and examined it. For several moments he was quiet. His expression changed—softened. The heat of his anger tempered into something more pensive. "This symbol, etched onto the metal of the blade...."

"I know not what it is," Mouse replied. "I have tried to find its meaning but cannot."

Garron nodded gently, looking thoughtful. He handed the knife back. "I believe you," he said. "I have no need to hold the knife."

Mouse took it back, unable to veil his surprise. He had great confidence in his own power to influence but still expected some uncertainty from Garron, some resistance surely. He did not expect blind acceptance on his word alone. Garron seemed the trusting sort, but not foolish or naïve.

Garron seemed unfazed as he returned to the crate and leaned his head back into Mouse's lap without a word.

Neither spoke while Mouse resumed the task.

Feeling the weight of him against his legs and the supple skin of his cheek against his hand, Mouse felt an inexplicable sadness well up from inside his gut. He knew not where it came from, but it swelled quickly and settled like drying resin around his heart. What could have caused Garron's quick trust in him? It felt undeserved. Unearned. Mouse had jeopardized everything with a single flippant comment, an amateurish mistake, and Garron had no reason to believe it was only a joke. But he did. Mouse was comfortable with the suspicion and distrust from others. Someone trusting him at his word was… unsettling.

And why did it matter so much what this noble thought of him?

GARRON MADE a quick rinse of his face with water from the bucket. "Now I really do wish I had a looking glass. If only to make sure you didn't make me look like a buffoon."

Mouse climbed off the barrel and put his ear to the door. For the moment, it seemed quiet out there, but that could change quickly. "Don't be vain," he replied dryly.

In truth, he looked dashing. Mouse was a little concerned that his good looks were going to attract too much attention. People were going to notice and remember seeing him. He lifted the leather sack of supplies from the floor and dropped it onto the barrel. He reached in and pulled out long black vestments, a colored sash, and a black four-cornered hat. "Now, put on this."

Garron held the garment up by the shoulders in front of him to inspect it. "A prelate's robes? Do I strike you as someone to take up the righteous path?"

"Hardly, but who's going to question you?" In his experience, religious figures got unmitigated access around places like this.

"How in the seven heavens did you acquire it?"

"It's amazing what you can find lying about when you do a bit of snooping." Mouse pulled out a novice's robe for himself. "Found them in a trunk of some nobleman's antechamber. Likely costumes for some fetishy sex games. But they're authentic, which is important." He unclasped and peeled off his jerkin and shoved it into the sack. "Quick now," he urged with a double snap of his fingers. "Your tunic and trousers can stay on under the vestments, nothing more. Especially not the boots."

Garron paused from pulling on his tunic to give Mouse a questioning look.

"Shepherds only wear cloth slippers," Mouse told him. "No hard heels."

Garron nodded and pulled the black vestments on over his head. It hung loose around the neck. "I think there are latches in the back," he said, turning around.

"Right." Mouse fastened the clasps behind his neck and between his shoulder blades. He then helped him position the hat on his brow, tucking in the stray hairs. He arranged the purple sash over Garron's shoulder and down the front, making certain the runic symbol of each god was prominently and correctly displayed, then took a step back to scrutinize the finished product.

"How do I look?"

"Eh," Mouse replied with a shrug. "A little young to be donning the purple, but no one will question you."

"You certain of that?"

"Have I yet to lead you astray?"

"We've only been out for a maybe an hour. Not exactly the towering accomplishment you want me to believe it is. I could have lasted this long hiding in a broom closet."

Mouse was taken aback by the nobleman's sudden sharp tone and felt his shoulders contract toward his ears, but he disguised his ire by turning to retrieve his own costume. "Perhaps you would prefer to experiment with that particular stratagem and see if it gets you out beyond the walls." Not for the last time, he questioned the wisdom of taking on this job. Contraband never questioned your skills. "It will work, I assure you," he added, forcing a calmer tone.

Garron nodded. "All right. Where to now?"

"Somewhere they won't think to ever look for us. The wing of the royal apartments."

CHAPTER 14

THE GUARDSMEN stationed at the entrance of the apartment wing stiffened into attention as they approached.

"And if this doesn't work?" Garron grumbled under his breath.

"Stop fretting and keep walking." Mouse was striding two steps behind him on his right side, which was customary for a novice. "And look pompous and arrogant. Oh, wait. Look who I'm talking to."

Garron shot him a hard look over his shoulder.

"Yes. Just like that."

Prodding Garron was an intentional gambit. Anger would help overcome his nerves. And improve his performance. Prelates were notorious for their sour moods, judging everyone they encountered with sanctimonious fervor. No one outside of the calling could ever measure up in conviction and devotion.

"Good eve to you, Shepherd," one of the guards greeted with a quick and respectful bow.

The guards stood shoulder to shoulder at the threshold of the arched passage that led to the royal apartments, barring entry. Garron stopped a few paces from them, hands tucked into his sleeves, and offered a single nod in return. The motion was thick with condescension, stating in clear language that he had no interest in responding or acknowledging them but was being forced to by circumstance. He eyed each in turn, waiting.

"Is there something we can do for you, Shepherd?"

"I wish to return to my apartments," he replied as if it were obvious. "As was requested."

"I am sorry, m'lord, but this wing of the manor has been declared restricted."

Garron looked perplexed, giving each a chilling glare. He turned to give Mouse a similar look. Mouse took a step forward to take over, thinking Garron was stuck and didn't how to proceed. Garron halted him with his extended palm.

"Are you saying," Garron said, stepping closer to the men, "that I am being denied access to the apartments that the generous Duke Delgan has provided me?" He spoke softly, enunciating each word with the sharp staccato of a hammer on a nail.

"Lord Prelate, the orders came from the duke himself. I am only—"

"I have spent half the night providing the final rites for a dying man and comforting his grieving widow, and I return to find I am barred from my bed." Garron's voice rose in pitch. The incredulous look on his face was so authentic Mouse would have believed it himself. There was more to this young lord than he estimated.

The men eyed each other with worried glances. It was unwise to anger someone with a direct ear of the gods. Especially one wearing a purple sash. A Grand Prelate could be a powerful enemy. It hadn't occurred to either of them that a prelate of this level wouldn't partake in any final rites. It was a task clearly beneath him—but Mouse wasn't about to quibble about the details. Garron's quick thinking had provided a plausible reason to be away from his bed, and the guards were too flustered to overthink it.

They were nearing the point of caving in. Mouse could see it in their fidgeting stances. Neither wanted to be the one to deny the prelate, so each was waiting for the other to play the role of the brave one. But neither would—there was just too much personal risk involved. Not only for their immortal souls but the danger of some real damage to their corporeal forms as well. A prelate could order a lashing just as easily as any noble lord.

So instead the two of them looked to each other askance with raised brows and jerks of the head. They were seconds away from letting them through, but the sound of footfalls interrupted their silent debate.

From behind them, a figure marched up the corridor. A fellow guardsman but this one with red cords at the shoulder. This was no grunt, no witless moron. This was their superior.

Fuck.

It wasn't someone too high up the ranks. That at least was good fortune. A high-level officer might have had interactions with Garron and recognized him. This was some midlevel officer of nebulous rank—which, Mouse realized, could prove troublesome as well. Someone working his way up the ranks with something to prove tended to be overly decisive and less prone to intimidation.

The puffed-up officer marched up to them with purpose, looking self-important and swollen with authority. "What is happening here?"

The guards exhaled in relief at his timely arrival. They looked in danger of passing out. Luckily, they would not have to make this decision, after all. Both gave the officer a hasty salute. "The Grand Prelate wishes to return to his apartments," one quickly announced, the delight of passing on the responsibility evident in his tone, "but we were given strict instructions to not let anyone through."

The officer made a quick inspection of Garron, from his head on down. Mouse could not read the expression on the officer's face. To be safe, he moved his hand closer to where his dagger was hidden inside the sleeve of his robe, just in case this turned south. His promise to Garron of no killing would be null and void if they faced a risk of being dragged away in chains or slain here in this corridor. He would protect himself. And his charge.

The officer looked to the men, his expression shifting to annoyance. "Joltheads. Does this look like an escaped prisoner to you?"

"No, sir. But we were told—"

"My apologies, Shepherd," he said, putting his back to the guards and bowing low to Garron. "Their ineptitude never ceases to astound me."

Garron narrowed his eyes and made a conspicuous tilt of the head in Mouse's direction. "Oh, trust me, I understand completely."

The officer's stoic face cracked, allowing a small smirk to lift the corner of his mouth. "I've no doubt. I only wish they'd learn to use the good sense that the gods provided them."

"They are but a blunt tool to be wielded by those with the wisdom to use them properly. The hammer does not know what nail to strike, does it?" They both chuckled. Mouse felt bile burn the back of his throat and was dangerously close to vomiting. "We can all be thankful," Garron continued, leaning closer, "and sleep more soundly knowing that you are here and possess the necessary intellect to guide them."

The officer nodded at Garron's sage assessment. "We will delay you no further, Shepherd. I thank you for your patience in this matter."

Garron bowed graciously to the officer and with a very straight back, started walking. The two guards scrambled to get out of the way. Mouse followed at his heels.

Around a corner and well out of earshot, Garron finally slowed his deliberate march. He put a hand to the wall for support and slumped forward as he exhaled long. "Thought we were done for," he breathed.

While Garron recovered, Mouse listened at a nearby door, picked the locked, and peered inside. Dark and quiet. It was a small antechamber with a bedchamber beyond. With any luck it was currently unoccupied.

"Quick," he said, "in here."

They scurried in and shut the door behind them. Mouse put a finger to his lips, then tiptoed to the second chamber for a quick survey. As he feared, there was a dark mound in the bed, buried beneath a blanket. The shape was smaller, so a woman or a youth. He backed out of the chamber and pulled the double doors that separated to the two chambers closed.

"Quiet now," he said softly with a tilt of his head in the direction of the chamber.

Even in the dark, Mouse could see Garron's eyes widen. "Someone's in there?" he replied in harsh whisper. "What are we doing in here?"

Mouse held up his palm to quiet him. "The alarm didn't wake whoever it is. We aren't likely to either—as long as we keep our voices down," he added pointedly.

Mouse carefully negotiated his way over to the window and pulled back the heavy curtain. Moonlight streamed in to cast a pale silvery glow on the furnishing. It wasn't much, but it provided at least a little to see by. Already his eyes were adjusting.

"Rather impressive back there," he said. A side table had a pitcher of water and a tray of small round pastries. He poured himself a mug and helped himself to a couple of pastries.

Garron gave him a hard look as if he were somehow tarnishing the space. "I've had plenty of experience dealing with members of the prelacy. One acts much like another."

"You think fast on your feet." He popped a whole tart into his mouth, then handed the other off to Garron. "That's good." It sounded more like "das ood."

In the dim light, he saw Garron shrug. He took the pastry and turned it around in his hand a moment, then took a gentile bite from it.

"It certainly helped you didn't have to attempt your dreadful low speech again," added Mouse. "You could speak as your normal lofty self. Now we need to find you something else to wear."

"Again? How many costume changes are you going to put me through?"

"As many as it takes. Look, it only takes one person to hear that a Grand Prelate was allowed through into this wing and look into it. If no prelates are currently supposed to be here....." He lifted a palm in the air and let the thought linger. "We need to stay one step ahead of them."

Garron lifted a pair of riding britches that were left draped over the back of a chair and held them up for Mouse to see. They were small, even for Mouse. "Well, I'm not likely finding anything to wear in here."

"No, which is why I have to head out there again." He cut off a sudden protest with his palm. "I have more caches scattered around the manor. It will be easier... and decidedly less dangerous if I simply retrieve what we need and bring it back. Don't look at me like that. You're safe in here." He headed for the door.

"What if... if whoever is in there wakes up, or someone shows up at the door?"

"Stay in a dark corner, and don't make a sound. I won't be long." Mouse put a hand to the latch, but Garron grabbed his forearm.

"I'm sorry," he said. "About what I said earlier."

Mouse looked up at him, confused.

"I'd still be in that cell if it weren't for you. And I'd never have made it this far on my own, that's for certain."

Mouse caught himself smiling back, though Garron likely couldn't see it. The testy comment Garron had made earlier, a comment that Mouse had already dismissed and forgotten about, was evidently still weighing on him. Garron was concerned that he'd offended him.

Mouse couldn't help himself. He was inexplicably moved by Garron's naïve concern for his feelings. It gave him a strange sensation of warmth and a tightness in his throat—which he quickly choked back down.

"Worry it none," he replied offhandedly. "I took no offense. This is what I do." *And later we can discuss ways for you to thank me*, he added silently.

Then he slipped out into the corridor.

CHAPTER 15

MOUSE WAS glad to be away from him for a while. Garron's presence alone was mucking up his thinking.

This was unlike him. During a job, Mouse never allowed himself to be distracted by a pretty face. In that manner, he was the consummate professional. But something about Garron had disrupted his focus. Those emerald eyes were largely to blame. They had an uncanny sorcery about them, and Mouse had caught himself several times stealing glances at them. But Garron had other fine attributes that drew the eye as well, and he possessed an energy about him that seemed to fill an entire room.

Mouse wanted desperately to despise him. But he found he couldn't. Garron wasn't anything like the other nobles that Mouse had had the displeasure of encountering in his career. The nobility were all insufferable bastards—the entire lot of them. Pus-filled boils slowly poisoning the lifeblood of the kingdom. But Garron, he was different somehow. He acted... well, noble.

It didn't seem possible. Was this all some well-rehearsed deception?

Fraud and trickery were Mouse's forte. It was a large slice of what he did when on a job, so he could typically see right through it when attempted by others. A sustained deception was an art form, and in the hands of a novice, easy to spot. Mouse saw no crack in the man's quality. If this was an act, Garron was a true master.

That fucking kiss, he thought dourly. That was the problem here. The memory of it clung to his brain like cold porridge sticks to a bowl. He was allowing it to muddy his perception.

He needed a walk about. Yes, finding new costumes was necessary, but this excursion was more about clearing his head.

First, he needed to hunt down the nearest window that offered a view of the inner ward. He wanted to gauge the level of commotion around the manor, gather a sense of how aggressive the search was currently elsewhere. If he was going to devise an effective escape, he needed intelligence on the enemy's search strategy.

The layout of the noble apartment wing of the manor was a labyrinthine mess, a muddle of corridors and chambers that didn't follow any sense or reason. The result of centuries of alterations and additions by each successive duke putting his personal mark on the manor. It was a wonder that anyone was able to find a way to their apartment without a map or a guide.

Mercifully, the window he needed was only a short distance away.

It was tall and narrow and recessed into the thick outer wall of the manor. He had to hoist himself up to reach the shutter's latch. He swung the shutters back, pushed out the paned glass, and leaned out. He was on the third floor, and the window provided a clear view of the entire area below. The sky to the east was only just beginning to lighten from black to indigo. At this early hour, the ward should have been quiet and vacant. Instead, it was a hive of activity. At least two dozen torches burned brightly below. Groups of guards stood in formation, awaiting commands while officers pointed and sent squads off running.

Mouse heard no distinct voices rising up to his window. Orders from commanders were conducted in whispers or in elaborate hand gestures. They were hoping to have Garron apprehended before most of the manor rose from their beds.

A group of officers, and what looked to be the chamberlain himself, stood around a makeshift table covered in maps. Maps of the manor presumably.

He watched them for a short while, trying to decipher their strategy. It seemed like they were focusing on the exterior of the manor, setting up a perimeter on and around the wall. They assumed, as he'd hoped they would, Garron and he would be attempting to scale over the wall. Good. Because he had other ideas.

The question was how much manpower were they dedicating to dragging a net through the manor. And were the noble apartments going to be part of the sweep?

He left the window and began a casual survey of the corridors. More reconnaissance. So far, this part of the manor was quiet and still. If felt isolated from the activity outside. A few early risers were about—laborers slinking off to perform their duties before their masters were out of bed. They didn't show any signs of concern or urgency.

That would all change soon. News of an escaped prisoner would spread, sending the manor into further chaos.

Or would it?

That gave Mouse a momentary pause. How much would the people of the manor actually learn about the escape? Certainly, the guard presence in the manor would be out in force to apprehend Lord Green Eyes, but Mouse wondered how much the residents of the manor would be told of what was happening. Very little, Mouse surmised. Garron's internment in the tower was kept largely secret, for reasons Mouse had yet to tease out. That meant they would be wary about what details they revealed about his escape.

That could work to his and Garron's advantage.

The chancellor would spin some yarn to explain the ramped-up military presence around the manor. "A training exercise" was the most likely excuse they'd give. But maintaining a ruse like that fragmented resources and energy. It muddied the available information and slowed progress. The inevitable surge of rumors would further the turmoil. That could provide Mouse plenty of wiggle room to maneuver around in the confusion, and serve up the opportunity he needed to slip Garron out of the manor.

Mouse's confidence grew. He could still manage to make this work and get Lord Green Eyes out of here. But they were far from out of danger, and Garron's restraints on him were becoming a real hindrance. They would be out in the city streets by now if Mouse had been allowed to handle it his way. A simple matter of a few tactical incisions in their defenses… and done. Quick and efficient. As it stood now, it was nearly daylight, and Mouse was nowhere nearer to figuring out how to get him beyond the wall.

Mouse continued his casual stroll about the place, keeping his eye open for anything that would help them. Nothing seemed particularly out of the ordinary or alarming.

If fact, it seemed perfectly ordinary, as if this were any other morning.

Mouse swore under his breath—he was more distracted than he realized not to have noticed before. There was little to no actual security presence in the wing. Some guards lingered about along with the few laborers that were already up from their beds, but their numbers didn't match what he saw gathered down in the ward, and they didn't seem to be searching or even on alert. They must have viewed this wing of the manor as secure. They believed that the prisoner couldn't have made it past the guards—or wouldn't have tried.

But no… it was more than that. They had intentionally shielded the alarm from this part of the manor. These apartments would be filled with important political and economic guests, and a heavy military presence tended to put such dignitaries' teeth on edge. More so, news of an escaped prisoner could erode their confidence in the esteemed duke and sour some delicate negotiations.

Delgan was undoubtedly savvy enough to not jeopardize any sensitive deals he had in the works. An escaped prisoner could be construed at the very least as an unfortunate embarrassment and at the worst, a sign of weakness or a lack of control over his dominion. This meant a lower guard presence for the time being and a more surreptitious search of the area if they suspected the two of them had retreated here. This was welcome news.

He checked in on his caches. He selected what he needed and stuffed it into a canvas sack.

On his way back, he swung by the open window again and peered out. Little had changed, and he was about to duck back in again, but something caught his eye. Someone new had joined the men around the table. Female likely, based on the comparative size to the others, and she wore a flowing black robe. Not a Shepherd—she was not wearing the obligatory four-cornered hat. Mouse frowned.

The men surrounding the table all made respectful bows. She appeared to say one final thing to them, and then she spun from the table. Hands hidden in her sleeves, her chin high into the air, she marched across the ward toward the doors of the manor. A gust through the wards made the robes lift and flow in easy billows behind her. The robes were made of black silk.

No, he thought. Couldn't be.

Not here.

He leaned farther out the window for a better view, but the light was still too dim and they were too far away to see clearly.

Fuck!

There was only one possibility. He abandoned the window at a jog. He had to get back to Garron. And fast.

MOUSE PICKED the lock and lunged in. The room was still dark. Garron must have pulled the heavy drapes closed after he left, for they were drawn again. The weak morning light formed a pinkish line down the narrow gap between the curtains and did little to illuminate the chamber. Mouse stood in the open doorway, allowing the light from the corridor to spill inside. It took a moment for his eyes to adjust, but he spotted Garron in the corner straight away, leaning a shoulder against the wall. Garron straightened, clearly sensing Mouse's urgency.

"Quick," Mouse barked. "Pull off those robes now!"

"What?" Garron asked, confused. "Why? What's happened?"

"Just do it." Mouse made a scan of the room. He spied what he needed quickly—the fireplace. He dodged out into the corridor again. Halfway down, he found a burning lantern in a wall sconce. He lifted it out and sprinted back to the room.

Garron was still clothed in the black robe when he returned. He had pulled off the purple sash from his shoulders but watched Mouse scramble about, looking confused.

"What are you doing? Take that off!"

Garron was shaken from his inaction and started pulling the robe over his head.

Mouse tossed a number of logs from the hopper into the hearth and laid the lantern down on its side among them. Oil spilled from the lantern onto the wood, and the fire spread. In moments, the hearth was ablaze. He inspected the fireplace tools propped in a bucket, which clanged like a bell when he moved them about. He selected a poker, studied the tip a moment, then positioned it into the flames of the growing fire.

Garron had the robe off but clutched it in front of him as if reluctant to let it go. "Mouse, what's this about?" He was looking anxious. "What's happening?"

"Come over here. By the fire so I can see better. Just hope I'm wrong."

He joined him by the fireplace still clutching the robe. "About what?"

The fire was starting to crackle, eating up more of the logs. Mouse repositioned the poker in a hotter zone of the fire. He took the robe from Garron's grasp and flung it aside, leaving Garron standing there in his smallclothes. His flawless skin reflected the firelight like gold.

Mouse immediately started to inspect every surface of his skin, turning him about in a circle to expose different parts to the light. His chest. His back. His legs.

It would be somewhere Garron wouldn't be able to see it himself. There was no mirror in his tower prison. "Lift your arms," he said.

Garron obeyed. "What are you looking for?"

"A tattoo."

"A what? I don't have a tattoo."

"Let's hope you're right." He squatted low to inspect the back of his legs—his thick beautiful legs. He rubbed his hands along the silky surface hoping to catch the feel of raised skin. Some tattoos—if well made—were close to the color of the skin and hard to spot.

"Hey. What's going on?"

Mouse sprung up. Both he and Garron turned to double doors to find a lad of perhaps fourteen standing in the open doorway rubbing sleep from his eyes. For several heartbeats no one spoke. Everyone exchanged stares, not knowing what to do.

Fuck!

"Nothing," Mouse replied, recovering his wits. "Go back in your bedchamber and close the door."

"Who are you? Why are you here?"

Mouse marched over to him. He didn't have time for this. "No one you need to concern yourself with. We are here on important palace business." He took the lad under the arm and guided him back in the chamber. "Now just stay in here and don't make a sound." He gave him a pointed look after he released him that left no question that he meant what he said. "Understand?"

The boy nodded with short little terrified bobs of his head.

Garron cried out in sudden pain.

Mouse closed the bedchamber doors behind him as he dashed back. Garron was down on one knee, his face contorted. Damn! He was too late.

"Where?" he demanded. "Where is it?"

Garron sucked through his teeth as he put his fingers over his right buttock. Mouse crouched down behind Garron. "Undo the drawstring," he ordered. Garron reached down to his waist and pulled the end of the string. The waistband of his smallclothes went slack, and Mouse tugged the garments down, exposing one cheek of his ass. One perfectly round hemisphere.

There it was.

Low on the right cheek, the rune burned into his flesh.

"What is happening?" Garron hissed.

"Tracer ink," Mouse told him. "They put a tattoo on your ass to find you in case you escaped somehow. They have a fucking mage here."

"Tracer ink?"

"It's been activated. That's why the pain. It's to slow you down so they can catch up to you." The rune glowed red against his skin.

"Well, get the fucking thing off of me," he snapped.

"It's not that easy, Garron." He kept his voice low. Calm. "There's only one way right now. And it won't be pleasant."

Garron looked to the fireplace, which was crackling wildly now. Then back at Mouse, who was still crouched down at eye level with his buttocks. "Oh shit."

"Yes. I'm sorry." Mouse adjusted the poker again, placing it deeper where coals were glowing angry red. "And I've got to do it quick. Before they narrow down where you are. The good news is I don't have to burn off the entire rune. Just disrupt it. But it does have to burn deep enough into the skin so the ink is removed in that spot. It's almost ready."

Garron winced again. His forehead was beading with sweat. "Well, it burns now, so I'd rather it hurt and not have them tracking me. How much time do we have?"

"Not much. The incantation does take some time to prepare, but once evoked, the mage will pinpoint your exact location."

"How did you know? About the tattoo?"

"I spotted the mage. They obviously summoned her out because of the escape. Tracer ink was the only logical conclusion." He hated mages. In his line of work, mages got in his way. So he made it his business to know theirs.

"I don't follow."

Mouse fought the urge to sigh and roll his eyes. Of course he didn't follow. "If a mage was employed here in Har Orentega, with the principal motive of keeping you under lock and key, they have two options. One, put a ward around the cell, which requires a mage of very high level to craft. Since there wasn't a ward around your cell—which is no surprise—few other than the great king himself can afford a mage with the capability to create one and frankly, I doubt you warrant the expense—we can therefore conclude the second option. Tracer ink."

"How did they get it on me?"

"Drugged food's a possibility." Mouse scrunched his face, reconsidering that thought. "But that can have side effects you'd notice.

Probably went with a sleep spell. Something a mediocre mage could accomplish. Pull those off entirely. We don't need them catching on fire." He handed Garron a leather belt, part of his next wardrobe change. "You'll want to bite down on this."

Garron complied and stripped off his short clothes, allowing them to drop to the floor. He stood there completely naked.

Mouse pulled the poker from the flames. The tip was glowing angrily. He squatted again down on one knee behind Garron, poker positioned in front of him like a weapon. He closed his eyes and tried to think of something other than Garron's perfect form glistening in the firelight. He was stalling, he knew—not because he worried about inflicting pain, but he honestly didn't want to mar the man's perfection. It felt like throwing paint on a masterpiece. Or smashing a statue.

"Get ready," he said.

Garron put the belt between his teeth, leaned into a chair, and spread his legs apart a little more.

Dear gods! Mouse thought. If only this pose were for another purpose.

"I'm ready," Garron replied. "Do it."

Mouse moved the glowing tip of the poker closer, making sure it was positioned, then pushed the tip against the skin, right in the middle of the tattoo.

Garron's entire body stiffened. He arched his back and made a low grunt through clenched teeth. But he didn't cry out any louder. Smoke rose up from the contact point, and Mouse could smell the charred flesh. He held the point for a count of five, then pulled the tip away. The rune was no longer glowing.

"Okay, done."

Garron sagged against the chair. "Nothing to it," he replied between breaths.

Mouse dropped the poker back into the bucket. Already the skin was swollen, inflamed, and blistering. "We're going to have to hunt down some salve. That's going to start to seep, then stick to anything you wear. There's danger of it festering."

Garron nodded. "Do you think we got it in time?" His brow glistened with sweat.

"Only one way to know. But I don't want to stick around here to find out. We need to move." He dropped the canvas bag at his feet. "Start dressing." Mouse looked up to find the door to the bedchamber cracked open and the lad peering out from the other side. He let out an exasperated sigh and threw up his hands. "Ah shit! Boy, I told you to keep the door shut." He spun about on his heel. Garron had already pulled on his smallclothes and a white chemise with a lace collar. "We're going to have to do something about him now."

Garron's head popped up, his eyes wide. "Mouse," he said in a low voice. "You spoke an oath to me."

Mouse stepped closer to Garron and leaned in. "Gods!" he said through clenched teeth, part whisper and part growl. "What kind of monster do you take me for? I've no intention on harming him. He just can't be allowed to blab about us when we leave. He's going to have to join us."

"What? You're insane! We can't drag him along."

Mouse shoved the door open farther. The lad stumbled back into a corner, quaking. "We don't have a choice. Right, lad? Should have minded when you had the chance. Now, make your bed. We're going on a little stroll."

CHAPTER 16

"WHAT'S YOUR name, boy?"

The lad stiffened his spine and pulled his shoulders back. "Lord Nevon Rhee of Har Senestus."

Gods help him. Another noble brat.

"Mother is here visiting with—"

"Don't care," Mouse cut him off. "When does your nursemaid fetch you, Lord Nevon of Har Senestus?"

The lad scowled at Mouse. "My steward," he corrected pointedly, "shall be here shortly. He arrives shortly after dawn. He has strict orders to wait—"

"All right, shut up." Mouse put a hand on the hilt of his dagger at his waist and made sure Nevon saw him do it. "Despite what I said to my companion over there," he said in a low voice, "I will hurt you if you don't cooperate." He wouldn't, of course. He spoke true when he told Garron he wouldn't bring harm to a child. The young were off-limits. But Lord Nevon here didn't need to know that. "And if you answer me in more than five words at a time, I may just gag you and stuff you into a pickle barrel in some forgotten corner of the kitchen. Don't test me. Understood?"

Nevon's lips tightened in irritation, but he nodded.

Mouse shepherded the lad out of the bedchamber. In the adjoining chamber, Garron was now fully dressed. Mouse had chosen a more garish look for him this time, the conspicuous attire of a rich merchant. Someone new to wealth and needing to show it off. Mouse calculated that it was a look that would fit in well in this wing of the manor. But even in the foppish garb, Lord Green Eyes managed to pull it off surprisingly well and make it presentable.

"I feel ridiculous," Garron grumbled.

"You look perfect. Now, we have to move out before the young prince's nursemaid shows up—"

"Steward," Nevon put in sourly.

"—to pull his pants on for him and shake him dry after his morning piss."

Garron scowled. "Lay off him, Mouse. He's just a boy."

"I'm fifteen," Nevon protested.

"And just keep asking yourself if you want to see sixteen." Mouse pulled the novice robes off over his head and began tugging on his new garments—the simple garments of a merchant's underling and clerk. Innocuous and easily overlooked. "All right," he said once he'd stomped his feet into his boots. "Time to move."

Nevon looked at Mouse horrorstruck. "You cannot expect me to run about the manor in… in… this!" He pulled out the sides of his nightshirt like a curtsy. "It's unseemly."

"Unseemly?" Mouse was losing his patience. They didn't have time for this. "You'll run the corridors na—"

Garron grabbed Mouse by the shoulder and guided him backward, away from the boy.

"Look," Nevon said. He rolled his head back and exhaled, as if speaking to two simpletons. "If you don't want to be noticed, it makes sense that I'm dressed appropriately."

Garron and Mouse exchanged looks. "He's got a point," Garron replied.

Mouse was ready to argue that it was early enough that there wouldn't be many people up and out of bed yet, but he knew the lad was right—which irritated him. Mouse had to watch himself. He was allowing fatigue and frustration to cloud his thinking.

He elbowed Garron's arm away and stepped closer to Nevon again. "How much of our conversation did you overhear?"

"Enough to know you're in some trouble with Duke Delgan," Nevon replied with a measure of self-satisfaction. "I gather that he was imprisoned here, and you're helping him to escape."

Fuck.

Mouse glanced over his shoulder at Garron. "Excellent." He rubbed his eyes with forefinger and thumb and tried to think of what to do about this. Things were spiraling out of control.

"Well, I'm not going to say anything," Nevon said, "if that's what you're worried about."

Garron's eyes narrowed curiously. "And why is that?"

Nevon gave Garron a surprised look, as if it were obvious. "'Cause you're a nobleborn. Like me."

Mouse fought the urge to snarl and blow air through his teeth.

"I'm not certain I understand the connection," said Garron, sounding very much like a diplomat.

Nevon's arms dropped to his sides as if he'd lost control of those muscles. "If he'd been the one thrown into a dungeon," he said, indicating Mouse with a tilt of his head, "I'd say it was probably because he did something horrible and deserves to rot there. But everyone knows that nobles are not put in irons for the same reasons as commoners. That means it's something political. And probably unfair."

Mouse had to admit the logic was sound. The lad was astute.

Garron's eyes shifted briefly toward Mouse, signifying he had come to the same conclusion.

"I can tell you too that Mother doesn't trust Lord Delgan," Nevon continued. He leaned in conspiratorially and lowered his voice. "She's telling people she's here to visit a cousin, but is really here to conduct some business with the merchants in the province. Lord Delgan would try to prevent it if he knew, so she's meeting with the merchants in secret. Mother calls him an 'untrustworthy snake.'"

From the look on Garron's face, Mouse could tell exactly what he was thinking. He shook his head. "We are not leaving him here, Garron," he said.

"I think we can trust him."

"Absolutely not. Too risky. He's coming with us."

"I'll only need a few minutes, and I can be ready to leave," Nevon said.

Mouse turned and raised his eyebrow at the lad, unable to mask his surprise.

Nevon shrugged. "I've nothing else to do. Mother won't let me take any part of her negotiations. She only brought me along to cover for her when she's not in the manor. Frankly, I'm bored silly."

"One minute," Mouse agreed with a nod. The lad opened his mouth to protest, but Mouse held out his hand to stop him. "It's that, or I pick out garments for you."

Nevon looked horrified at the very idea of it. "Very well," he said with an eye roll, and then he strode back into the bedchamber.

"This is a terrible idea," Garron grumbled once Nevon was out of earshot.

"We have no choice, Garron."

"He's just a boy."

"All the more reason not to trust him. A boy that age can lie to your face as effortlessly as farting."

Garron looked as if he might argue but frowned and said, "I don't like it. I fear we are putting him in danger."

"He will not come to any harm," Mouse said. He looked up directly into Garron's bright emerald eyes. Garron still looked dubious. "I promise," he added, then glided to the open doorway to keep an eye on the lad, if only to make sure he didn't try to signal someone from a window or attempt some other foolhardy notion of escaping. Nevon rummaged through a trunk beside the bed and pulled out random items.

In the other chamber, Garron leaned heavily against a chair with his hip pushed oddly in one direction, presumably to keep the fabric from touching the wound.

Nevon pulled out trousers and a silk chemise and set them aside, then selected three different jerkins and arranged them side by side on the bed. He stepped back and considered each one.

"Pick something," Mouse growled.

"I'm working on it!" the lad testily replied.

"Choose, or I'll choose for you."

"I won't be spotted wearing something that makes me look like a street beggar. I'd rather you killed me."

"A tempting offer!" Mouse sniped.

"Look, it's not that simple. Ashimnae always selects my daily wardrobe for me."

Mouse sighed. He was losing patience, but he dug deep and forced a calm in his voice that he didn't feel. "The blue one. That one looks nice. Wear that."

Nevon looked over at Mouse as if he were a troll that had strayed into the room. "Of course you'd pick that one," he said, and grabbed the green-and-gold jerkin next to it. He started to squirm out of the nightshirt, but stopped and glared at Mouse. "A little privacy, if you don't mind."

Mouse folded his arms and looked up at the ceiling. When he looked back down again, Nevon was buttoning up the front of his jerkin.

"Wait!" the lad suddenly exclaimed. "I've no boots! Ashimnae took my boots with him last night to polish them. I've no others."

"Then you leave without any."

Nevon froze, eyes wide with shock. "And run about the manor like a street urchin?"

Mouse turned to Garron. "Are all you noble types as ignorant as this? Perhaps someone should inform your ilk that there is more to street poverty than a lack of proper footwear." Garron made a wry face and turned away. Mouse threw up his hands. "Fine! If this moves things along." He sat down on the edge of a chair and pulled off his boots again. Mouse's own feet were small and wouldn't be much larger than the lad's, so the boots would suffice. He chucked them across the room with some force. Nevon had to leap out of the way or be struck by them. "Here!" Mouse said. "I'll run about like the urchin, then."

A merchant's assistant without boots would look peculiar, but Mouse didn't have time to worry about it now. They needed to be out of the room before the brat's nursemaid arrived.

"Something you're accustomed to, I suspect," Nevon said as he scooped up each boot and tugged them on. He stamped his feet a few times, his lips twisting down in a grimace. "These aren't very well made. They pinch my toes."

"Can we leave now, Your Highness?"

"Hold on!" Nevon said suddenly. Mouse threw up his hands again as the lad dashed to the bedside table. He pulled open the drawer and rummaged through it. "I'll leave him a note. I'll tell him that I went to go get something to eat in the kitchens." He pulled out paper, a quill, and an ink well and dashed over to a desk by the window. He scribbled out a quick note, folded the paper in half, then considered the room with pursed lips. He settled on the table by the fire, and placed the note next to the tray of sweets, propping it against a chalice.

Mouse grabbed the note and opened it.

Nevon scowled at him. "You can read?"

"Better than you. And I can apparently spell better than you as well."

"I was writing quickly," Nevon replied, sounding a little wounded. "It should keep Ashimnae from growing suspicious, for a while at least. He'll wait here for a time before he decides to look for me."

The note said exactly what the lad claimed it would say. Mouse kept his face neutral and replaced the note on the table. "So maybe I won't have to stuff you in a pickle barrel today after all."

Nevon pressed his lips together and gave Mouse a level stare. "I think you're all talk." And he marched for the door.

CHAPTER 17

THE SUN had nearly crested the horizon when the three of them exited Nevon's small apartment. The eastern sky had lightened to sapphire and was painted with streaks of pink clouds. Pale light filtered in through the occasional window, illuminating the eddy currents of dust and giving the corridors a strange, dreamlike air.

Mouse had Garron lead the way while he moved Nevon along with fingers lightly pinching the back of the lad's neck. They moved at a deliberate pace, careful not to appear too hurried and draw attention. Mouse also made certain they did not run headlong into Nevon's manservant en route. The lad pointed the direction Ashimnae would come, from his temporary residences, so Mouse led them along a different route but was cautious all the same in case he was lying.

The corridors were more occupied than Mouse liked. Unlike earlier, it was the dignitaries and aristocrats now roaming about, looking haughty and official. Most were either local luminaries or guests from neighboring duchies, but he spotted the livery of a well-connected family from the capital. Delgan was showing his ambitions, clearly attempting to expand his influence. As for the laborers and servants that Mouse encountered before, they had done what was expected of them when their masters were about; they disappeared from sight entirely.

No one paid them any mind, but Mouse caught himself tightening his thumb and forefinger on Nevon's neck each time someone walked past.

"Ow! That's not necessary, you know," Nevon grumbled.

Despite his proclamations of willing cooperation, Mouse still didn't trust him. "Just reminding you that I'm here."

"Your odor is doing a superb job of that already. You realize if we were in Har Senestus, you would be drawn and quartered for just laying your hand upon me."

"Just keep moving, little prince."

The lad's shoulders clenched under his hand, and he grinned in satisfaction. He needed to get them out of the corridors as quickly as possible, before someone recognized Nevon or started asking questions.

Still, no one about seemed in any particular hurry or on edge. That could all change quickly enough if the mage had managed to isolate Garron's whereabouts before the ink was disrupted. At any moment, these corridors could be thick with guards.

Mouse herded them into a seldom-used stairwell toward the back of the manor. They descended two flights and hurried through another maze of corridors.

As they rounded a corner, Garron nearly collided with a cluster of three guardsmen. Mouse's heart lurched into his throat, and on reflex he moved his hand close to where the dagger was hidden. But Garron offered a quick apology and a bow, and the three marched off without a backward glance. They may have been on the lookout for an escaped prisoner, but not two men and boy.

The lad might turn out to be a surprising asset, after all.

"There, to your right," Mouse said to Garron. "Turn."

They ducked down a short hall to a small unassuming door that would have been easy to overlook. "This will lead us to the lower levels."

"Servants' passages?" Nevon said with sudden alarm.

"Easy, Your Highness. You won't break out into open sores by communing with the common folk."

Nevon's face darkened in irritation. "I know," he grumbled. "And don't call me that."

Garron threw him a look. "You sure know how to win people over."

"I can be charming," Mouse retorted. "When need be." And he wasn't going to waste his time kowtowing to some entitled snob that he was going to ditch somewhere at the first opportunity.

Garron pressed his lips together in a sardonic snarl. "Warn me when it's about to happen so I know to keep an eye open for it."

Mouse pulled open the door, peered in, then stepped inside, flagging the other two to follow. The passage beyond was dark and narrow, forcing them to proceed in a single file. A single tallow candle burned in a small wall sconce, providing just enough light for them to see their way, but its black, sooty smoke hung in the air like a specter and made the air thick and foul.

"How did you know this was here?" Garron asked.

"I told you. I'm a good planner. I learned everything I could about the place before I came to fetch you."

"It's creepy in here," Nevon grumbled. "And it smells."

Mouse bit back a sharp reply. Yes, brat, this is how most experience the world—so you can enjoy silk sheets and the smell of rose petals. Garron was in a more generous mood. "We won't be in here long," he replied in a gentle tone.

The passage continued for a ways, then rounded a corner. They could hear murmurs echoing against the walls from up ahead. Servants of the manor going about their morning business. A stairwell seemed to materialize from the shadows on their left. Mouse clicked his tongue at them and signaled with his head for them to keep up with him. With palpable trepidation, Garron and Nevon descended behind him. The stairwell was hardly wider than Mouse's shoulders, and it twisted in a tight spiral as if following the tread of a screw. The front edge of each step was worn down—eroded away by centuries of boots owned by those locked into a life of servitude.

Mouse felt a measure of guilt for what he was about to do. This was a private sanctum, a place where the servant class could escape the eye of the elite for a time, a place where they could relax and mingle freely with members of their kind. Now he was bringing two nobleborn into it.

"Why are we traveling deeper into the manor?" Garron asked. "Instead of trying to get out?" He spoke in hushed tones, as if in a shepherd's chapel. He felt it too, Mouse sensed. His movement down the steps was awkward and clumsy, and he hissed a little each time he lowered his right foot. It was clear the burn on his ass was bothering him.

"I'm working on it," Mouse answered. He tried to sound confident, like he knew what he was doing, but his voice betrayed him. Escape for the moment was secondary. Right now, he was more focused on not getting them captured. The mage obviously now knew the tattoo on Garron had been discovered and the rune's power disrupted. There was no way of telling how precisely she had pinpointed Garron's exact location before Mouse burned it off, but Mouse was willing to bet she could at the very least provide a general vicinity. He wanted to be well clear of the noble apartments if and when a sweep began.

Gods burn him! This fucking mage was going to be trouble for them, no mistake. There was little that ever caught him flatfooted, but he certainly didn't anticipate having to contend with that.

What other little tricks did she have planned? He'd be a fool to think she had nothing else.

And what could warrant the amount of coin required to hire the mage in the first place? What was so important about Garron?

The stairwell dumped them into a space that was too wide to be a corridor but too long to be considered a chamber either. It had low walls but a high arched ceiling that ran its entire length. They were deep in the bowels of the manor. More tallow candles burned in carved-out niches in the stone wall, but they barely pushed back the dank gloom of the place. Its purpose seemed eclectic—part storage, with barrels and crates left stacked about with no discernible order, and part gathering place. Makeshift tables surrounded by stools and benches were clustered about one end like an abandoned tavern, plates and mugs left in haphazard piles.

Nevon looked around with wide-eyed fascination, as if amazed that such a place could even exist under his feet. It was clearly his first exposure to the underbelly of a keep, his first glimpse at how the meat became the sausage that appeared on his silver plate. "What is this place?"

Three women emerged from a doorway. They each bore a stack of folded linen sheets in their outstretched arms and giggled among themselves. Mouse caught only a fraction of their conversation, but it was clear it was about a boy one of them fancied. As they tumbled into the space, relaxed and carefree, they all became aware simultaneously that they were not alone.

The change was immediate. With a start, the conversation was severed and backs stiffened. Smiles fled with such immediacy it made Mouse fume. Their faces turned to Garron in unison.

"M'lord!" one of them exclaimed as she fought to recover herself. She lowered her gaze from him and curtsied. The other two followed her lead. "Forgive us. Are you in need of something?" In a single heartbeat, the three of them had recognized Garron for what he was. Their unease and surprise was palpable.

"No, good ladies," Garron replied in gentle speech. "Forgive the intrusion." Mouse could sense that he recognized the effect his presence was having and was shamed by it. He had stepped into their realm and altered it, claimed it by just being present.

"It is no intrusion, m'lord. How can I assist you?"

"You cannot. Please, I insist, go about your work and pay us no mind."

Fat little chance of that happening, Mouse thought.

"As you wish, m'lord." With a solemn march not unlike a funeral procession, the three carried their neatly folded burdens away, all the joy from moments before suffocated away.

The room from where the women appeared was lined with washing tubs along one wall and tables for folding along another. The pungent smell of lye and lavender choked the room. At the opposite side, a stairwell led up, likely to an outside courtyard where the lines were tied for drying. Two other women were elbow deep in washtubs, hard at work scrubbing sheets against a washboard. They too already knew of Garron's presence, for their chins were tucked low, and they said not a word.

Mouse considered the stairs to the outside, but to keep such workings out of sight from the gentle class, clotheslines were kept in closed-off areas typically with no access to the rest of the manor or manor grounds. Gods forbid the nobility catch a glimpse of their smallclothes flopping about in the breeze.

"This way," Mouse announced with conviction, as if he knew the way, and led them away from the laundry. The two followed without question, like sheep lost in an unfamiliar wood. Mouse poked his head into the various doorways, scanning each chamber. In short order, he discovered what he was searching for. He snatched a tallow candle from the niche and ducked inside.

A food store. His nose told him they were getting closer to the kitchens, which set off his stomach. The chamber was deep and dark and filled mostly with crates of vegetables and dirty tubers, but a quick survey revealed a crate of decent apples in the corner and a wheel of wax-covered cheese on the shelf. Mouse wasted no time pulling it down and cutting off thick slices. He passed the sections around.

Garron leaned against a stack of crates as if winded. He pulled the fabric of the trousers away from his skin with a hiss and positioned his hip so it didn't come in contact with the wound. He took the wedge of cheese offered him but just held it. "We're resting here, I gather?" He looked drawn and pale. The change in him seemed sudden, like a lantern about to exhaust the last of its oil. The night had taken its toll on him. Not surprising—after weeks of lethargy in a cell and a questionable diet, this had been a taxing spike of activity. And the initial adrenaline of his escape had worn off.

"For a bit," Mouse replied. "I'm going to survey the area." He put a hand on Garron's arm. "Keep to the back and rest. You'll be safe here."

Garron nodded.

Nevon climbed up on a crate and chewed on his hunk of cheese, looking content and unflustered. This was all just an interesting distraction for the lad. An unexpected adventure. He must have felt Mouse's eyes on him, for he looked up suddenly.

"What?"

Mouse pursed his lips in thought. What to do about him?

Garron seemed to read his mind. "I will ensure he stays put, Mouse," he said.

Mouse made a single affirming nod. He had no choice but to trust him. "I'll be back soon."

MOUSE WAS back in less time than it took to skin a rabbit. He half expected when he slipped into the storeroom to find Garron asleep and the lad gone, but they were both in the back, lounging on crates as if seated on thrones and conspiring quietly like old friends. Mouse dropped the sack he carried on a barrel top and rummaged through it.

Garron looked up. "That was quick."

"Just getting a feel of what we're up against."

"And?"

"There are guards about, sweeping the area. Nothing too aggressive, but they are actively looking. My guess is they believe us elsewhere, but they're not leaving anything to chance."

He pulled out a loaf of bread and handed it to Nevon, who grabbed it with both hands and put his face into it to smell it. He made a groan of pleasure.

"It's still warm," he exclaimed. "How'd you manage that?"

Mouse shrugged. "Trade secret." The reaction to good warm bread was universal. No matter how much coin was in the coffers, or how rich your diet, everyone responded the same to freshly baked bread.

His quick tour had surveyed the kitchens and some of the workshops buried down there in the belly of the manor. He located where foods and supplies were carted in too—a potential exit point from the manor. It now had guards stationed there, but he could figure out a way past them if need be. It was worth considering, but it would put them out into open ward and no closer to being on the other side of the wall.

"Now if only I had some butter and jam," Nevon lamented.

Mouse pulled out two small earthenware crocks and handed them over too. "Any other requests, Your Highness? A roast duck, perhaps?"

Nevon attempted an annoyed look, but he was too happy about the bread to pull off anything believable. Even Garron smiled.

"I didn't leave you out, Lordship. I come with gifts for you as well." He pulled out another small earthenware container and held it up for Garron to see.

"What's that?"

"I happened upon the manor apothecary. Should help with your burn." In truth, it was what he set out to look for, but Garron didn't need to know that.

Garron took the jar, relief visible on his face. "Thanks, Mouse." He pursed his lips and held on to it a moment without moving. "I... uh... might need some help getting it on."

Mouse noticed how Garron leaned to one side favoring his right cheek as he sat. Mouse nodded and took the jar back. "Stand up, then."

Garron complied, carefully lifting himself off the crate. He turned his back, then propped one arm on the crate to brace himself. It didn't take Mouse long to learn why Garron wanted him to do it for him. The wound had begun to seep, and his smallclothes had stuck to the burn.

Mouse carefully began the slow process of peeling the encrusted linen from the wound. Garron stiffened but didn't utter a sound.

"Why does he call you Mouse?" Nevon asked.

"That's my name."

Nevon scrunched up his face. "Your parents named you after a rodent?"

"It was not the name they gave me." Mouse's lips tightened at the memory. He hadn't thought about his other name in a long time. It was there, tucked in a dusty bin in the back of his mind, waiting to be recalled. It seemed somehow alien to him now, as if it belonged to someone who didn't exist anymore. The distraction caused him to pull the linen too quickly and Garron flinched. "Sorry," he told Garron. "Mouse was another name given to me. When I was older. I chose to use one and not the other."

Garron looked down over his shoulder at him. "And how does one come to be called Mouse?"

Mouse intended to dodge as he always did when that particular question arose—as it inevitably did. But the look in Garron's eye weakened his resolve, and before he was even aware, heard himself answering truthfully.

"It's not terribly complicated," he began. "I have always been small. And… perhaps caused some measure of mischief around the village. From time to time."

"So far, nothing particularly surprising," Garron replied with a smirk.

Mouse scowled at him. "You may want to wait until after I'm done down here to insult me." He tugged on the fabric a little harder to make his point.

Garron stiffened. "A valid point. Proceed, then."

"In time, it would appear, I inadvertently developed a rather… inimical reputation. Which turned out convenient for all the other children of the village when they had done something particularly impish. I had become an easy scapegoat."

"And an easy target for ridicule and harrying as well, I imagine," Garron added.

Mouse was momentarily tripped up by Garron's insightfulness but forced his face to not let on. "Which is how I learned how to defend myself, incidentally," he said. "I don't know how it started, but some villager began referring to me as that 'pesky little mouse.' As things happen, the name stuck." Mouse plucked the last of the fabric from the wound and sat back on his heels. "There. Tricky part's finished." Mouse tugged the short clothes farther down Garron's hip to keep it out of the way. He peeled the wax seal out of the earthenware jar.

"Those days are far behind you. Why continue to use it?"

Mouse dug two fingers into the yellow paste and began to gently apply a thick layer over the wound. He was amazed how little the flesh beneath the skin gave in to the pressure of his fingers. It was like massaging a ripe melon. "I grew to like it. It suits me. Plus, a name attached to a reputation can have its uses."

"No doubt. It's a name people will remember, and I'm certain your reputation precedes you aplenty."

"Is that why you left?" Nevon asked. "Were you forced out? Did the villagers run you out with pitchforks at your back?" The lad leaned in, captivated with this glimpse into the lives of commoners. Especially sinister ones like himself. The whole morning had been an exciting peek under the rock for the lad, seeing how the rest of the world lived their sad lives.

He felt his expression darken. "Nothing so dramatic." He pushed the wax back into the opening and rose to his feet. "All right, that's done. Should be good for a while. But it'll have to be reapplied before too long, or it'll start to stick again."

"The pain is subsiding," Garron noted with some surprise as he carefully pulled his short clothes and trousers back over his ass.

"Reagents in there for pain, I imagine," Mouse told him. "Should stop the wound from festering too. But let me know if you feel a fever coming on."

Garron put his hand on Mouse's shoulder just below the neck and squeezed. "Thanks, Mouse." His thumb and forefinger pressed directly against skin above the line of Mouse's jerkin. The gesture was gentle and familiar, intimate in a way that Mouse was unprepared for. It sent shock waves of heat through his flesh, and his torso and shoulders tightened involuntarily. It wasn't until Garron pulled his hand away that Mouse found he could breathe again.

What the fuck was wrong with him?

Mouse nodded to appear casual. "We need to be going," he said.

"I could use a moment longer," Garron replied. "I feel I am just starting to catch my breath again." He leaned back and rested his head against the wall.

Mouse wasn't entirely certain what their next move was anyway, so he agreed. "Very well."

Garron lifted his head again and gave Mouse a narrow look. "Then I have one more question, if you don't mind."

Mouse raised an eyebrow.

"Your father. Tell me about him."

That was not the question he expected, and he did little to hide his surprise. "My father? Garron, we hardly have the time—"

"Indulge me. Please."

Mouse gave a small shrug of acquiescence. "What is there to tell? He's a simple man. Uncomplicated. Kind. Nothing like me."

"Was he military?"

Mouse chuckled lightly. "Gods, no. He's a tanner. Wanted me to follow him in his craft... but both fate and I had other plans. He still has a shop in the village and carves out a good living there." What power did Garron possess over him? Mouse found himself defenseless, spilling information he hadn't disclosed to anyone in years. "He is well known, actually. Many are known to travel quite far to commission his work." Mouse could not help but crack a smile of pride. His father was a master, and Mouse could never understand why he stayed in that small town instead of heading to one of the bigger cities. "He's from the south originally, I think, but met my mother in the north—Entenund, I believe—so he decided to settle near there in Hallowridge."

"And your mother?"

"Died when I was very young. Look, what's this about. Why all these questions?"

"Curiosity," Garron replied. "I cannot help but wonder how your father came about owning such a spectacular dagger."

Mouse's hand unconsciously moved to the hilt of the dagger. "I don't really know," he said. "Never thought about it. I found it the night I left. I was searching for a bit of coin to take with me, and I stumbled upon it at the bottom of a chest. I took it, not knowing its value, but needing a weapon."

"And now? You don't find it strange that he should have it, hidden away?"

"Perhaps it was given to him as payment."

Garron made a slow nod. "Perhaps." Then he let the subject drop and said no more.

A wave of irritation washed over Mouse. What was that about? What was he trying to imply? He folded his arms and looked across the storeroom at nothing in particular.

But something caught his eye. Movement. In the corner. And his heart tightened.

Fuck.

Slowly his hand moved back toward the dagger. His father's dagger. And he slipped it out of his belt. With deft practiced fingers, he positioned it for a throw. But even as he did it, he knew it was too late.

Fuck. Fuck. Fuck.

CHAPTER 18

IN ONE fluid motion, Mouse pulled the dagger back behind his ear. With a quick flick, he sent it spinning across the storeroom. The dagger made a soft whistle as it flew and a moment later, from the darkened corner, came a satisfying single high squeal. Then silence.

Both Nevon and Garron flinched. "Shit, Mouse!" Garron exclaimed, irritation in his voice. "Strange time for target practice."

"Gather up our supplies," he answered with cold seriousness as he crossed the storeroom. "Time to move."

"Why? What's happening?"

Mouse located the dagger. His aim had been true. The blade had completely skewered the rodent's body. He grabbed the hilt and lifted it off the ground, keeping it horizontal with the carcass still on the blade. He looked over the body and frowned. Exactly what he feared. He carried it back to the others.

"Ew!" Nevon exclaimed, recoiling. "What are you doing? Get rid of that!"

Mouse held it a little higher for Garron to see. "Look closely. What do you see?"

"It's just a rat!" Nevon said.

"No," Garron said, leaning in to inspect it. "Mouse is right. There's something on the fur. A symbol of some sort."

"A mage's rune. Burned into the flesh. This is one of the mage's spies." He flung the carcass into the corner. It hit the wall with a small thud and slid down to the floor. Dammit. He knew she would try something else. How could he have been so careless?

Nevon looked in horror in the direction where the body had been tossed. "A spy? A mage can do that?"

"She was watching us through the creature's eyes. They know where we are, Garron. We have to go. Now."

They fled the storeroom and sprinted down the corridor. In short order, the entire area would be flooded with guardsmen. He had to get them someplace quickly, or it could all end in disaster.

"Where are we going?" Garron asked behind him.

"Away from here," he replied—but he really had no idea. They were heading in the direction of the kitchens, which would have too many people about. His mind ran a quick inventory of their options. He had to lead them somewhere else. But where? The mage had discovered that he and Garron were still deep in the manor, hiding out in the servants' tunnels, which meant they could dedicate all their resources and concentrate their search. They would send in guards from every direction to block their escape.

And it was likely that the mage had other four-legged spies about.

Following the main artery through the manor's substructure was too risky. Not that any of the servants would deliberately turn them in, but self-preservation was powerful. Someone would sing if pressed. He led them down the first side passage they came across—a narrow, low-ceilinged route that looked promising. But ten steps in, Mouse heard voices farther ahead, so he shooed the other two back again and sought a different route. A different passage branched off to the right. This time, Mouse turned an ear to the opening and waited. Hearing nothing, Mouse trotted ahead on the front of his feet, dagger gripped tightly in his hand.

The passage was short and ended at an ironbound door. Mouse knew immediately what he'd stumbled upon. There was only one thing that would be kept this tightly locked down here among the manor's drudges.

He sent Garron off to fetch a light while he squatted down and pulled out his small leather case of tools. Garron returned moments later with one of the fat tallow candles from the wall niche. He shaded the flame with his hand as he scurried back. He handed the candle to Mouse, who set it on the floor underneath the lock. It smelled of rancid fat. The weak flame gave off just enough light for Mouse to see by, but also black smoke that billowed upward and quickly formed a sooty cloud near the ceiling of the tight space. Nevon coughed and covered his nose and mouth.

The door had two locks. Kneeling before the door, leaning in and squinting from the poor light and the stinging smoke in his eyes, Mouse slipped his tools into the first lock. The process didn't demand too much by sight. While it did help to see how far the tools were in, their angles into the lock, and so forth, it was a job accomplished mostly by feel and instinct. He moved his tools around to sense the interior. This lock was unlike all the others in the manor. No surprise. It would have been commissioned special from a locksmith of some prestige.

"Can you do it?" Garron asked.

"Of course I can do it," he snapped, his hands freezing in place as he looked over his shoulder. "Though it would go quicker without interruptions."

Someone had spent a good deal of coin on this lock. It was well made and did not provide him a lot of room to maneuver about inside. Plus it had two release pins instead of the typical one. He felt the first mechanism within catch on his tool and start to release. Then....

Snap.

"What was that?" Garron asked.

"My tool broke."

"What?" Panic was rising in his voice. "You have another?"

Mouse teased out the broken end from the hole, tossed it aside, and returned to his leather case on the stone floor. "One more." He slipped it out and began again.

Voices came from down the passage. Shouting.

Nevon started bouncing and fidgeting with his hands. "Mouse?" he said in a frantic whisper. "I think they're coming." Garron put a hand on the lad's shoulder to calm him.

How odd, thought Mouse, while he felt around again with the tool. How odd it was how invested their captive was in their escape. The lad was more anxious than any of them. This had been a strange day indeed. "Hurrying is what broke the first tool," he replied flatly.

The tool caught the mechanism again. He gave it more a gentle pressure this time and could feel it—almost see it in his mind—move. Holding the first tool steady, he positioned the second tool and dug deeper for the second release. Behind him, the voices were getting louder. Someone was barking orders. He could hear movement too, footfalls on stone and the clunky sound of armor.

He maneuvered his hands deftly and felt the lock mechanism obey his tender coaxing. He could feel the strain on the tool. He held his breath until he heard the soft click.

"One down."

"Mouse, they're going to be upon us any second."

Garron was right. He could hear them working their way down the corridor, making a thorough sweep.

Mouse set to work again. The lock was similarly constructed…
luckily. But it was made for a different key. Two separate keys for one
room. A fail-safe way to prevent the contents of the room from walking
off. Two different people had to unlock the door. Mouse shut out the
sound of the guards drawing closer, and the sound of Garron's foot
anxiously tapping on the floor, and focused his entire attention on the
tiny hole in front of him. He allowed himself a full breath, and then
he inserted the tools, orienting them as he had before. He twisted his
hands, feeling the force of the pins against his tool. Slowly. Smoothly.
He closed his eyes and constructed the lock in his mind as he guided the
two slender iron rods.

Click.

Mouse pushed the latch, and the door swung open.

"Quick, now!" he ordered. Garron and Nevon dashed into the
room. Mouse scooped up the candle and his tools and followed.

Just as he predicted. The room was rows and rows of stacked
wooden kegs. The wine cellar.

He closed the door—softly, for guards were no more than ten strides
down the main passage. He handed the candle to Garron and waved him
away from the door. It would not help if the guards saw a light coming
from the gap under the door.

Nevon grabbed Mouse's sleeve. "I can distract them," he said in a
whisper. "I can lead them away from here. Tell them I escaped and know
where you are hiding. That could give you an opening to escape."

Garron looked at Mouse with a raised brow.

Mouse herded the two of them away from the door, deeper into the
cellar. "A good idea, Your Highness," he said. "But it wouldn't work."

The lad's face darkened. "You don't trust me," he said sharply. "You
still believe I'll cross you and tell the guards where you are. What's stopping
me from screaming out right now, huh?"

Mouse put a hand on his shoulder and with a gentle look, held up
his other palm to slow the lad down. "I do trust you," he answered. And
he did, surprisingly. For whatever reason, the youth had attached himself
to their struggle. "But they wouldn't believe you. The mage witnessed
you too and knows you aren't in any danger from us. But she also doesn't
specifically know who you are, and I want to keep it that way."

"Maybe we should let him run off, then, Mouse." Garron offered.

Mouse considered that but shook his head. "Not yet. A young noble down in the servants' passages? Dressed like that? They'll work out he was with us in an instant."

He moved on the front of his feet toward the door again, knelt in front of it, and went to work relocking the door from the inside. He reinserted the tools, this time to trigger the lock, which was always easier. In seconds he had both relocked.

The three of them crept down one of the long aisles of stacked kegs until they reached the back wall. Mouse heard someone try the latch. Muffled voices came through the door.

"This here's the wine cellar… gonna require two keys. Should we get the chancellor to unlock it so we can check?"

"Don't be daft. Place's locked up like a vault.…"

For the moment, they were safe. Cornered yes, but safe. But there was the danger that someone would eventually decide to check it out. For now, their best option was to wait out the initial sweep and sneak out when the trail went cold and they expanded the search to other areas again.

They sat on the floor and leaned against the wall. Mouse took a moment to close his eyes and catch his breath. He could still hear the muffled shouts out in the passageway, but the relative quiet of the cellar gave him a chance to think and plan. The rich smell of oak from the barrels reached into his brain and calmed him, clearing his head. He sat there for a time, leaning back against the cold stone of the wall. He could easily drift off, he realized, so he forced his eyes back open.

"What would happen if Delgan discovered I aided in your escape?" Nevon asked.

Mouse frowned. The lad spoke matter-of-factly, with the same intonation that he might use when asking what soup was being prepared that day. But there was a disquiet layered beneath his tone, a prickling concern. Apparently it had begun to seep into the lad's brain that dangers are inherent in adventures.

"He won't," Mouse replied.

"Suppose he does."

"You yourself pointed out that there are different rules for the noble class than for us rabble." He attempted to sound casual. Blasé. "It's unlikely Delgan would throw you into any of his dungeons."

Garron considered that, then made a small shrug and lifted his brow. "That is not to say there wouldn't be consequences, Mouse."

Mouse threw him a hard look.

"What does that mean?" Nevon asked, his voice rising a degree.

Mouse sighed. He hoped to spare Nevon that added worry. They didn't need the lad panicking and causing a problem for them. But there was no avoiding it now. "Just what he said. There would be consequences. Direct punishment would be unlikely—at least from Delgan's end—but the knowledge of your involvement would sour the relationship between Delgan and your family. And your dukedom."

Nevon was quiet a moment. "I hadn't thought of that."

No, of course you didn't, Mouse thought, but held his tongue.

"I don't want this to cause problems for Mother," Nevon added. The concern was more evident in his voice now. "She's worked hard to establish her contacts here. I don't want to be the cause of it failing."

"Don't worry about it, Your Highness. I won't let it happen."

Nevon's lips scrunched into a pout. "Stop calling me that. I'm not a prince."

Garron swatted at Mouse's arm, which made Mouse chuckle. "Look," Mouse told the lad, "if we run into any trouble, I'd have you just hide out in here until it all blew over. Once it's quiet again, you can sneak back to the noble apartments and find your way back to your posh little room. You can then spend the rest of the day eating caviar and roast grouse and ordering servants about at your whim. No one need ever be the aware of your involvement."

Nevon seemed to accept that and nodded.

They fell into a silence again. Mouse looked down at his hands and systematically tugged at the knuckles of each finger until they cracked. His fingers were sore, the muscles resisting when he tightened his hand into a fist. There were small abrasions and scrapes that had scabbed over on the pads and sides of his fingers. The climb up the tower, he realized. His hands were recovering from that still. Had that really only been nine or so hours ago?

When Mouse lifted his head up, Garron was glaring at him narrowly. "What is it you have against nobles, Mouse?"

He almost laughed. "You cannot be serious!"

"It is not as if Nevon or I had any control of our status in the world. You cannot blame us for who our parents are. We are each born into our own circumstances."

"And I was born with nothing."

Garron's face darkened into a mix of sorrow and fatigue. Not surprising. It had been a very long night. "I think your life was far richer than you realize." He sighed. "Yes, my sheets are satin and meals obscene compared to most. But, honestly, the life of a noble is...."

"Dull!" interjected Nevon.

Garron laughed. "Yes. Dull is indeed the word I'd use."

"I could go for a little dull now and then," Mouse replied. "And the satin sheets."

"You'd be clawing your eyes out from boredom in less than a fortnight, and you know it."

Mouse didn't know how to respond, so he said nothing.

"You know," Garron added, "we aren't all terrible people."

So I've come to learn, Mouse thought.

THE SILENCE settled on them for a time. Each slipped away into his own thoughts. Nevon seemed fixated on a spot that appeared on his fine jerkin and tried to scrape it off with his fingernail. His dresser was going to have a fit when she saw the amount of dirt under his fingernails and how disheveled his hair was. He was one shabby tunic away from passing as a commoner.

Which, Mouse realized, could be the lad's way out of this mess.

"Garron?" he said.

Garron lifted his head from the wall and opened his eyes. "Huh? What?" He had obviously fallen asleep.

"I should probably reapply the salve," Mouse told him.

"Oh, right."

While Mouse dug out the jar from his pack, Garron climbed to his feet and dutifully tugged down his trousers and short clothes. This time, the linen pulled cleanly away and did not stick to the wound. Mouse scooped more of the yellow cream on his fingers and applied it to the burn, taking more time to massage it in than probably necessary.

"Look, Garron...," he said as he put the earthenware jar back in his pack. He wasn't certain how to proceed, and the pregnant pause that followed did not escape Garron's notice. The nobleman pulled up his trousers and turned about. He remained quiet with a questioning look, inviting Mouse to finish.

"This escape of yours," Mouse began tentatively, "has grown... progressively more complicated." Mouse was trying to approach this gently. But in truth, the ordeal was a fucking disaster.

Garron glanced around at their surroundings. "We do appear to be moving in the wrong direction," he agreed with a nod. "Moving deeper into the manor rather than closer to any exit. What are you saying, Mouse?"

"Nothing specific, I suppose. The mage's presence here is forcing me to recalculate our options. It all means that getting you beyond the walls will prove more difficult than I initially thought."

Garron seemed to digest this a moment, his expression unreadable. "Impossible?"

"Not even improbable. I wasn't lying when I said that I've never failed a job I was hired for. Today will not count as my first."

"But you are having some doubts. That is plain enough."

Mouse rubbed one eye with his forefinger and middle finger. "No, it's not that. My ability to see you freed is not in question. But I cannot see how we are going to get out of this now without... without some measure of bloodshed."

Garron's gaze lowered as he considered this, and he was silent a moment. "You have held strongly to your word so far. I am grateful, truly. Whatever happens from this moment on, I trust you will do what you can to not cause any unnecessary harm or death. But....." He took in a long breath and exhaled slowly. "But should it come to that... should it come to violence, know I will surrender before harm comes to any man."

Mouse's heart tightened. "And they will likely kill you." *And me.*

Garron nodded. "If that is the case, so be it. I will not live out my days with the blood of innocents on my hands."

"They are hardly—"

"Have they any choice, Mouse? Yes, they pursue us, but their will is not their own. They follow orders they do not dare question, and cannot be held responsible."

Mouse looked away and was quiet.

"You think I'm weak," Garron said to Mouse's silence. It wasn't a question. It was more of a challenge. "You view my forbearance from violence as flaw of character." Garron's eyes were narrow and his lips thin. It was the closest Mouse had seen him to anger.

Mouse shook his head. "No," he said. "No, quite the contrary actually." In truth, he wondered if he would ever have the strength to risk his own life on any such conviction. "A question, though. What of the one giving the orders?"

"As in Duke Delgan?"

"Or the chancellor."

A coldness passed over Garron's features as his eyes narrowed. "If we face him, do with him what you will."

Mouse nodded. He could live with that.

Garron studied Mouse's face a moment. His lips pressed in a thin line of concern. "There is something yet on your mind."

Mouse turned away, his mouth turning downward. He was not accustomed to being read so easily. "A personal matter," he answered quickly out of reflex, then reconsidered. He felt compelled to say more, though he didn't know why. He told himself the information might be relevant to the mission but knew it was something else. "The mage certainly heard our entire conversation when I spoke of my father. I said too much…."

Garron looked back at him quizzically. "How so?"

Mouse shook his head. "It was foolish of me. I should never have spoken so freely of him. Now… I have put him in danger. Based on what I said, it is possible they can locate him. They will find him and—" He stopped himself. The words were spilling from him in a rush like a leaky keg, and he needed to regain control of his tongue. "Garron," he continued, more slowly this time, more mindful of his words. "My past… well, I've had to survive, you know. I won't apologize for that. I did what was necessary, but… my crimes are many, to say the least."

"Ah," Garron replied with nod. Mouse could see on his face he understood. "Your fear is that they will hold your father responsible for your crimes in your absence."

Mouse nodded. "That is the law. I've managed so far to hold off the king's guard from taking him." Garron's brow lifted at that. "Bribery," Mouse put in, answering Garron's unasked question. "Delgan now presumably has a substantial ax to grind with me. I have stolen his prize. He is a dangerous man, Garron, and I fear I may no longer be able to protect my father."

Garron considered this a moment, then said, "We can get a message to him. Warn him."

"Assuming there's time. They are already making efforts to locate him, certainly. We would have to find our way out of here soon if we are to get a messenger to him in time."

"We will," Garron replied, but Mouse didn't think he sounded all too confident. Garron pressed his lips together as he thought a moment. "You realize, of course, I can provide some aid in this. Beyond just sending him a warning. Once we are free from here, I'll have access to resources—"

"A kind and generous offer," Mouse cut in. The typical response of the wealthy and powerful—the solution to any problem is to throw coin at it. "But that won't be necessary. It is my affair." And he would manage it himself, as he had always done. "I've no wish to drag you into it." He felt himself pulling back and regretted having even mentioned it.

"I would be happy to help, if I can. Considering all you've done…."

Mouse made a sad little chuckle. "All I've done," he repeated. In truth, all he'd managed to do so far was to get him locked into a chamber far grimier than his previous cell. Garron was forgetting that Mouse wasn't doing this for any altruistic reasons. He was to be handsomely paid. And the coin he earned would in theory solve the issue anyway with the purchase of a king's pardon. But all the gold in the king's coffers wouldn't mean shit if he didn't get out of this keep. "Thank you," he said, attempting to lift his tone and put an end to the topic. "We can discuss it further, perhaps. Once I've actually accomplished what I was hired to do." Mouse doubted that Lord Green Eyes would even recall the offer or the conversation once he was safe beyond the keep's walls. Garron would surely not want to sully his breeches wading through the complications of Mouse's life. "Until then, we should plan our next move."

As if on cue, Mouse heard the sound he most dreaded. The click of the lock. Then a second click followed shortly after.

"Hide," he told Nevon in a heavy whisper. The lad gave a sharp nod and moved quickly. He crawled up the shelving that housed the rows of kegs and lay down on the top row near the ceiling. He was completely out of sight. Mouse reached over and snubbed out the candle, thrusting them into darkness as thick as pitch. The door to the passage beyond crept open, the hinges protesting with a high-pitched squeal, and warm light from a lantern crashed into the room. It lifted over the row of barrels like a sunrise over a horizon.

Hopefully, it was just some lackey fetching a requested keg of wine. The door was shut and light moved. Aisle by aisle it moved closer. It would stop for a time at each aisle as if searching. From the footfalls, Mouse determined it was only one person—which confused him. Two keys were needed to open the door, and they wouldn't likely give both to one person. Was this some high-ranking courtier entrusted with both keys to hunt down a specific vintage? Mouse pulled out his dagger from his belt and gingerly moved his feet underneath him into a low squat. He was ready to spring if necessary.

Regardless of what he told Garron—he would protect him. At all cost. And he would cope with Garron's outrage afterward.

The light rounded the end of the last aisle and for a moment, Mouse was temporarily blinded by the sudden intensity. He lifted the dagger, prepared to throw at the first sign of a threat. He could only see a dark silhouette.

"Well, shits on a stick! There you are!"

CHAPTER 19

MOUSE PULLED back his arm, fully prepared to release the dagger, but some unknown motive stayed his hand. Some deep part of his brain told him to wait—and a single heartbeat later his intellect caught up to his instinct. This was no guardsman, clearly. The silhouette was too small, and the shape implied no armor was worn. And the voice was clearly that of a woman.

But that did not mean she wasn't a danger.

She stepped forward down the aisle at an unhurried pace, lifting the lantern higher. "Don't bother lobbing that lovely thing my way, dear. No good will come of it." She was dressed in the simple attire of a maidservant and wasn't either particularly pretty or homely. She would be someone easily overlooked and ignored by most. But Mouse recognized the signs that she was much more. She held herself with too much self-assuredness and willful authority and spoke with an ease that was far above her alleged station. This was no common drudge. And Mouse knew immediately who she was.

He lowered his arm and lifted to his feet. But he kept the blade firmly gripped in his hand nonetheless.

Her brow lifted a fraction as she raked her eyes over him. "My, my. They weren't lying. You are rather… undersized, aren't you?"

"Size isn't everything."

"Apparently. Drux is still recovering from his encounter with you."

"How did you find us?"

"Wasn't easy. I've been combing the manor an entire day. When I caught an ear that you had been discovered hiding out down here, I decided to check out the places I'd hunker down."

Garron climbed to his feet. "Mouse? What's going on? Who is this woman?"

Mouse did not pull his eyes from her. "I wondered if we would eventually meet," he told her. He kept his tone neutral. "I could have used your help earlier."

"By my estimation, looks like you can use some help now."

Garron joined him at his elbow, his body nearly pushing against his. Mouse could feel his heat against his bare arm. "You know each other?"

"We've not had the pleasure of meeting, no." He chanced a quick glance toward Garron. "But I knew she was here somewhere. This here is the guild's mole stationed in the manor."

The woman curtsied. "Yensia, at your service."

Mouse bowed politely in return—but kept his eye on her the whole time and his hand firmly around the hilt of the blade. Any furtive movements on her part, and he would act. "Mouse, at yours," he replied with a thin smile. "I assume this gentleman requires no introduction."

"Indeed he does not." She made a respectful nod to Garron. "M'lord."

Garron replied in kind with a simple bow.

"Whoever you have hiding up on the stacks might as well come down as well," Yensia added casually.

Mouse was about to proclaim he had no idea of what she was talking about, but the lad's face poked out from atop a barrel.

"Well, Master Nevon, as I live and breathe," she said with a widening smile. "This is certainly an unexpected pleasure."

"Good day, Yensia," Nevon answered sheepishly.

Yensia clicked her tongue and shook her head. "Your garments are going to be frightfully dirty from being up there, you know. I imagine your mother is going to be quite cross with you." She looked over at Mouse, and her eyes twinkled with delight at Mouse's surprise. "His mother and I are acquainted, as it turns out. We have had some business dealings together during her visit here."

Curious, thought Mouse. He was beginning to think he'd like to meet the lad's mother after all. "Please don't take this wrong way, Yensia. But why have you come to find us?"

"As I said, you could use my help. It appears the cat has you cornered, little Mouse."

Mouse very nearly groaned. Everyone thought the cat and mouse references were so clever. He shrugged and attempted to appear unconcerned. "Nothing I can't handle." She didn't look like she believed him but had the courtesy to not say so. "But," he continued. "I cannot help but wonder who you are presently representing on this visit."

Yensia's genial demeanor faltered some. The warmth behind her eyes cooled. "Ah. You refer to the guild's arrangement with Lord Delgan. Heard about that, did you?"

Garron's body stiffened beside him. "And what arrangement is that?" Garron asked. He was quick to recognize the danger they were in, Mouse noted.

Mouse answered for her, just to make sure she understood how much he already knew. "The guild has been given broad license to conduct their business both in the manor and on the streets in exchange that Yensia here provide Delgan with useful intelligence about the guests and residents of the manor. He is essentially ignoring her presence as long as it's beneficial to him. I'm certain the arrangement also includes a favor or two where the guild is to take care of some unofficial and less pleasant tasks for him as well. Delgan has managed to expand his network—and sphere of influence—to include the city's cabals. He now controls both the legitimate and illicit forces of the region. Accurate?"

"More or less." Yensia's face discarded any pretense of good humor. "Delgan only just has his foot in the guild door, but we all see where this is heading. He is starting to push, demanding more by small degrees so as not to generate too much discontent too fast and trigger an internal coup. Keeler is losing control of the guild. Though he's too blind or pigheaded to see it."

Keeler. The same oaf he encountered at the soup stall. It was no surprise to Mouse he was making a mess of it.

Yensia shook her head. "It's only a matter of time before he—and the rest of us—are answering to one of Delgan's men. Specifically, it'll be the chancellor."

"Elasiar," Mouse replied, unable to keep the disdain from his voice.

"Ah, I see you've had the pleasure. He's an ambitious worm, that one, and has a keen insight of the criminal underground here in the city. Too clever by half and bloody ruthless besides. I hear he's set his eyes onto the Shadow Elite now too. Seizing up businesses. Putting members in irons that don't play by his rules. Piece by piece he's dismantling their power." She shook her head. "Bet the Elite are wringing their hands raw."

Mouse nodded. "So, I'll ask again. Who are you working for now? Delgan? Or the guild?"

Yensia stepped closer, her fist clenched. "I don't work for that fat cur, Mouse. I am loyal to the guild. And a guild does not heel to any aristocracy."

A good answer. Mouse had been a guild man for a time himself. It turned out that working with others wasn't necessarily his strength, but he understood the sentiment that kept people in. And the zeal behind it. It was all very intoxicating—the ripe feeling of having power over your destiny, the love of the city that you worked tirelessly every day to carve up like a holiday roast, and the sense of belonging the guild provided to all the lost and indigent that the city shat out. "The brotherhood before all" and all that rot. And, of course, the fervent contempt and distrust of anyone with a title sitting before his name.

Yes. It was the appropriate response. But nonetheless, he studied her face, her eyes. Garron was watching him.

"Can we trust her?" Garron asked.

Mouse read the intensity and determination. And the intelligence. But he did not see deception. "Yes." He loosened his grip on the dagger and let the tension in his shoulders subside. He felt Garron ease next to him as well. Strange how quickly the man had come to trust him so explicitly. They'd known each other less than a complete day.

He nodded to Nevon, and the lad climbed down from the shelving. As he rejoined Mouse and Garron, he wiped the front of the jerkin with his hands, self-conscious now of the amount of dirt and grime that stained the fine fabric.

"How did you know where to find us?" Mouse asked.

"Part luck. Could tell they thought you were down here somewhere, so I was working my way through all the hiding places I'd consider. This was my third choice."

"How did you get in here so easily?"

She waved her hand in front of her dismissively. "I've had copies made of every key in the manor. There's no chamber I can't get into. Delgan has greatly underestimated me and my skills."

You hope, thought Mouse. Delgan was no dolt and seemed to be keeping one pace ahead of everyone in this city.

"He's convinced I'm his loyal puppet," Yensia continued. "That took some patient work, I can tell you. No thanks to that simpleton Keeler. But I'm very selective as to what information I pass on to him.

Nothing too valuable. Exhale, boy, before you pass out. I've told him nothing of your mother's dealings. Her work here in the city is safe."

Nevon's shoulders lost their tension, and his torso slumped forward.

"Anyway, it's a fine line I straddle here. I work harder to oppose him than benefit him, so I have to be careful. When word came to me from the guild what you were attempting, I started keeping eyes open for you." She gave Garron a pointed look. "Delgan's to benefit greatly from your internment. So, if helping you escape sets him back a pace, I'm in."

"How's he to benefit?" Mouse asked.

"Don't know the details. But he sure was happy with the deal he struck."

"Any idea who he struck the deal with?"

"None whatsoever. Never saw him before, or since. An obvious intermediary."

Mouse glanced over at Garron, who had turned and stared off into the darkness of the cellar, unseeing and lost in thought. Garron's mouth was pressed in a tight line, his lips all but gone. Was he trying to figure out who was behind this? Or did he already know?

"You have a plan?"

Yensia laughed, her easy disposition returning. "Of course. I'll have you out of here in the time it takes a flea to piss."

YENSIA CHECKED the corridor first. The other three waited just inside the cellar. She returned moments later. "Looks like they've completed their first sweep. Since they didn't find any sign of you, they'll conduct another, and soon. This next one will tear the place apart." She shook her head. "I don't envy the servants and laborers down here. This will not be a pleasant afternoon for them."

She was right about that. The guardsmen would assume they'd seen something, so they would likely be heavily interrogated.

"So we don't have much time," he finished for her.

"Yes. So, follow me quickly and do exactly as I say."

She led them past the manor kitchens, circumventing the more active regions. Warm savory-smelling currents flushed into the cooler passages. Guardsmen loitered about by the ovens, but they didn't seem to be actively searching. They were more likely taking advantage of the search to score some buttered rolls or flirt with the kitchen wenches.

Without a good reason to be there, the guardsmen would have been chased out by the manor cooks with large wooden spoons. The lantern brandished in front of her like a weapon, Yensia took them down a series of unlit passages in an area that Mouse hadn't yet explored. From the shuffle marks in the dirt floor, Mouse could tell guards had swept through here, but it was quiet now. The three of them followed close on Yensia's heels. Mouse trusted she knew where she was going—she made her way through the labyrinthine network with practiced ease.

Deeper in, the corridors grew cruder, the walls roughly hewed right out of the bedrock the manor was built on. The latest passage ended abruptly in a space that was more cave than chamber. A hodgepodge of items had been dumped there—a broken iron weapons rack, a cracked stone vat, and some old crates, probably forgotten about for generations and likely to disintegrate if ever moved. Yensia went right to the corner and dragged a rotted old tapestry out of the way to expose a hinged trap door in the floor.

"Where does this lead?" Mouse asked.

Yensia's eyes twinkled as one corner of her mouth lifted in an impish smile. "Straight out of the manor."

"You certain?" Garron asked, his voice betraying a resurgence of fresh hope. "Why is this here?"

Yensia and Mouse exchanged a quick glance, both taking a bit of pleasure from Garron's naiveté.

"Well," she replied, "lords with a shiny reputation can't exactly parade their whores right through the main gates, now can they? Or should they want to sneak out for a night of wicked behavior and don't want their wives to know…." She trailed off with a single brow raised.

Both Garron and Nevon made the same disapproving face that made Yensia laugh.

Mouse bobbed his head approvingly. "How many know of this?"

"Very few." She grabbed one of two iron rings attached to the portal and indicated with a tilt of her head that Mouse grab the other. "The nobles and the occasional merchant who use it still keep it very quiet. Guards would not know to check here."

Perfect.

Mouse and Yensia heaved, and the door begrudgingly swung open on its stiff hinges. Underneath was a hole that descended into darkness with a wooden ladder fixed to the side.

"Here." She handed Mouse the lantern. "Go quick now."

Mouse took it from her. "How will you get back?"

She swatted the air in front of her. "Ah, don't you worry. I can find my way through these passages blindfolded."

"But what about him?' Garron asked, leaning his head toward Nevon.

"I'll get him back safely, don't you worry. And he won't say a word, will you m'lord?" She smiled down at the lad. "I know too much of his mum's recent activities for him to wag his tongue about."

"I wouldn't say anything anyway," he grumbled back at her. He looked up at Garron. "Can't I go with you? I could help."

Mouse and Yensia exchanged glances again. What was it about Garron? The lad was willing to abandon the safety of the manor, abandon his mother, and travel down a dark hole with him to some unknown place. He was strikingly handsome, of course—but that was only part of it. His nature had an intoxicating magic. Was anyone immune to his charms? Himself included?

Garron put a hand on his shoulder and smiled warmly down at him. "You have done us a great service already, Nevon. But now it's time for Mouse to get me to safety, and it'll be dangerous."

"I can handle myself."

"I've no doubt," he answered with a laugh. Not a condescending or mocking laugh, but an affirming one that made Nevon's cheeks color. "But should the unlikely happen, I would be unable to forgive myself. I would be denying the world a strong future leader, and there are precious few of those." With his hand still on Nevon's shoulder, he guided him over to stand with Yensia. He then took the lantern by the handle from Mouse. "I will send word to you when I am safely away. And I would very much someday like to meet your mother."

"I have a few tasks that he can do from here," Yensia replied. "If he were that strongly inclined to assist."

Garron nodded to her. "Thank you. For everything."

"Oh, I'm not helping you, darling. I'm hindering that sleazy bastard."

"All the same," he said. Then he lowered himself onto the top rung of the ladder and descended into the hole. The darkness gradually consumed the chamber as the lantern sank with him.

Mouse positioned himself to follow but paused. "Your guild deserves a better leader than Keeler."

"I've often thought so. We're in a bit of flux at the moment. He's the third in a year. Lasted longer than the other two, but still not worth a floating turd."

"I may know someone better qualified."

"Is that so?" In the dark it was hard to read her face, but he thought he saw amusement light her eyes.

"Interested in the position?"

"The thought has crossed my mind," she said. "On occasion. Can't do any worse."

"Well, should you wish to pursue that course, I'd be willing to offer my services in helping you achieve that end. Free of charge, of course."

"Nothing in our vocation is without a price, love."

"Then consider my price marginal. A favor or two, perhaps."

She folded her arms. "Is this some clumsy attempt at showing gratitude? I told you, I'm not doing this for him. Or you."

"No," he replied. "I just despise seeing a poorly run guild."

"Wouldn't want it for yourself?"

"Not my style. I'd rather pull strings from the shadows." He stepped down onto the first rung. "One more thing. Should you happen on any evidence as to the who or the why behind this business...."

She shrugged. "I'll see what I can do. Won't promise anything."

That was good enough for him. As Mouse moved to follow Garron, Nevon sprang forward, waving his hands. "Wait," he said. "I still have on your boots."

"Keep them," Mouse said.

"You can't go down into that hole without boots!"

"I've been in worse places with less, lad. I assure you."

Nevon shook his head as he dropped to the floor. "Here." He tugged each boot off with a grunt and tossed them over. Mouse considered reminding him of his earlier comments about running around like a street urchin but chose to hold his tongue. He sat down on the edge of the square hole and pulled the boots on.

"Thanks."

As he lowered himself down the ladder, he heard Yensia say, "Help me with this."

"It's going to be black as pitch in here," Nevon replied over the angry screech of the hinges. "How are we going to find—"

The trap door dropped with a bang above him, shutting out the rest of his protest.

CHAPTER 20

MOUSE FELL in behind Garron. The tunnel was dank and foreboding… and very narrow, forcing them to walk single file. Garron's larger form blocked the light from the lantern he carried, shrouding Mouse in shadow. The air was noxious and stale. It felt more like a sewer than a passageway. Water seeped in from fissures in the stone and trickled down the rough walls to form pools on the uneven floor. At times it was as deep as their ankles, and Mouse discovered that the boots he had reclaimed from Nevon had substantial cracks in both soles. Icy water leaked in, numbing his toes.

It was hard to picture any parlor girls making this trek up from the city, or noble dandies venturing out, risking a soiling of their finery. They would have to be quite randy indeed.

"Mouse, I so enjoy our time together," Garron said dryly. "You introduce me to the most extravagant places."

"Only the best for His Lordship. What do you think about exploring a coal mine later? Or we could rent a wagon and collect the dead from some recent plague."

Garron laughed. A hearty laugh bigger than the gloom of the place should allow. His shift in mood was palpable. He was energized, giddy even. Even the murkiness of the tunnel didn't seem to dampen it. Now that they were out of the manor proper, his escape must have seemed like a reality for the first time. They weren't entirely out of danger yet, Mouse knew, but they were getting closer. Mouse couldn't help himself and laughed along with him.

The laughter died away gently, and they fell into the quiet task of traversing the tunnel. In the silence, Mouse caught himself thinking about the end of the mission. It felt close now. All that remained was the task of smuggling Garron out of the city. No small feat surely, but Mouse predicted it would prove easier than getting him out of Delgan's keep. And after that, once he delivered Garron safely to his protective entourage, well… that was it, wasn't it? Mouse would get the rest of his payment, and Garron would be escorted back to Har Dionante. He would return to his life as son of

Duke Braddock—a life of satin sheets, ten-course meals, tennis in a private courtyard, and watching tournaments from box seats safely distanced from the smell of horses and the unwashed rabble below.

It all had a peculiar finality that tugged at Mouse unexpectedly. He and Garron would never cross paths again. They existed in two very different worlds, and there was little chance of those worlds ever crossing paths again. It wasn't as if they were going to ever meet up in a tavern one night to share a pint and laugh about their adventure together.

He shook his head.

What the fuck was wrong with him? Garron was a job. Another object he was hired to steal. Nothing more. Any sense of a companionship he felt between them was nothing more than an illusion. Mouse knew well he was not the gentle sort. He was crude and undisciplined, not the sort that mixed well with the gentility. He was simply confusing Garron's affable nature and civility with genuine amity.

The tunnel angled downward for a while, at times steeply and at other times becoming roughly formed stairs. It didn't seem to hold to a single path but would sway and turn as if avoiding unseen obstacles in the surrounding rock. The deeper in they traversed, the drier it became, but Mouse's feet were already soaked and gone numb, so it didn't much matter.

"Do you have a plan?" Garron asked, breaking the long silence.

"I always have a plan," Mouse replied. That didn't, however, mean it was a good plan. He had a few ideas brewing but wasn't ready yet to settle on one yet. He wanted to wait to gauge the climate when they arrived outside. "Getting out of the city will still be dicey. It won't take them long to figure out that we gave them the slip. There will be plenty of guards sweeping the streets."

"It gets low up ahead. Careful," Garron said, looking over his shoulder. "Oh wait," he added, "never mind." He tried to hold a steely face when he said it, but a smile cracked through. Mouse made a face back at him. "Well, if anyone is to get me out of this shithole town, it's you." Mouse nearly laughed out loud at that. He couldn't explain it. Something about Garron cursing, or even acting bad-tempered, brightened his mood. "Just tell me what you need me to do," he added.

"You needn't worry about that," Mouse replied. He paused, hesitating to proceed. His father still weighed on his mind. The more time that passed, the more danger he was in. He needed to act. "Actually," he added slowly. "With your indulgence, I'd like to seek out a messenger to hire straight away."

"To warn your father," Garron said, nodding. "Of course, Mouse. I agree. He should be warned."

"It will not take long nor endanger you."

"I know," Garron said. His expression changed then. The levity of earlier fled his eyes, and his mouth turned down on one side. "But…." He stopped and turned around to face Mouse directly. "About that."

Mouse looked back up at him with a suspicious raised brow, not at all clear where this was heading. "Yes?"

"I think you needn't worry about him. I'm fairly certain your father can take care of himself."

Mouse felt his cheeks flush and lips tighten. "Needn't worry? What can you know about the danger he may be in? I may well have doomed him by—"

Garron put a hand on Mouse's shoulder to stop him. "That's not what I meant." He smiled gently, while his eyes revealed that he was carefully considering what to say next. "I agreed, remember? We'll send warning. It's just that…. Let me see that dagger again. The one that belonged to your father."

Mouse rolled his head to the side. "That again?"

"Indulge me."

His shoulders fell some in reluctant compliance. "Very well." He slipped the dagger out of his belt and handed it hilt first to Garron, who took it from him with gentle hands as if holding an ancient relic. "Honestly, I can't comprehend your fixation with it."

He smiled then, strangely and inexplicably, as if some mystery had been answered. "It feels heavy to my hand. Clumsy even."

"Then you're an idiot, because it's the lightest and most evenly balanced blade I've ever held." He reached for it again, to take it back, but Garron twisted and moved it out of his reach, and held up his lantern between them to interfere.

"A moment yet. I'm not done."

"You just don't know a good blade when you hold one."

Garron chuckled. "I've held some of the very best in all the kingdom, actually." Gripping it by its hilt and holding the lantern close, he angled the flat side of the blade to face the light. He looked closely. "This symbol."

"I already told you. I've tried to identify it, but I've not seen the emblem ever before."

Garron was very quiet for a moment as he studied it. "But I have."

Mouse's heart froze solid. He wanted to speak, say something, ask anything, but found for once in his life, he could not utter any words.

"How did you come to have it again?' Garron asked.

"I told you," Mouse said in quiet voice. "I found it among his things. I took it the night I left the village."

"Where? Where did he keep it?"

"He had it in a chest, hidden under a false bottom. Wrapped in a velvet cloth. Garron, tell me. How do you know that symbol?"

"I have seen this symbol when I've visited the capital, when I've gone to the keep and the king's palace. And I've seen it in my studies. This weapon… it would have been too valuable for someone to give up as payment for services. I'm certain your father was good at his craft, but this could have purchased an entire town. Several, in fact."

Mouse listened, waiting—a feeling of dread creeping over him. A part of him knew the knife was more than just a knife, even when he took it. But he had blocked those thoughts from his mind.

"Mouse, this is the emblem of the Black Guard."

Mouse inadvertently took a step backward. He shook his head. "I'm sorry… did you just actually say to me that this belonged to the Black Guard?"

"The symbol is undeniable. I'd recognize it anywhere."

"That just isn't possible." He had not heard them spoken by name in a very long time. The Black Guard were famed throughout the kingdom. Famous for their skill but also infamous for their terrible failure.

"I'm certain this must come as a shock. But there is only one way this dagger has come into your father's possession."

"No. That is patently ridiculous. My father is a tanner. He is not— nor ever was—some royal guard." Not just any royal guard, either. The Black Guard. Mouse wanted to laugh. His father, the quiet-spoken, gentlest man he'd ever known, a highly skilled and deadly protector of the royal family?

He knew little of them, only what he picked up from tavern stories, which were mostly rumor and hearsay—and likely exaggerated. The legion disbanded before he was even born, so there were fewer around now who could vouch for these tales. It was always a company of twenty men, as the stories went, and it was claimed that the brotherhood existed for generations beyond counting, since the dawn of the realm and the very first king. To be chosen was said to be the greatest honor bestowed upon someone of common birth. Each had been hand selected by the king himself, and membership insured a life of respect, honor, and some said great riches and land. But acceptance meant a life dedicated fully to the service and safety of the king and his family, never to marry or father children. And from the day a warrior took the emblem on his skin, no one but other members of the brotherhood and the royal family would be allowed to gaze upon his face again.

But the Black Guard was no more....

"There were survivors, Mouse."

"Three," he replied, his voice barely making a sound. "As the story is told."

"Yes. There were three who lived that day. Three members of the brotherhood... and the young prince."

The prince who would become King Harus V.

The tale, regardless of the narrator, had enough common threads to hold at least some truth. A rival family attempted an assassination of the king and his entire family, with the aim to end the royal line. An advisor close to the king betrayed him, and an entire legion of soldiers breached the palace in the middle of the night. The Black Guard fought off the onslaught against incredible odds and succeeded in putting each would-be assassin to the sword, but not before the king, his queen, and two of his children had been butchered... along with seventeen of the Black Guard. One heir remained.

It was told that the three survivors were so distraught at their failure to protect the king, they left the palace in disgrace, never to return again. Many believed that they had taken their own lives.

Mouse touched his own forearm absently, thinking of the burn that marred his father's arm. He'd fallen into a fire after too much drink. That was the story he'd always told. It was what would have been his sword arm, the arm where such an emblem would have been inked into his skin.

Garron extended the hilt to him, and Mouse hesitated before taking it back into his hand. "The dagger is enchanted," Garron said. "Spelled to recognize your father's hand. You, having his blood, are close enough to satisfy the enchantment. Which is why the dagger has always felt so natural to you. It has, in a manner of speaking, accepted you. But," he added with a tilt of head, "it would somehow know your father, should he hold it. Or perhaps even if he were near show some sign. Such enchantments are like that."

"This cannot be real," Mouse said.

"It explains much. Your uncanny skill, most of all. You apparently take after you father more than you realize. Come. Let's get out of this place so we can send that warning. I would very much enjoy being there if any of Delgan's thugs try to apprehend him. They would be little match for a member of the Black Guard."

Mouse nodded and followed Garron in a stupor as if his head swam from drink. *Only if they get the warning to him in time*, he thought. Forces were certainly already on the move against him.

CHAPTER 21

THE TUNNEL came to an abrupt end not unlike it began, with a ladder rising to a trap door. Mouse climbed up and lifted his ear to the door. Hearing nothing, he tested it with a light push. It lifted easily, unlocked and unobstructed. Which was a relief—he half expected this underground journey to be for naught, and they'd be forced to return. A pale light stabbed in from the crack, but still he heard nothing. He pushed the door up farther and climbed out.

The chamber he found himself in was small and cramped. The walls were unpainted planks of wood, and the ceiling had rows of roughly hewn beams. Bright afternoon sunlight streamed in from two barred windows near the ceiling. Crates were stacked neatly against one wall, and clay amphorae of lamp oil and bolts of textiles were arranged on large wooden shelving that stood along another. A small desk and stool were positioned in the corner, with a chaos of invoices and legers blanketing the surface.

A warehouse, Mouse realized. Small-scale merchants with limited cargo rented storage chambers such as these. They were often used as quiet hiding places for various contraband as well. Mouse wondered if the merchandise here was just props to disguise the true purpose of the place, or if the renter received a discount for allowing people to parade through his stockroom.

He leaned back over the hole. "Stay there a moment," he said. Garron nodded from the bottom.

He made a quick loop of the tiny chamber. It was always best to be overcautious. Another of the mage's four-legged spies could end their escape plan quickly. He listened at the storeroom's lone door—a standard plank construction with three horizontal iron bands. It hung on a track bolted to the wall above it. Again, no sound came from the opposite side. So far, they seemed safely away, but that didn't mean a legion of men weren't outside the building, waiting for them to emerge.

Mouse tested the door's release and pulled. It slid to the side with a small squeak of protest from the wheels as they rolled along the track, but it moved easily. Someone had made certain the whole apparatus was well oiled. Outside was a wide corridor, plenty wide for merchants to cart in their goods, and either side was lined with identical doors spaced equally apart.

He signaled Garron up.

"Looks clear," Garron said but turned to Mouse for affirmation.

Mouse gave a slow nod. "So, here's what we are going to do. Just walk on out of here as if you belong. Appear as if you've been here before and know where you're going, so don't walk too fast so you can get a look around. You're already dressed as a merchant, so no one has cause to stop or question you." He grabbed a ledger off the desk. "I— your dutiful clerk—will be right behind you."

"What if they ask for papers or something? Like an invoice or lease."

"They won't." At least he hoped they wouldn't. Some hired watchmen enjoyed the authority and could be difficult, but most were indifferent and lazy. By now, it was past midnight, which meant the warehouse would be quieter. Mouse would be surprised if they found anyone about that was awake or sober. "If you just act important, most will leave you be. I've seen you look that way before, so I know you can do it."

Garron made a rude gesture, but it was half-hearted. The skin encircling his eyes was dark while the rest of his face was ashen and drawn. It had been more than an entire day since either of them had had any sleep, and now with most of the excitement hopefully behind them, it was catching up to him.

"All right, then," Garron said. "Let's get it over with." He took a deep breath and marched down the center of the corridor with a straight back and his chin up. Mouse slid the door closed behind him and followed.

The corridor led to another, which then deposited them into a high-ceilinged open area: the space where merchants brought their carts in to be loaded or unloaded. Two crane arms affixed with a block and tackle were mounted to opposite walls to lift freight to or from the platform on the second floor. Garron marched right through the center of the open area with Mouse close on his heels, the clap of his footfalls on the wooden floor echoing around them. No other merchants were about, but a few unattended carts had been wheeled into a corner. No one was about to operate the crane, apparently. At the far end was a set of wide double doors, also hanging from tracks. Larger versions of the doors at each storeroom. One of the doors was slid partially open.

Garron made straight for the open door, his pace quickening.

Mouse scanned the area for the hired watch. He knew they had to be somewhere. He spotted them along the side wall—three of them, sitting around a wooden drum turned on its side. They were throwing dice in a wooden tray and talking quietly among themselves. A woman in a simple green shift leaned against the wall behind one man's shoulder. A wife or favorite whore. She glanced up at Garron as he strutted past, then returned her attention to the dice game. None of the men took notice.

Garron and Mouse stepped out of the warehouse and onto the streets of Har Orentega. No ambush awaited them. No guards were canvassing the street. The citizens milling about paid them no attention as they walked past.

They had escaped the manor.

"Where to now?" Garron asked.

"Somewhere I'm fairly certain I won't be welcome."

"WHAT THE fuck is the matter with you?"

Taurin paced the floor of his bedchamber, red-faced. With one hand, he tugged at the clasps of his surcoat as he stomped back and forth in front of his massive bed, while he swung a chalice of wine about with the other, splashing the crimson liquid all over his very expensive rug, making it look like the recent scene of a murder. Their arrival had interrupted the entertaining of important clients, and Taurin had dressed well for the affair. But moments after they'd entered the chamber, he'd transformed into something considerably less urbane.

Mouse had never seen him quite this angry—but then he'd never brought a fugitive to his doorstep before either. He took a seat in one of the chairs by the fireplace, leaned back, and brought one leg over the other knee as if enjoying fine theater.

Garron on the other hand moved to stand very quietly against the wall trying not to bring attention to himself. He too threw harsh glares in Mouse's direction.

"I have half the mind…. No. Three-quarters of the mind to send for Delgan's men immediately and have you arrested, and him"—he made a dramatic point of the finger at Garron—"turned over."

"But you won't."

He spun about. "Oh, won't I?" Nothing terrified Taurin more than the notion of his little empire collapsing. He had grown powerful, certainly. And Mouse had never known anyone to enjoy the fruits of power more unabashedly. But no one's ongoing success among the Shadow Elite was ever assured. Just as Taurin had shouldered his way to a better position when some titan fell, some young villain would do the same to him.

Mouse knew that Taurin was dangerous in this state. But a part of him didn't care.

"You are overreacting, Taurin," he said.

Taurin stumbled back as if struck. "Overreacting? You brought an escaped political prisoner here! In my establishment! Do you have any idea—" He stopped himself and shook his head. "Of course you do. You just don't fucking care." He tugged at the neck of his fine white chemise to loosen the lacings of the thong over the chest and wiped the sweat from his brow with the sleeve of his surcoat. "Did I not make myself clear before that I did not want any part of this on my doorstep? I have a fucking business to run here. And that business does not include helping Delgan's personal little trophy escape from his dungeons."

"Taurin, you know as well as I do they'll be searching every inn and tavern in the city tonight."

"Leave the city tonight, then!"

"Don't be daft. Both bridges leading to the city gates have already been drawn." The decrees were posted in every public square. An unnamed threat to the citizens of Har Orentega had forced the city to keep both bridges raised until the threat was neutralized. Even now, Delgan wasn't willing to admit his secret prisoner had escaped. "Until we arrange passage on a ship, we need a discreet place to stay out of sight." Mouse moved both feet to the floor and leaned in, resting his elbows on his knees. "One night. That's all I'm asking."

"You ask too much. This could ruin me."

Was nothing more important than the power and influence he brandished about in this city? Yensia was right. The Shadow Elite were running scared here in Har Orentega.

He dropped his forehead into his palm. "Gods! The Taurin I once knew would leap at an opportunity to thwart the aristocracy. When did you become so gutless?"

"Fuck you, Mouse!"

Mouse dragged his hand down his face to cup his chin. "Look," he said. "I'll make it worth the risk you're taking. Fifty crowns."

Garron straightened. "Mouse—"

He held up his hand to stop Garron from saying anything further.

Taurin glanced inside his chalice, saw it was empty, and threw it on the floor. He folded his arms, and his eyes shifted toward Mouse. For several moments he held them on him, and Mouse could see the calculations working in his mind. The businessman had risen up through the cloud of anger.

"One hundred," Taurin said finally. "And you owe me one job. No limits. No turning it down."

"Mouse, no!" Garron exclaimed.

"Done," Mouse replied, louder to drown out Garron's protest.

Garron stepped away from the wall. "Two hundred crown," he said to Taurin. "And Mouse owes you nothing."

Taurin slowly swung his gaze over to Garron as if noticing him for the first time. The anger had evaporated completely, and his eyes narrowed with interest. "And how will I get my coin, fugitive?"

"You will get it. You have my word as a nobleman."

Taurin smiled thinly like one does when a child says something charming. "Darling, I run a brothel. I know firsthand the market value of a nobleman's word." He held Garron's hard gaze for several moments before breaking it off with casual disregard. The corner of his mouth twitched. He seemed to realize something about Garron at the moment, and it amused him. "Still," he continued with a slight shrug. "You seem an honorable sort. Perhaps worth the risk. Two hundred crown would go far in making any damage you potentially cause to my business disappear. Plus...." He swung his gaze toward Mouse and the expression turned colder. "I would enjoy the added bonus of not having to suffer this rat-faced bastard again."

Mouse sneered back. "Well, then. Everybody wins."

"Do we have a contract, then?" Garron pressed.

Taurin's chin lifted as he considered. "Yes. One night. No more."

"We'll be gone by morning," Mouse replied.

"See that you are." Taurin strolled over to a long table against the wall and selected a new chalice, then poured wine from the decanter. "I regret that the accommodations I have available currently are probably not what you're accustomed to, Your Lordship. The night has turned out to be surprisingly busy."

"I have spent the last three weeks in a cell. Whatever you have, I'm certain it will be more than adequate."

"We'll need a meal, though," Mouse put in.

Taurin sighed and his shoulders drooped. "I will have something brought to you."

"And I need to hire a messenger. Someone I can trust. I'll need you to arrange that for me."

"Fine."

"And I need my gear retrieved from the inn I was staying at. Have one of your lackeys run that over."

Taurin waved a hand in the air like he was having an attack. "Fine, fine, fine! Just get the fuck out of here before I change my mind." His cheeks were flaring again, and Mouse fought the urge to smile.

CHAPTER 22

THE BEDCHAMBER Taurin provided was certainly not one used for entertaining clients but likely belonged to one of the entertainers, or perhaps one of the other staff that occupied the brothel. The furnishings were utilitarian at best—a small wardrobe, a table and stool, and bed against the wall under a shuttered window. The quilted blanket that covered the bed looked generations old and was the only visible color in the entire space. An attempt by Taurin certainly to make some point, but Mouse didn't care. The room was clean and quiet, one might even say cozy. Mouse had often had worse accommodations, and Garron seemed not to mind either. He seemed ecstatic to be free of the manor and somewhere he could finally relax. Within moments of being in the room, Garron had kicked off his boots and tugged off the merchant's jerkin.

A knock on the door revealed a young boy burdened with a tray of food. Garron relieved the lad of the tray that threatened to capsize him, and Mouse tossed him a half royal. Mouse hadn't realized how hungry he was until the smell hit him, triggering his stomach to twist in sudden complaint.

Together, he and Garron dragged the table next to the bed and shared the meal of mutton sausage, beans, roasted tubers, and wedges of hard bread all loaded unceremoniously onto the tray. They were provided a flagon of wine as well, but no mugs, so they passed it back and forth. They ate in silence, both leaning over the tray and shoveling in food as fast as their mouths could chew. The brief times Mouse lifted his own head, he had to suppress a laugh. Garron's table manners were anything but noble. He imagined how mortified his fellow aristocrats would be if they saw him now. In short order, they were sopping up the juices with the remaining bread.

Garron fell back with a satisfied groan. "I don't recall ever eating so much in one sitting."

"Impressive, I'll grant you," Mouse replied. "You would have fit in well among us ruffians."

Another knock came at the door, soft and tentative. Mouse lifted from the stool and, out of habit, lay on his belly to see under the bottom of the door. One set of boots was visible. He rose to his feet again and opened it cautiously. Another lad stood waiting with a canvas sack slung over his shoulder. His gear. So far, Taurin had kept his end of the bargain. All that remained was the message to his father, and there was no way to confirm that Taurin had indeed sent it off. He had no choice but to take Taurin at his word, and although he'd given Mouse no reason to doubt him so far, the notion did not put Mouse at ease.

He dropped the sack on the bed next to Garron and began inspecting the contents. One by one he pulled items out and arranged them on the bedding. There was something gratifying—comforting even—about having his familiar gear with him again. Garron sat up and took an interest too. He picked up one of Mouse's boots.

"Careful with that," Mouse said.

Garron made a face. "I'm not going to damage your boot, Mouse. It's not made of glass."

"It's not that." He took the boot from him and turned it around so the heel was facing up. "See this release?" He pointed to a small round button on the side of the heel, then depressed it with his thumb. There was a sharp click, and a blade the length of a forefinger stabbed out from the back.

"Oh," said Garron, his brow lifting in surprise.

"Yeah," he replied with a chuckle. "Didn't want you to skewer your hand."

Garron pulled his hands away, palms out. "I leave you to that, then." The look on his face was one of distaste, which made Mouse's stomach tighten. What a thug he must seem.

Garron pulled himself farther onto the bed and reclined, resting his head on what was a sad excuse for a pillow. Mouse took the hint and moved everything to the floor. He made an inventory of his gear, making certain it was all accounted for. One could never be sure that the lad sent to fetch the sack, or some curious lackey at the inn, didn't paw through his equipment and select some prize for himself. Everything seemed present, so he took a few moments to organize it for the next day.

He looked up at the bed. Garron's eyes were closed, and his breathing had slowed to a steady cadence, his chest rising and falling.

Mouse couldn't help but grin. Free of the manor, and with a belly full of food and wine, his body had finally had enough.

Mouse closed the shutters on the small window to darken the room. He arranged his pack on the floor into a makeshift pillow, then pulled off the page's uniform he'd worn all day and threw it into the corner, happy to never have to wear that again. He stretched himself onto the floor. Only moments after he rested the back of his head on the pack and closed eyes, he felt himself drifting off.

"What are you doing?"

Mouse's eyes popped open, jolted awake. He rolled onto his side. In the pale light of the room, Mouse could just make out Garron's shape seated on the edge of the bed. The fading light of evening that filtered through the shutters reflected off the skin of his shoulder, arm, and leg. He had stripped out of tunic and breeches and wore only his smallclothes.

"What does it look like?" he said. "I'm sleeping. Or was rather."

"Why are you on the floor?"

"Despite what you think about me, Lordship, I can be nice. I was letting you have the bed."

"You're an idiot. The bed's big enough for both of us."

Hardly, thought Mouse. "Not when you're passed out like a drunken sailor." He worried that in the dark Garron wouldn't pick up on his sarcasm, so he lightened his tone. "I didn't want to disturb you."

"Well, I'm not going to let you treat me like the entitled prig you think seem to think I am. I'm willing to share the bed with a commoner."

"Prig may have been a bit harsh, I'll admit," Mouse said. "Fop, perhaps. Or a dandy."

Garron threw the small pillow at him.

Mouse laughed and tossed it back. "I've slept in worse places, Garron. I assure you."

"Get up here," he said. "We can share the bed."

Mouse's entire body tensed. The last thing he wanted right now was to lie down so close to him. Were it anyone else, Mouse would not have thought twice about it. But now, the idea filled him with cold dread. Mouse could no longer deny or ignore his draw to Garron. It had been growing steadily since he first met him, and only now was Mouse able to face what was happening.

Aside from the fact that Garron was a nobleman, and the target of a job—two strong reasons why he should stay as far away from him as possible—there was also no reason to think that Mouse's growing affection would ever be reciprocated. Even if he did share Mouse's attraction to men—which was unlikely—there was no chance that a sophisticated gentleman like Garron, accustomed to refined things, would ever have interest in a base scoundrel like himself.

Despite his resolve, lying next to him would feel too close to what he caught himself longing for. His mind wrestled against an onslaught of emotion, but his body had already surrendered to the idea. He wanted it too fiercely for any good to come of it. He considered turning the offer down again, but would refusing only raise more questions? Or was that just his way of justifying his answer?

"All right," he said.

He lifted himself slowly from the floor. Garron pulled the quilt back and slipped his legs and body under it, then shuffled closer to the wall to give Mouse more room. Mouse sat on the edge of the bed. The room was warm, but he left his tunic on to reduce the chance of their skin touching during the night. He slid his legs under the quilt and turned on his side with his back to Garron.

"See?" Garron said cheerfully. "Plenty of room."

"Yeah. Much better," he replied.

They weren't touching, but Mouse could still feel the heat of Garron's body radiating against his back.

This job needed to be fucking over. He needed to get Garron safely out of Har Orentega and to the meeting place so he could collect his coin and be on his way, putting the whole thing behind him. This boyhood infatuation he had with Garron was getting out of hand. Once he was gone, it would get better. He'd forget about him.

He closed his eyes and took a deep breath, trying to ignore Garron and just go to sleep. But Garron's presence seemed to fill the whole room and envelop him.

As he lay there hoping for sleep to take him, images flooded into his mind unbidden—memories he had locked away and not thought about in years. Memories of his crime. He tightened his eyes against them, willing them away, but they would not be deterred. They came, and Mouse's heart twisted.

It had been a day of exploring the wood south of the village, wrestling about, and swimming naked in the lake. The day was glorious. Just he and Marcan, two inseparable friends. However, Mouse had misread Marcan's affection for him as something more. At a moment that seemed perfect, while they both warmed themselves in the sun, Mouse rolled over and kissed him.

Gods, it seemed so ridiculous now. How could he ever have thought Marcan shared his feelings? But he was young, and the young see only what they want to see.

As soon as Marcan came to realize what was happening, he shoved Mouse off him. There was a stunned silence between them, several heartbeats of them staring. Mouse wanted to say something, anything, but couldn't find the words. Then Marcan was angry. Terribly angry. His face flushed and he lunged. Mouse was knocked back, sprawled on the sand, and Marcan was on him in instant. The punches flew at him with a frenzied desperation, and Mouse brought up his arms around his head to protect himself. But a fist caught his brow above the eye and then his jaw. His head reeled from the impact, and the metallic taste of blood filled his mouth. And still Marcan swung.

Mouse pushed him off, but Marcan was on him again. Shouting at him. Again and again.

A fist crashed against the side of his head. The pain was fantastic, and the edges of Mouse's view tightened with blackness.

Panic set in. He squirmed to escape, but Marcan was bigger and forced him back to the ground. Mouse pushed him back again, enough to bring up his knee and plant a foot at Marcan's waist. He kicked, putting all his strength behind it.

Marcan flew back, arms flailing, none of his body in contact with the ground. He hit the ground, and a great cry of agony exploded from his mouth.

Mouse lifted himself onto his elbows. Through a fog of tears and blood, he tried to make sense of what he saw.

"Renn, help me." Marcan's voice was no more than a choking whisper.

Mouse wiped his eyes clear. Marcan lay on his back, leaning against a driftwood log. It took a moment for his brain to piece together the gruesome scene. There was blood—Gods, so much blood. He'd never seen so much. Then he saw it. A long jagged branch protruded from the center of his chest.

Mouse could only stare in horror.

"Renn... get... help." Blood gurgled out over his chin. He tried to say more, but it was lost in chokes and spits. Then Marcan's head fell back and his body went limp against the log. He was dead.

And Mouse had killed him.

That was the last time anyone had ever called him by his given name.

"Good night, Mouse," Garron said behind him.

Mouse hadn't thought about that day in years, but all the pain came crashing in around him as fresh and raw as when it first happened. He didn't trust his voice, so he said nothing in return. Maybe Garron would think he was already asleep.

MOUSE WOKE with dawn's pink light squeezing through the slats of the shuttered window. Warm and comfortable, he allowed himself to lie there a moment while the fog of sleep evaporated. He had slept deeply, not waking once as far as he could remember. But as consciousness returned, he was aware of Garron's body against him. No, not just against him—on him. Garron's leg was bent at the knee and draped over Mouse's thigh, and his thick arm came over his waist and snaked up his tunic. Garron's palm lay against the skin of his chest, gently cupping the curve of his pectoral.

Mouse's entire body went rigid.

"Good morning," Garron said into Mouse's shoulder, a smile in his voice. He squirmed a little, snuggling in tighter and moving his hand in small circles on Mouse's chest.

"What... what are you doing?"

"It's called spooning," Garron said.

"Yeah, I know what it's called."

Garron lifted himself onto his elbow to see Mouse over his shoulder. He had a big wolfish grin splitting his face. "Now you have a problem with it?'

"What do you mean 'now'?"

"Well, you started it."

Mouse felt his eyes pop open wider. "I didn't!"

Garron chuckled and tilted his head a little to the side in a gesture that said he had conflicting evidence.

"I didn't!" Mouse insisted. He tried to wiggle his way up to a sitting position, but Garron's arm prevented him from moving. That was what he told himself anyway.

"Well, then you're rather handsy in your sleep."

Mouse felt his face flush with embarrassment. "Oh gods!"

"Relax. I rather enjoyed it," Garron said with a widening smile. He leaned in closer to Mouse's face, a wicked look in his eyes. "Saved me the trouble of making the first move."

Then his lips were against Mouse's lips. They were just as soft and warm as that first time they kissed. Garron began with gentle pressure, moving his lips around and tenderly pulling Mouse's lips into his mouth. The intensity grew, and the pressure against Mouse grew harder. With his strong tongue, he probed the opening a moment, then forced Mouse's mouth open farther and thrust the tongue deep inside.

Mouse closed his eyes and his head lifted to meet the kiss. Every sensation he was aware of centered on that tongue penetrating his throat. He even pulled the tongue in farther with his own suction. He was dimly conscious of Garron adjusting his body over him, his weight bearing down on him, the warmth of his flesh radiating into his own like a hot bath. And the swell of Garron's cock against his thigh.

Mouse felt himself slipping, sinking deeper into the kiss, deeper into the passion that pulsed out of Garron like a furnace.

He pushed Garron away.

"No," he gasped. "No, no, no, not this." He pushed harder, forcing Garron off enough for him to slip out of the bed and cross the room.

Garron leaned back against the wall, flummoxed. "Wait. What just happened?

"Nothing. I'm sorry. I... I don't want this."

"You don't want this?" Garron repeated.

"No."

"Well, your cock is telling a different story."

Mouse looked down. Sure enough, his body had betrayed him. He was fully erect and protruding straight out, forcing his small clothes into a sizable tent. He tried to adjust it, to somehow disguise it, but it was no use, so he held his hand over it instead.

"Look, this just can't happen," he said.

"And why not?"

"Gods! You're a nobleman, Garron, first of all!"

"What does that have to do anything?"

Mouse rolled his head back. "You cannot be serious!"

"It doesn't matter to me," Garron replied, his voice softening as if he was wounded by Mouse's insinuation. "Mouse, I know you don't think highly of us nobleborn—"

"Stop. It's not that."

"Then what?"

"You know my life, Garron."

"Is this about your status, then? You're somehow embarrassed? I wouldn't have thought you'd care about that. I am free to choose my partners, if that's what you're worried about."

Mouse shook his head. "You know the work I do. You don't want to keep company with the likes of me. You have a reputation to consider—"

"Don't be ridiculous." Garron moved to sit on the edge of the bed. "I'll decide who I spend my time with. And no one will dictate otherwise."

"How very noble," Mouse sneered.

Garron fell quiet a moment, holding Mouse's gaze with an expression close to sadness. "You're noble too, you know," he answered gently. "In your way. Though you don't want to believe it."

"Oh, sod off!" Mouse groaned, rolling his eyes.

"I'm serious, Mouse. There is a quality to you that I have never encountered in anyone... of any class. I'd like the privilege and opportunity to know more."

Mouse put the heels of his hands against his eyes. Garron knew nothing of the dark deeds of his past. If he but glimpsed Mouse's history, he would change this pursuit in an instant. "You don't know what you're saying," he said quietly.

"I know that the thought of not seeing you again makes my heart ache. A part of me doesn't want this to be over. I'm dreading it, in fact. But it doesn't have to be that way."

"Stop right there. Don't you even dare suggest it, Garron."

"Why? Does that frighten you?"

Mouse stared at him imploringly. Why did he not understand? He felt the sting of tears in his eyes. "There's no point in pursuing it. It's a fantasy. A mirage."

Garron's head jerked back as he'd been struck. "Mirage? Mouse, I am genuinely and deeply drawn to you. That is no illusion, I promise you."

"Of course it is. It's just...." He waved a hand about as he struggled for words. "Just postliberation infatuation. You're misinterpreting your feelings about being freed."

"Stop being ridiculous. There's no such thing. What I'm feeling right now is… is…."

"If you say 'love' I swear I'll punch you in the head. I'm no silly fourteen-year-old maid that is going to swoon from your attention."

Garron chuckled dryly. "A sense of anticipation, actually," he said. "Hope." The corner of his mouth lifted impishly. "Desire. And I would wager good coin that you feel the same. Do you think I have not noticed your affections? The way you look at me when you think I cannot see."

Was he that obvious? "But it doesn't matter! Don't you see? I would never be accepted in your world, Garron. And you certainly don't belong in mine."

"We would figure something out," Garron replied with a shrug.

Mouse threw up his arms. "Gods! Would you listen to yourself? I'm not going to become some pet kept in some out-of-the-way gilded tower, if that's what you're thinking."

Garron's eyes narrowed. "I'm not suggesting that. But shouldn't we at least give it a go? See where it leads?"

"To what end?"

Garron opened his mouth to respond but was interrupted by a knock at the door.

Flustered by the conversation, his head swimming with so many conflicting emotions, Mouse broke one of his own cardinal rules of his craft. He opened the door without checking it first.

"What?" he demanded, flinging it open wide.

Chancellor Elasiar stood on the other side, flanked by two of Delgan's helmed guards.

"Well, isn't this cozy," he said. "I pray I'm not interrupting anything."

CHAPTER 23

CHANCELLOR ELASIAR glided into the room as if he owned it, followed by two guards, which put them all directly between Mouse and all his gear on the opposite side of the small bedchamber. Mouse, standing in his smallclothes and a tunic, calculated the odds of getting to his dagger. There was little chance. The room was now very crowded, and there was no room to maneuver. Both guards, fully armored and with helms covering their faces, had their weapons drawn and ready. One would surely strike before he made it around them. If not at him, at Garron.

His mind whirled, searching for a solution.

Garron slowly moved off the bed and stood against the wall. His face had gone ashen.

"How did you find us?" Mouse asked.

Elasiar's mouth spread to expose his teeth. "Oh, we had a little help from a friend."

From the corner of his eye, Mouse caught movement. Another figure moved into the doorway but remained at the threshold of the room. Taurin.

Mouse felt his face burn with sudden rage. With a sharp intake of breath, his jaw clenched, and his fists tightened into white spheres. Every muscle was ready to lunge at Taurin. It took the entire strength of his will to not give in to it.

"You fucking gutless backstabbing rat dick!" he growled through his teeth. From his periphery he could see Elasiar's grin lengthen with satisfaction.

Taurin matched Mouse's glare with steely defiance. "It wasn't me, you imbecile," he said.

"I will gut you from ass to ear, you pusillanimous, pig-fucking louse. Your best hope is that they kill me right here and now."

"That is one possible outcome," Elasiar sneered.

"Mouse, it wasn't me."

Something in Taurin's tone needled its way through his fury and made him take note. He didn't know what yet, but something tapped into his rational mind. Through the thick haze of anger, he forced himself to look deeper into Taurin's expression for signs of… anything. Deception? Guilt? Taurin was a crafty bastard and a cunning liar, but Mouse knew his tricks. Taurin's face was as solid and unwavering as he'd ever seen it. It was then he noticed that a third guard stood behind Taurin, weapon drawn. In his sudden willingness to believe Elasiar, he hadn't seen him there at all. And Taurin was still wearing his nightclothes. Under no circumstances would that vainglorious fop leave his bedchamber not fully dressed and his hair not perfectly coiffed.

And his hands were behind his back. Shackled.

Mouse's rage began to leak from him at a slow dribble, like a wineskin with a pinhole. Some measure of control returned to his muscles, and his fists unclenched. "No," he said. "It wasn't you, was it? But I know who did." He swung his acidic gaze at Elasiar. "It was one of his girls."

Elasiar raised a single brow.

Taurin's face lit with surprise. "Wait. What?" He lurched forward into the room, but the guard grabbed him from behind and pulled him back to the threshold. Elasiar rolled his eyes and nodded to the guard, who struck Taurin from behind, forcing him to his knees with a grunt of pain.

"The woman at the warehouse," Mouse continued, "with the men throwing dice. You must have suspected we would use the tunnel, so you sent her there to watch the exit. She recognized me from when I was here before, knew we'd likely head here, and reported it to you."

Elasiar lost all sign of his earlier smugness. "You are as clever as they say," he answered in a tone that held both ire and fascination. "I must admit until this moment, I couldn't figure out how you got past the outer walls and into the manor. But now I recognize you, Lord… Yazura was it?"

"It was."

"A masterful deception. But I saw you leave with your carriage. Accompanied by my guards. Mind telling me how you accomplished that?"

"I will happily explain it to you over a pot of tea someday."

"Or with you stretched to your limit on a rack," Elasiar replied with an indifferent shrug. "Begging for mercy. Whichever suits me when the time comes. As for your friend, Hawken… well, now that I know he was complicit in this business, I will sadly have to rescind my offer to return him to his old office."

Fuck. Mouse stiffened. "Hawken had no knowledge of—"

Elasiar waved his hand in the air. "Oh, please don't insult me. If it makes you feel better, I can throw the two of you in the same cell. You can reminisce about how you very nearly outwitted me." He closed his eyes and shook his head as if saddened. "I always thought no good would come to that paunchy lummox. Troublesome, that one. Unruly and undisciplined. I don't know what I was thinking when I offered him that position again."

Elasiar swung his attention toward Garron, then. His smile broadened as if seeing an old friend. "And, Lord Garron. What a merry chase, yes?"

Garron stared back with hard eyes but said nothing.

"You very nearly slipped through our fingers," Elasiar said, "and thwarted the duke's grand deal."

"And what is this deal?" Mouse asked.

"Ta-ta," said Elasiar, waving a finger at him. "That's the big secret to be revealed later. But I suspect Lord Garron has already figured it out." The chancellor's eyes looked askance at Garron. "Hmm?"

"I will not return to your prison, Elasiar. You will have to kill me right here."

Elasiar's smile turned sinister as his eyes narrowed. "I'm happy to hear we are of like minds on that, my lord. You see, it was the duke who didn't have a big enough cock to have you killed straight away. I recommended it, but he got squeamish. Nobleborn just aren't accustomed to making those kinds of difficult decisions. I happily don't suffer from such weaknesses. With you dead, there is nothing to prevent the deal from proceeding." He looked over his shoulder. "Guards. This is where you come in."

The guards raised up their swords as Elasiar moved to get out of the way.

Mouse's mind was a whirlwind. Ideas spun through his head in dizzying loops, each rejected as they flew past. He had to do something. Anything. He watched in horror as the guards moved into action. Unarmed and nearly naked, if he tried to intervene he would be cut down easily, and the outcome would be the same. The door was blocked by Taurin and the third guard, his gear was on the opposite side of the room, and there was nothing in the room he could remotely use as a weapon. He scanned the room searching for something—anything—he could use.

He lunged. In one swoop of his arm, he grabbed the food tray from the floor as he put himself between Garron and the guards. He braced himself, brandishing the tray as a shield. But as he leapt into position, something else was happening.

One helmed guard lifted his thick sword arm for a broad backswing. Mouse quickly calculated the attack. Where he stood, he was well out of range of the blade. The arc of it wasn't nearly close enough to reach him. Mouse watched as the blade spun about. The sweeping horizontal swing whizzed through the air with terrible force to strike the neck of Chancellor Elasiar. The blade cut deep, nearly severing the head entirely. The body buckled and hit the wall with a thud, and there was an eruption of blood like a ruptured wineskin. Elasiar dropped into a disturbing crumpled heap.

At the same time, the second guard grabbed Taurin by the nightshirt and flung him in the room, then thrust his sword into the unprotected neck of the third guard in the corridor.

What followed was a strange kind of timeless silence. No one moved or said a word. The guards, Taurin, Mouse, and Garron all stood frozen while two bodies bled out on the planked floor. Mouse, with his back to Garron, felt fingers curl around the curve of his shoulder. The first guard glanced in Mouse's direction, then looked down at his handiwork on the floor through the visor slit of his helm. He considered the bloody sword in his hand before tossing it onto the body of the chancellor. Then he pulled off the helm.

Hawken shook his head from side to side to loosen the sweaty tendrils of hair adhered to his forehead. "Fuck it's hot in there!" He turned to Mouse with a knitted brow. "Paunchy lummox?" With a scowl, he kicked the motionless lump.

Mouse let out the air from his lungs in one rush as he dropped forward and propped himself up on his knees. "Gods burn me, Hawken! Couldn't you have given me a signal or something?" He wanted to scream but was too light-headed at the moment. His heart pounded furiously against his rib cage.

"Always hated that pompous bastard," Hawken grumbled down at Elasiar.

Garron's hand remained on Mouse's back. "Mouse? You know this man?"

Garron's rapid breath burst in hot waves against the back of Mouse's neck. "He was instrumental in helping me get to you in the first place."

The second guard tugged off his helm, unveiling a mane of red hair and bushy beard to match. Mouse recognized him immediately, though he was cleaned up better the last time he'd seen him. Mouse had hired him to play one of their bodyguards when they borrowed the carriage to get in through the manor gate. He was a dockworker by day but took the occasional coin for work that required a different kind of muscle. Hawken had apparently been busy networking in his absence.

Hawken smiled and gestured to the man with his head. "You remember Reginus Fenn, yes?"

"I do indeed," said Mouse, certain he had a perplexed look on his face he couldn't wrestle under control.

"Good to see you again, mate!" Fenn replied with an easy grin, as if they'd just gotten reacquainted in the market square. Fenn tossed his helm onto the bed, then ducked out into the hall again. He grabbed the body of the third guard by the ankles and dragged it into the room, leaving a gruesome streak of red across the planked floor. Hawken moved aside as Fenn shuffled in to deposit the body next to Elasiar. He dropped the legs with a satisfied flourish and dusted off his hands as if pleased with a job well done. His face scrunched when he noticed the long stain from the hall. He looked down at Taurin, who was still on the floor in stunned disbelief. "Mate, you might want to consider a rug or something for out there."

Taurin recovered. His face flushed with sudden anger as he struggled to his feet using the wall for support. "Hawken, you had better have covered your tracks. If this butchery gets traced back here—"

"Oh, relax, Taurin," Hawken replied. There was something significantly different about the man. He seemed at ease, almost cheerful. What had happened during Mouse's time in the manor? "The idiot told no one about coming here. He wanted the glory of parading the prisoner back to Delgan all to himself. The only other person who knows is your girl that was working for Elasiar. I suggest you see to it *she* doesn't sing."

Taurin's eyes darkened with a dangerous intensity. "You can be certain of that." He turned to show that his hands were still shackled behind his back. "Can someone take these fucking things off me?"

Hawken shrugged and tossed a ring of keys to Mouse. Still sore about the deal he made with Garron the night before, he grabbed Taurin by the nightshirt and pulled his face close.

"Looks like Hawken did you quite a service, Taurin," Mouse growled. "Word is Elasiar had his fingers wiggling about in a lot of different pies here in the city."

"If he's right, and no one knew he was here, then yes. None of my associates will be sorry to hear he's gone, certainly. The man was a pain in everyone's ass."

"Won't be any tears shed in the guild either, I wager," Fenn added.

"Forgive me if I don't start a jig just yet," Taurin grumbled. "It's my floor that he's bleeding all over. All it takes is one witness that saw him entering my establishment—"

Hawken shook his head. "He had his cloak up over his head the whole time. No one could identify him. He didn't want anyone tipping off Mouse."

"Think, you idiot." Mouse tilted his head toward the body. "There is the mastermind behind Delgan's power grab. Dead. As should now be Delgan's ploy to seize control of the city's underground. Now it's time for the Shadow Elite to get their thumbs out of their collective asses and take back the power you generously handed over to him." Mouse pushed Taurin against the wall and brought his face so close their noses nearly touched. "I want Delgan punished. You understand? Not only for what he did to Garron, but also for his fucking overreach. Make him suffer so he and every other greedy nobleborn with a scheme thinks twice."

Without waiting for an answer, Mouse spun Taurin around. He unlocked the shackles from Taurin's wrists, and they fell to the floor with a clang. Taurin didn't say a word. With a tight scowl on his lips, he stared at the floor as he flexed and rubbed at his wrists.

Mouse raked his fingers through his hair and found the hairline wet with sweat. He tried to wrangle in the thousand questions whirling through mind. "Hawken, how—" He held out his arms in a wide shrug. "How the fuck did you pull this off?"

Hawken laughed. A big, hearty laugh. "I've been keeping my ear to the wall since you got in there. Caught word that they believed you might have found a way out of the manor and beyond the wall, and that they had a new plan. I knew Elasiar would want his hand in it, so...." He shrugged. "I may have used my newly restored respectability to talk my way back into the manor and position myself as one of Elasiar's personal guards. Unbeknownst to him, of course. All said and done, it was all fairly easy, actually."

"But you realize you just butchered your employer, right?"

"I have a letter signed by the duke himself that I have been restored to my former office. This bastard's death—or unexplained disappearance, anyway—will have no bearing on any part of that. Seems his position's open now, anyway." He shrugged again, grinning this time. "Who knows? Maybe I'll be recommended for that office instead."

Mouse couldn't help but chuckle. He couldn't picture the brute in the robes of a chancellor, playing the diplomat in the court.

"Besides," Hawken continued, "there's a solid chance I won't be taking up the position anyway."

Mouse raised his brow. "Oh?"

Hawken's expression sobered some as he nodded. "I've been doing a fair share of thinking over the last couple of days, Mouse."

"Always a dangerous pursuit, you ask me," Mouse replied.

"Well, you're to blame for that. I was perfectly satisfied with my life until you came around to muck it up."

Mouse knew that was horseshit, but he didn't challenge it. "You've received a better offer, I gather?"

Hawken scratched the back of his head. "Not exactly. May just see where the winds take me."

Mouse knew exactly what that meant. He was off to seek adventure.

"The wife and kids are heading north to live with her sister and assist on their farm," Hawken continued. "A mutually agreed upon decision," he added with a hand up to ward off Mouse's next question. "So... that leaves me free to chase other interests. Perhaps His Lordship here would consider something for me in Har Dionante. It seems a more amiable town than the one I currently reside in."

"I am certain," Garron replied, "we can come to some agreeable solution to your needs. The least I can do, considering."

"Excellent news!" Hawken said with a widening smile. "I look forward to discussing that with you." He seemed a liberated man, to Mouse's eye. Relieved of some invisible oxbow that had once burdened his shoulders. He now stood straighter and smiled freely, like a smitten boy. "But first, let us conclude our current business of getting the two of you out of this damnable cesspool." His expression shifted as if he was less confident about what he was about to say next. "If you'll forgive me, I took a bit of initiative."

More than a bit, Mouse thought.

"Yesterday, when Delgan decreed the bridges be drawn up, I knew it meant you'd accomplished the deed. It was why I started poking about for information. But it got me thinking too. It was going to be a challenge for you to get His Lordship out of the city and have it done quickly. My time spent at the Blue Stag did put me in acquaintance with other members of your variety, so I reached out to some I knew. I thought I could arrange some quiet passage out for you. Well, I'll cut to the quick. I was visited by a man named Keeler. I'm told you know of him."

"We're acquainted," said Mouse dryly.

"Well, Keeler made it clear to me he is anxious to see you on your way and out of his city. Those were his words. So, it's been arranged—on his coin, mind you—that you are to board the River Falcon, a cargo vessel at the docks. That ship has agreed to smuggle you out of the city and awaits you both now. We just have to get you to the docks and on board that ship."

As if it was going to be that easy.

"So… as much as I enjoy the both of you standing there in your smallclothes," Hawken added with a single brow raised. "I suggest you pull on your gear and we head off straight away."

Garron made a sharp glance Mouse's way with a surprised look, but Mouse pretended he didn't see it. He wasn't about to get into any of that at the moment. He considered offering Hawken a reminder that he was, in fact, speaking to a nobleborn, but taking into account that he'd just saved their skins, Mouse figured that any umbrage Garron felt would be short-lived. He looked at Taurin and indicated the bodies with a tilt of his head. "You'll handle this mess?"

"I have a choice?" Taurin sneered. "Yes," he added with a small shake of his head. "I'll take care of it. Just get out of my place. Get out of my city. And the next time you are in town and are considering a visit—think again. I am henceforth unavailable."

"Seems to be a theme with you," Garron noted.

Mouse shrugged indifferently. "I have a way with people." Anyway, he was more than happy to oblige him. He had no intention of ever returning to this shithole town again.

CHAPTER 24

THE FOUR of them—Garron, Hawken, Fenn, and Mouse—left the Scarlet Unicorn as a unit. After borrowing yet more from Taurin's extensive wardrobe and the uniforms of the slain guards, they hit the streets with Garron dressed as a rich foreign merchant followed by his scribe and guardsmen, who were graciously loaned to him by the duke himself. The guards led the way, parting the crowd with shouts and the swing of forearms while Garron made a haughty march behind them, unaware of the throngs of people he inconvenienced as if they were beneath his contempt. Mouse trailed the small company, with a ledger book tucked under one arm while he gripped the bridle of a donkey with the other. The lumbering and uncooperative beast pulled a small two-wheeled cart loaded with textiles. As they progressed down the center of the street, causing no small disruption, Mouse kept checking under the cart for drips of blood leaking through the wood from the bodies stowed beneath the mound of fabric.

"This isn't going to work," grumbled Garron over his shoulder.

"Losing faith in me already, Your Lordship?" Mouse answered.

"We couldn't be making ourselves any more conspicuous."

"But who, mind you, is going to stop and question two of the duke's own personal guard?"

The gambit was perhaps a bit of a risk. If anyone bothered to look at the merchandise in the cart, they would find the textiles to be moth-eaten and cheap in quality—old unused scrap from Taurin's storehouse—not nearly the quality that Garron's performance was selling. And it was highly unlikely that the duke would loan off his own detail even for the most favored of suppliers. But his argument stood. Who would risk checking? Theater was always the art of illusion.

They traversed the narrow streets and worked their way steadily toward low town and the docks. They cut through the crowd like a ship cutting through ice sheets in winter. And as Mouse suspected, no one thought too much about it and just stepped to the side long enough to let the dandy and his small entourage pass, then went about their business.

The boundaries of low town were marked by the leveling of the ground beneath their feet as they entered onto the flat flood plain of the river. Gracious homes, sprawling inns, and storefronts gave way to tenements and warehouses. Winds raced the byways and carried the odors of the river docks—fish, tar, and the smell of freshly cut wood. Ahead of them, the top of one of the drawbridges reached over the roofline. Raised, Mouse knew, specifically to prevent them from leaving the city by one of the two gates on the opposite shore of the river. The river was the only way out of the city now. There was no chance the duke didn't know that as well. The place would be a hive of guard activity.

Any zig or zag up ahead could put them at the shore of the river. Mouse kept his eyes open for signs of the city guard. Some would certainly be in plain sight. Others would be covert. He kept a careful eye on each person they passed by, searching for any indication they were not who they seemed.

Then someone stepped out of a shadowed corner to stand in the middle of the street as they approached.

"Gods," grumbled Mouse.

Keeler stomped toward them and was clearly heading directly toward Mouse, ignoring Fenn and Hawken—two men dressed as the duke's personal guard. Mouse shook his head in wonderment. What an imbecile.

Hawken was looking his way, waiting for the go-ahead to intervene. Mouse sighed and gave a single nod. "Get him someplace."

As Keeler marched between Hawken and Fenn, seeming blind that they were even present, the two scooped up the guild leader from under his arms and dragged him off backward in the opposite direction. Keeler sputtered in rage and waggled about to free himself but was no match for the two of them. People on the street very quickly glided away to give them the widest possible berth. They had no interest in getting mixed up in the Duke Delgan's honor guard's business.

Keeler was shuffled into a small merchant's shop. From the street, Mouse could hear a small series of crashes from within the shop; then the distressed vendor scurried out in a rush.

"This will only take a moment," Mouse told Garron, and strolled into the shop himself.

It was a small storefront, and Fenn and Hawken took up the larger share of it. Keeler was on his backside, sprawled against the shop's counter with pewter and silver dinnerware scattered on the floor around him. His face was crimson with rage, but he made no attempt to get on his feet when he saw Mouse enter the shop. A pewter goblet rolled off the counter and landed on Keeler's head with a dull clang.

"Stay with Lord Garron," he told Fenn, who immediately ducked out of the shop. Mouse turned his hot gaze to Keeler. "What the fuck are you doing here?"

"Making sure you get on the ship and leave my city," Keeler spat back, attempting to sound like he was still in control. He managed to get his feet under him with the help of the counter and stand back up.

Mouse rubbed the corner of his eye with the heel of his hand. "How did someone with the brains of a fucking bale of rotting hay manage to take control of this city's guild?"

Keeler's brow knotted. "Say, what now?" He leaned in with his fist clenched. "I arranged your transport—"

"You very nearly sabotaged our cover. Because why would a thug approach a rich merchant's apprentice while the duke's own honor guards just stood by idly and watched? You nearly just told everyone out there that we are not what we seem and that I'm the one in charge. If a city guardsman had seen you, we'd all be fucked."

Keeler's face contorted as he processed that. He at least had the grace to look a little sheepish.

Mouse stepped right up to Keeler until their torsos nearly touched. He stared hard up into the larger man's eyes. "I'm going to speak very slow and use all small words to make sure you understand," Mouse told him in a gentle tone as if speaking to a child. "Gather up your men, get them to the docks, and be prepared."

"Prepared for what?"

"*Anything*, you moron. Honestly, how do you dress yourself in the morning without someone pointing out to you what goes where? The city guard will be there in force looking for us. They know as well as we do that the river is the only way we're getting out of the city since the drawbridges are raised." Keeler's eyes opened a fraction as comprehension sparked to life. That obviously had never occurred to him. "Yes, Keeler. Understand now? Get your fat ass to the docks and be ready to cause a little mischief when the need arises. We will need distractions if we are to get Lord Garron on that ship unseen. Can you handle that?"

Mouse didn't wait for an answer. He turned back to the door, but before he exited to the street again, he glanced over his shoulder at Keeler once more. "If this goes sour," he said, "I'm holding you responsible. And I will see to it your days of running the guild are over." Not that it mattered, Mouse knew. His own idiocy would bring about his downfall in short order anyway.

With Hawken on his heels, he rejoined the others. He grabbed the donkey's bridle and gave it a tug to get her moving again. Hawken and Fenn took their place in the front, and the four continued on their way. Mouse looked behind them one last time to see Keeler stumble out of the shop and stomp off down the street in the opposite direction.

"Do you want to run the guild here?" Mouse said to the donkey. "There's sure to be an opening soon, and you're better qualified." The donkey raised its ears as if considering the offer.

"Will he do as you asked?" Garron asked.

"Probably not. But I can't worry about that. We'll get you on that ship. Don't worry."

Hawken dropped back a bit. He looked at Garron as he spoke, but Mouse knew he was talking directly to him. "We're nearly to the river and the docks," Hawken said, his voice muffled from inside the helm. "What then?"

Mouse approached and spoke as if to Garron. "Don't lead us out into the open just yet. I want to see what we're dealing with first."

Hawken bobbed his helmed head, and they marched on.

They reached the edge of low town and crossed into the warehouse district. Mouse directed them into a quiet alley to wait. If Keeler was going to aid them, as unlikely as that was, Mouse needed to give him time to get his men into position.

After a time, he ventured out alone into the wide-open region along the river. The docks. The area was a sprawling industry that hugged the shore upstream from the two drawbridges. Tall ships with tied sails and broad, flat-decked barges, about a half a dozen or so in all, claimed the available dock space this side of the river, while three other vessels were moored up on the opposite bank. Cranes levered the freight off their decks and stacked them in neat little mountains on the wide cobbled plaza that stretched from the boardwalk by the river to the row of warehouses that lined the edge of the city.

It was past midday, and the docks were in full chaos as sailors, dockhands, and merchants hurried to make use of the remains of the day. But their efforts were hampered by the choking presence of the city guard—poking around, asking questions, and generally putting themselves underfoot and making a nuisance of themselves. Their numbers were staggering, actually. Delgan had put his guards out in force. It looked more like an army assembling for an invasion. Many of the city guardsman brandished sheets of parchments as they circled the docks.

Were those renderings of Garron?

Some of the guardsmen stood at intervals around the perimeter of the wide area, while others milled about trying to look official and imposing. They snooped around the piles of stacked freight, as if they thought Garron might be smuggled out in a crate of onions. Or they were just looking for something to pilfer for themselves while they pretended to care about some unknown escaped prisoner. More guards were on the docks themselves, searching the ships and interrogating crew and captains.

But none of the streets leading out to the city were blocked, and the traffic heading in or out of the docks were not being detained or questioned. It was a strange, conflicted sort of tossing the net. The duke's forces were making a clear presence at the dock, obviously trying to hunt someone down, and at the same time people were freely passing in and out of the area. A blockade would bring activity to a standstill, and Delgan knew anything that disrupted commerce would chafe the ass of the merchants and shippers who brought substantial coin into his own coffers. So the guards attempted a casual but aimless sweep of the area.

Mouse made his own loop along the margins of the docks. Within moments, he spotted a group of guild members loitering about. They were easy enough to identify. Their thuggish garb and ink-covered arms were enough to flag them, but they were the only ones not involved in any industry. They leaned against walls and stacks of crates, spitting brown globs on the cobbles and scanning the area for any trouble to cause. Then he eyed another cluster farther up. So, Keeler had wised up after all and put his men to action.

Mouse had to admit he was surprised. Keeler wanted to be the one giving orders, not taking them, and Mouse had treated him like an errand boy. Keeler could have just as easily stormed off and left Mouse to slip through the net on his own. But he really wanted Mouse out of his territory and was willing to swallow his pride this one time to make sure it happened.

He approached the outer boundary of a cluster of brutes and made eye contact with the craggiest among them, the one likely to be the leader.

The man nodded back to him. "You the one they call Mouse?" There was a noticeable edge in his tone.

Mouse bobbed his head while looking out toward the river.

"You have a plan?" asked the thug.

"More or less. Just be ready. Await my signal, then set out to cause as much turmoil as you can."

The thug grinned, exposing his four teeth. He clearly liked the sound of that. "What are we looking for?"

"You'll know it when you see it." Mouse never slowed his pace as he strolled past the scruffy group. He marched on and noticed still more groups of guild members peppered throughout the area. Mouse made a point of holding his gaze on them until they noticed him in return and nodded in acknowledgment.

Then he looped back, venturing closer to the river this time. It took him no time to locate the barge they were to be smuggled out on. However, a half dozen guards were pacing the dock that led to the barge's gangplanks, and one guardsman was even standing on the vessel's deck speaking with a member of the crew. Even with what he had planned, getting aboard was going to be dicey.

He veered his trajectory toward the alley where the others waited, but something caught his eye. He happened to look out at another of the docks, and he saw her. The woman in the black robes he'd seen in the courtyard two nights ago. The mage.

Fuck.

He hurried back to the others, but not before he lifted three oil lanterns from outside a warehouse.

"You find the ship?" asked Garron.

Mouse nodded. "It's a barge moored at the end of the second dock. Red paint on the hull, a red falcon head on the flag. Hawken, I'm going to need you two to get him there and on board."

Hawken and Fenn had taken off their helms and held them under their arms. Both nodded. "Easy enough," Fenn replied with a shrug.

"It won't be. Guardsmen are on the boardwalk and on board some of the vessels as well."

"I know these docks, mate," Fenn told him. "I know the men that work them. Dressed like this, who's going to stop us? They're going to think we're just part of the search. We'll get His Lordship aboard."

Garron's brow tightened in concern. "What about you?" he asked.

"I am going to make sure no one pays any attention to you." Mouse pulled out his dagger and started to cut the bindings on the donkey's bridle, careful not to sever it completely. He left a thin section still connected.

Garron gripped Mouse's arm. "But you're going to be there, right?"

Mouse gave him a reassuring smile. "I'll catch up to you." Seeing Garron's anxiety deepen, he added, "I promise." He turned to Fenn and Hawken. "Get out of the area as soon as it's done. Ditch the—"

Fenn waved him off. "We know the routine, mate! Let's just get it started." Then Hawken and Fenn fitted the helms back over their heads.

They needed to position themselves closer to the docks first. Mouse took the donkey's bridle and guided her out of the dark alley and farther down the narrow street. It was a quiet channel without shops or much traffic, which was one of the reasons Mouse had chosen it. Once the docks were in view, Mouse, one by one, opened the lanterns and poured the contents of oil over the bolts of textiles in the cart. He pulled out his flint kit from his pack.

The other three, piecing together what was about to happen, put more distance between them and the cart.

"Well, my friends," he said to Hawken and Fenn, "appears this is farewell. If you're ever in Har Terrena, call on me. I won't be hard to locate if you look under the right rocks."

"I may at that," said Hawken. "Just don't fuck this up. I won't be able to save your ass a second time."

Mouse laughed and clasped both their hands.

He struck the flint stone over the fabric. It took only three strikes before a spark caught and set it alight, and fed by the oil, it surged into a healthy flame.

The flame spread quickly, eating up more and more of the fabric in the cart. The donkey began to pace and stamp nervously, but Mouse held her bridle firm. In moments the cart was engulfed. The flames crackled and roared. Black smoke billowed upward in a twisting column. The donkey lunged about, eyes white in panic. Mouse held on as long as he dared.

As the donkey started to rear and kick, he let go and jumped clear. Finally freed, the panicked beast sprang away at speed.

"Now for the show. Get going, Garron." He took off across the docks at a sprint.

The flaming cart careened across the dock, spilling black smoke in its wake. Screams and shouts erupted all around as people dodged and lunged out of the way. The terrified donkey brayed as she galloped in wild frenzy. She bucked and kicked, trying to break free from the inferno behind her. The cobbled plaza was not made for such speeds—the cart bounced and tilted to the side precariously.

Mouse ran across the area as fast as his legs could take him. He caught glimpses of guild men spilling from hiding places. Some set upon groups of guardsmen, while others began scampering off with crates of merchandise. Other guards ran over to assist their comrades in the widening brawl while merchants and dock workers hollered for help and chased after the thieves making off with their profits.

In moments, the entire area had descended into chaos.

The bindings keeping the donkey attached to the cart finally gave way and snapped, freeing the beast. The cart listed onto one wheel and bounced into the air. Carried by momentum, it twisted and rolled. By now, the cart itself was fully aflame and coming apart. It hit the cobbles on its side and tumbled in a terrifying, unpredictable fireball. It struck the corner of a large stack of earthenware vats and exploded apart, sending flaming debris in all directions. But the impact destabilized the neat order of vats. The ones at the top teetered, then toppled and fell to the ground.

The first to hit the stones cracked open like an egg, and viscous dark liquid oozed out.

Pitch.

Mouse winced—he hadn't planned for it to go quite this far.

Others saw what was happening and scattered in all directions, waving their arms and shouting for people to get clear as more clay containers were dropping from the top. The result was extraordinary. Within seconds, the entire pile erupted in a fiery blast. People closest were thrown to the ground. A black mushroom of smoke boiled up over the docks, and flaming debris rained down over everything. The flames reached higher than the row of warehouses.

The danger of this becoming a true conflagration was suddenly very real, and everyone knew it. The crowds occupying the docks now had a unified purpose. If just one of the surrounding buildings went up in flames, if one burning coal landed on a warehouse roof, there might be no stopping the fire. All of Har Orentega could burn to the ground.

As Mouse drew closer to the boardwalk along the river, he slowed to a jog. Dockhands and ship crew alike were dashing past him with buckets and shovels. One of the barges was throwing off its lines and pushing free from the docks, the captain on the deck barking orders. He was not taking chances with the vessel or its cargo catching fire as well. Among the chaos, Mouse spotted the mage, still on the dock and shouting to the guardsmen around her. Her voice was lost in the cacophony, but Mouse was certain she was ordering them to ignore everything else and continue their search.

Mouse waited. Everyone around her had sprinted off at her bidding and left her alone and unattended on the dock. He walked up to her.

Arcane symbols were embroidered along the hem and sleeves of her robes. The cloth was elegant silk that shimmered like the dark surface of a lake at nighttime. Her hood was pulled back to expose her single tight braid of black hair that hung down over her left shoulder. She had pale skin, and her face was gaunt and eyes deeply set—likely the cause of too much time spent in dark cells studying spells by candlelight. Mages were not prone to physical vanity, but this one was pretty in her own way, with full lips and bright yellow eyes that sparkled with intelligence. It took her a moment to notice him standing there and realize he was not part of the surrounding bedlam. She looked at him, confused a moment as to why he was there staring at her, and then comprehension and recognition widened her eyes.

"Your handiwork, I presume?" she asked.

Mouse allowed himself a satisfied grin.

"I almost didn't recognize you, Mouse," she said. "A rat's vision isn't so clear, you know, but its hearing is astounding."

Mouse ignored the veiled threat. He smiled at her. "You're too late," he said.

She raised a single eyebrow at him.

"Thought I'd let you know and save you the trouble of searching in vain," he continued. "He's out of the city. And outside of your reach."

She smiled condescendingly. "Is that so?"

"It is." He turned to look out at the river. She turned too, following the direction of his gaze. The barge that had pulled away from the dock to protect itself from the fire was now drifting away downstream. "Appears I won, mage."

The exchange was a strange contrast from the wild commotion that surrounded them. They spoke calmly, almost civilly, as if the two of them sat in a parlor sharing a decanter of wine, while the world around them unraveled.

Her face gave nothing away as she swung her eyes back toward him. "Hardly." Her voice was cold. "You see, even though you cleverly figured out about the tattoo, you didn't remove all the ink. I may not be able to track his specific location with it anymore, but I can still sense its presence."

Mouse too kept his face rigid and unreadable. "What does that matter?"

"I feel it now, my dear. The ink is close. Closer than that barge out there, certainly. I know that Lord Garron is still here." She took a step closer. "Foolish little mouse, thinking you could outwit one of us. We will find him soon enough, despite your pathetic attempt at distraction. He will be found and returned to Duke Delgan… and you will be hanged by the neck before the day is concluded."

"You know," he replied, "I've never cared much for mages. For a number of reasons really. I don't really understand your power, but to my mind you possess an unfair advantage in the natural world. I find it abhorrent. But secondly, I find the arrogance of your lot to be insufferable."

"Is it arrogance? Or do we just better understand the universe and embrace our place in it, more so than the likes of you? I would argue instead it is you who is arrogant, thinking you could best me in this contest."

"I've done well so far. I'll remind you Garron is not yet in your custody."

"You've given us a merry chase, I'll admit. But that ends soon." She tilted her head and lifted her shoulders a fraction. "But," she said, "should you somehow manage to slip him past us yet again—as unlikely as that is, but you've surprised me before—" Her face darkened in new intensity. "I'll have you know that I will not quit my pursuit until Lord Garron is either recaptured or dead. It will be a personal mission of mine. I cannot allow someone like you thinking there is any hope in resisting us. You will never be allowed to win."

Mouse nodded with pursed lips. "Exactly what I feared."

And he lunged.

With reflexes she could not hope to counter, he sprang forward. His shoulder rammed against her midsection, and he threw his arms around her. The tackle caught her unaware, and the impact knocked the wind from her in a startled cry. Mouse pushed with his legs using all the strength he could muster, and drove her back… back… back. She flailed about to gain her footing again, but the force of his push was beyond her strength to oppose. He drove her to the end of the pier, and they went over the edge together into the river.

AFTER THE initial crash into the water, a strange silence followed. The din from above the surface was instantly just a distant hum. It was now just him and her, spinning into the depth as if dancing.

The water was shockingly cold. Mouse's entire body constricted. He fought against the impulse to exhale the air he held in his lungs. Against him, the mage flailed about to free herself but only managed to tangle herself in her own robes. He tightened his grip on her anyway. The cloth absorbed the water as they sank and clung to her body. It twisted into knots around her legs as she struggled. Before the impact, Mouse had pulled in a full breath. In her surprise, the mage cried out instead as they fell and emptied her lungs. Panic was already setting in, and she clawed at him in a desperate attempt to break free.

Deeper and deeper they sank.

They were near the base of the pier. The thick wooden pylons reached up through the greenish gloom like the pillars of a sunken temple.

Mouse released his grip on the mage. She tried to kick away from him and swim for the surface, but he grabbed her long braid before she could escape. With his free hand, he reached into his boot and pulled out a dagger. Not his father's—but an old one he carried about.

He dragged her by the braid closer to the pylon.

The wood of the pier was very old—it had stood here for centuries, and in places, the wood had split. Cracks ran vertically along its length. At some point, the city had attempted to repair the problem by fastening thick iron bands around the pylons to prevent the wood from splitting apart further.

Fueled by terror, she fought wildly to break his hold on her, kicking and waving her arms about. But already her strength was flagging. She'd lose consciousness soon. He pushed the blade through the weaves of her hair, then thrust the tip of the blade into one of the cracks in the pylon. He wedged and wiggled the dagger in as deep and as tight into the crevice as he could manage. Satisfied, he pushed off with his legs and swam away.

As he kicked toward the surface, he glanced back down into the murk one last time. The mage was tugging vainly at the blade's handle, but she did not have the strength to break it loose.

CHAPTER 25

THEY WERE provided a small cabin below deck and told in no uncertain terms to stay put and out of the way of the crew. Mouse was happy to oblige.

As soon as the door was closed behind them, Garron dropped onto a large shipping trunk and leaned back with his head on the wall. He closed his eyes, and his entire body sagged. He looked like he was a heartbeat from being asleep.

"Quite the diversion," he said without opening his eyes. "More than you intended?"

"A tad, perhaps," Mouse replied. "It worked, which was the important part. Hawken got you aboard easily enough."

"At the risk of sounding ungrateful," Garron said dourly, "I didn't want you to burn down the fucking whole city."

"They'll get it under control. Everyone was pitching in." Mouse wanted to believe that, but he didn't sound as confident as he wanted. Frankly, he didn't give a shit. Delgan was a rat-fucking bastard, and his city could burn to cinders as far he was concerned. Garron would judge him harshly for such thoughts, so he kept them to himself.

He peeled off his wet clothes and hung them on wall hooks to dry. Mouse had climbed onto the barge from the river, and Garron thankfully hadn't asked him why. Mouse had no interest in revealing what had taken place in the depths of the river. He sprawled himself out naked on the narrow bunk that was nestled into an alcove. He allowed himself a full deep breath and released it slowly—his body accepting the deed was done now and he could finally relax. It was done. The barge now lumbered its way down the river, and Garron was beyond the reach of Delgan.

This should have been a time of celebration. Garron was safe, and Mouse's part in this was finished. All that remained was to deliver him over and collect his reward. Mouse's flawless record remained intact, and he could return to his old life of lifting trinkets and baubles from rich prigs that didn't appreciate or deserve them. And now, with the payoff he'd receive, he could purchase the king's pardon and conduct his work without the added complication of having to pay off His Grace's men. Coin could stay put in his own purse for a change.

But the encounter with the mage left him feeling uncharacteristically morose and with the sensation that he was somehow indelibly stained. Fatigue was largely to blame—it cut deeply into his muscle and bone. And, of course, he couldn't shake the festering sentimentality that was gnawing at him from within.

He told himself he looked forward to this business being concluded, but in truth, his stomach twisted at the thought of passing Garron on to his entourage and then walking away.

Garron's words from that morning were still hot in his mind, like a steaming kettle fogging up his thoughts. Such tempting and compelling words. Mouse could almost see his willpower collapsing and giving himself over to them. But Garron had spoken with the passion of the moment—not with reason, and Mouse knew he'd be a fool to take any of it to heart. Garron had been intoxicated by his unexpected freedom, nothing more, mistaking gratitude for attraction. And now that he was truly free, the words he said were likely already forgotten.

Mouse closed his eyes and wove his fingers together behind his head. As he lay there trying to push all such thought from his mind, he was suddenly aware of Garron's eyes on him. He pretended not to notice. Or care. But a part of him wondered if he had displayed himself naked on the bunk on purpose.

Mouse heard Garron rise off the crate and then felt him sit with one cheek on the edge of the berth next to him. Garron pulled his leg up, and the round of his knee brushed against Mouse's thigh. The gentle rocking of the barge moved Garron's hip against Mouse's side in soft waves. Mouse opened one eye to look up at him, but he couldn't read his expression because his face was in shadow.

"How long will we be aboard, do you think?" Garron asked.

"Hard to say," Mouse answered. "Until morning, certainly. At the speed we're moving, it'll take a while to get beyond Orentegan borders. Depends on where they plan on docking. Har Senica, perhaps, but I doubt they'll wait that far. The captain will want us off as soon as possible in case there's trouble. He'll deposit us off at one of the more remote villages. Renoa would be my guess."

Garron nodded, seeming more to buy time and collect his thoughts than in understanding. Mouse could tell he had more to say and was working his way around to it but hadn't decided on the best route. "Never was much a man for the water," he said. "I swim well enough, and I don't get the sickness like some. Just prefer the ground beneath to be more firmly settled."

"Haven't had much cause to be aboard ship much either. But I understand you grow accustomed to it."

"Not sure I ever would," Garron replied pensively. He leaned back against the wall. "What happens then? When we are off the ship?"

"I will send out a courier to my contact the first chance we get and let him know I have you safe. And then we buy a couple of horses and head north to the established meeting place. West Dughnum, at an inn called the Trident Arms."

Garron nodded thoughtfully. "Then you accept your reward, and you're on your way."

"Something along those lines, yes."

Garron looked down at his hands and for a moment seemed distracted by a fingernail. He looked uncomfortable. Mouse could tell he had something to say and was trying to figure out how to broach the subject.

Of course, Mouse knew what was on Garron's mind. He wasn't naïve, and he wasn't an idiot. He'd already seen this coming. Garron was regretting the words of passion he'd said at Taurin's and was trying to figure out a gentlemanly way of retracting them. Now that he was free— truly free—and could once again envision his life back in Har Dionante as a reality, Garron had come to realize the folly of that earlier proposal. He'd come to realize at last that the worlds they lived in were just too different. And whatever attractions they felt for each other, nothing could ever realistically come of it. Mouse knew Garron would see it that way eventually.

Still looking at his hands, Garron pursed his lips. "So, about this morning," he said. "About… the conversation before we were interrupted."

Mouse steeled himself for what was coming next. It would sting certainly, for there was a part of him that ached to be with Garron. But holding on to some fantasy that this nobleborn gentleman would want him in his life was nothing but an absurdity. Mouse knew better.

He was about to save Garron the trouble of saying it, but Garron spoke first.

"I meant every word I said, you know. That hasn't changed."

Mouse's eyes sprang open. That was not what he expected to hear. "Excuse me?" His heart jolted into rapid beats.

Mouse could feel the smile light Garron's face even though it lay in shadow over him. Instead of saying more, Garron leaned in, and Mouse felt soft lips press firmly into his own.

This time, Mouse was powerless against it. Some corner of his mind thought about fighting, pushing him away, but the notion of resisting was pointless. He didn't have the strength of will. Instead, Mouse sank deeper into the warmth of the kiss. Garron's mouth pulsed against him, sending waves of passion coursing through Mouse's entire body. His jaw relaxed as Garron's tongue prodded the opening of his mouth. As the thick muscle thrust inside, he was aware of nothing else—and pulled the tongue in farther with his own suction.

Garron pressed in even harder. Suddenly, the weight of Garron's torso was against his own, and Garron's soft hand explored the contours of Mouse's chest and abdomen, pinching chest hair between his fingers and tugging gently. Then the hand moved south. Past the belly. The muscles of Mouse's abdomen tightened in response. Past the waist. Fingers brushed the line of hair that ran vertically downward until the fingertips combed through the edges of his tuft of thicker hair.

Mouse's sensual awareness was now fully on his cock as it swelled to life, lifting upward like a crane's boom and springing back against the back of Garron's hand. Garron chuckled softly but didn't pull off the kiss. Instead, he curled his fingers in a tender embrace around his swollen girth. Mouse involuntarily moaned his approval.

Never had he felt so consumed by his senses. Each breath through his nose brought Garron's heady scent directly into his brain like an apothecary's physic. It sent his mind whirling. Eyes closed, he could see everything with his skin. The soothing rolls of the barge on the waves rocked Garron's firm body against him again and again in an intoxicating rhythm while Garron's hand guided the foreskin upward over the head in cadence with the ship's movement.

His face flushed with sudden heat, and he felt his sac tighten.

"Gods!" he whispered against Garron's lips. "Please stop."

Garron pulled back from the kiss, and at the same time slid his hands down to cup Mouse's scrotum. He rolled the wrinkled skin between his fingers. "Plan on protesting some more?" he asked. There was a wicked sort of delight in his voice. "Going to tell me some more how you don't want this?"

"This is such a bad idea, Garron," he said, but there was no conviction in it. He spoke between gasps, and his hips continued to respond to Garron's touch. "I'm not the one for you."

"Shouldn't that be my call?"

Even though Garron's face was fully in shadow, Mouse turned his eyes away. "But you have no idea the kind of man I am." The words barely formed, and each consecutive one that passed his lips made his heart twist tighter. A part of him hated himself for even saying the words. Part of him burned to just give in to the desire and worry about the consequences later. But he couldn't allow himself. Fear and practicality always won out.

He could feel Garron smiling down at him, which irritated him. Why didn't he fucking understand?

Garron moved his hand from Mouse's groin and caressed his knuckles down the length of Mouse's jaw. "Gods, you are such an idiot! Adorable... but an idiot."

Mouse's eyes widened, taken aback. "Excuse me?"

"Do you think me so naïve? Of course I know your past is not filled with philanthropy and pacifism. But in the short time I've known you, Mouse, you've proven yourself to possess more integrity and honor than most of the so-called noblemen I know."

Mouse pushed air through his lips. "Me? Honorable? You are naïve."

"You have convinced yourself you are wicked and incapable of redemption. I'm here to tell you you're wrong."

Mouse opened his mouth to protest, but Garron put two fingers over his mouth. "Let me finish. Do you think you alone have committed heinous deeds? We have all done terrible things, Mouse. No one can honestly say otherwise."

"Except you."

"No," Garron replied softly, breaking his gaze. "I am not as virtuous as you would paint me. I've done my share as well, believe me."

Mouse didn't believe him, but he didn't argue.

"I've seen men," Garron continued, "who claim themselves to be good and honorable do wicked things with ink and parchment. A most cowardly act, because they never have to face the ones they've wronged or feel the consequences of their deed. I have seen those who rail on about their own compassion willfully ignore those in need or treat those beneath them with contempt.

"We all justify our dark behavior in some way, mask it behind some twisted form of truth that gives us license to do what we will. In my experience, people can rationalize the most reprehensible acts and sleep soundly through the night as if no blame rests upon their shoulders. Take Delgan. He has certainly justified my imprisonment and death sentence as something for the betterment of his city and his people."

Garron held Mouse's eyes with intensity. "But you," he said. "You face your demons directly. You do not try to disguise them behind some false truth or rationalize them away. That doesn't make you wicked. It makes you honest."

Mouse was quiet a moment. "But what difference does that make?"

"All the difference in the world. The events that led you down this path you're on are behind you now. From here on, everything can change."

"You don't understand my past, Garron."

"Your past doesn't matter. What matters is what happens now. You can now choose a new path, Mouse. Perhaps a new path that includes me."

Mouse wanted to laugh, but his heart wouldn't allow it. "So... am I to put on tights and surcoat and join you in your manor? Parade about as your concubine, join the other ladies of the court in their sewing circles and afternoon tea?"

Garron laughed out loud. Heartily. Warmly. "No. Nothing like that, you idiot. I would never subject you to that slow torture. I had something else in mind."

Mouse raised his eyebrow.

"Let's disappear," Garron said.

"What?"

"You heard me."

"Well, now who's being ridiculous!"

"I'm serious, Mouse. We'll go off together and build a new life for each other. We go to where you agreed to meet for your payment, we take the coin and instead of heading off to Har Dionante, we head somewhere else. Anywhere. A new city—or a small town, whatever we want. But just us."

"And do what?"

"I don't know. Buy an inn. Buy a farm. Buy a tall ship and sail the seas to the east."

Mouse shook his head, not believing what he was hearing. "You're telling me you'd give up your station and leave your posh life behind? For me?"

"Without a second thought. Without ever turning back."

"Garron…." he began, but stopped himself.

"Are you telling me you wouldn't do the same for me?"

"It's not as simple as that," Mouse replied quietly.

"It can be." Garron too fell quiet for a moment, then said, "Mouse, I have never felt this way about anyone before. Have never known anyone like you before."

"And what if it turns out in a month we despise each other? Or you snore terribly and I can't spend one more night with you? What then?"

Garron shrugged. "You go back to your old life. And I will go back to mine."

Mouse turned away and looked up at the ceiling.

"If you don't feel the same way," Garron added, mistaking Mouse's silence for something else, "then say so. And I will leave it be."

Mouse's gut twisted. A part of him screamed out to push Garron off of him, tell him he didn't feel the same way—not because it was true, but for Garron's own sake. To protect him. How could he ask Garron to give up his life for him? How could he subject Garron to the life of a commoner? But try as he might, he couldn't form the words. He couldn't bring himself to say them out loud. The notion of sharing a life with him was too exhilarating. Though he couldn't bring himself to believe it was even possible, he couldn't reject it either. Giving in to Garron was just too dangerous—more dangerous than anything he'd ever done before. But he couldn't resist it either.

In a very quiet voice, he heard himself say, "I do feel the same."

Then Garron was kissing him again. It felt different this time. It felt deeper. Stronger. As if some veneer between them had stripped away. But it was more than that too. The kiss wielded a potency that Mouse had never experienced, one that transcended some unseen boundary he hadn't thought possible. He felt it everywhere. It seeped into his bones and made his toes curl. And the last remnants of doubt he clung to dissolved away.

Garron broke off the kiss only long enough to pull off his tunic and strip off his trousers. Then once again he was lowering onto the small cot next to Mouse, ready to resume. His naked body pressed against Mouse's. The touch of their skin together was electric and sent waves of passion coursing through every muscle. But as Garron leaned in again, a thought wormed into Mouse's brain, and he held Garron back with a hand to his chest. His beautifully formed chest. "Garron, why did Delgan imprison you in the first place? Who did he make the deal with and why?"

"That doesn't matter anymore," Garron said.

He's right, thought Mouse. What did it matter? None of it would ever matter again. And he once again gave in to Garron's intoxicating lips. And a great deal more after that.

CHAPTER 26

"HOW LONG do you expect?" Garron asked.

Mouse adjusted the fat hare he had positioned over the fire. Juices dripped out and sizzled on the hot coals beneath. He wasn't sure if Garron meant dinner or their destination. "Soon," he replied, covering both answers.

Mouse stole a casual glance at Garron. He sat opposite him, on the other side of the fire, his face illuminated by warm yellow light. He sat cross-legged on the ground, wrapped in a blanket, and stared into the flames, mesmerized as if it was his first experience with fire.

His first taste of a commoner's life.

The River Falcon had docked at the village of Renoa in the hours before dawn. The captain had his crew unceremoniously deposit the two of them on the pier, and then they pushed off again without a word or a wave.

Mouse made certain their time in Renoa was brief. He straight off hired a messenger to run word to his contact regarding Garron's liberation. Then he hunted down the village farrier and procured two horses, saddles, and plenty of provisions for a few days of travel. The farrier had a weapon for Garron too—an old military-grade short sword, crudely made but well tended and still sharp enough. Garron would need something to protect himself. The road could be dangerous.

They were immediately off on the north road before the sun had barely broken the horizon. They traveled the entire day at a fair pace, with Mouse constantly looking behind them to see if they were being followed.

"Do you suspect we'll arrive by tomorrow?"

Ah. The journey was the topic, then. "Hard to say," Mouse answered. He caught himself, reluctant to tell Garron that it was unlikely they'd reach West Dughnum by the morrow. Garron might well romanticize the joys of a simpler life, but he had yet to experience its true charms, like spending a night out in the chill air, trying to sleep on a cold hard ground with a root poking you in the back. After one night of that, Garron could well be put off on the idea of running off with him if that was what life would be like.

He looked up at the sky. Most of the stars were obscured, meaning clouds had rolled in. "Depends on the weather," he said. "And the condition of the road."

Gods! Mouse dreaded the notion of rains coming in during the night. A night spent on the cold ground was unpleasant enough. A cold, wet night was infinitely worse.

"And what of your contact? How long before he and my escort arrive in West Dughnum after they receive the news?"

"Again, impossible to say. My guess is we'll enjoy a few days of quiet solitude at the inn before they arrive."

Garron nodded but didn't reply. His expression was hard to read in the dim firelight, but it seemed in that moment that he sank into a more pensive mood.

"Are you feeling anxious?" Mouse prodded. He wasn't at all surprised by Garron's inward mood of late. The closer they drew to West Dughnum, the closer Garron was to the decision of parting ways with his old life. Of course, Mouse was still unconvinced it would happen at all.

"A little," Garron replied.

"Well, understandable," Mouse said after a moment. He forced down his own tide of anxiety that threatened to rise up and shake him apart. Garron's tone was pregnant with deep unspoken thoughts that Mouse could not begin to read. Garron felt closed to him.

He added more wood on the fire and turned the hare on the spit again. He didn't know what else to say, so he said nothing. When he glanced again at Garron, he was watching the swirl of smoke that rose up through the gap in the canopy overhead. He must have sensed Mouse watching him, for he looked down again and caught Mouse's eye.

"Come over here," Garron said.

"I'm tending to dinner," Mouse replied, forcing a smile. "You want to eat, don't you?"

"The hare is fine for a minute. Come here and warm me up." He extended an arm to hold out one end of the blanket, suggesting Mouse should occupy the space.

Mouse dropped the branch he had just picked up and moved around the fire to join him. Instead of taking the seat next to him, he crouched behind Garron and wrapped his arms about his shoulders in a gentle hug. Garron's hand reached up and caressed the length of Mouse's bicep.

How quickly this feeling had become so familiar, so comfortable. The feel of Garron against him. His touch. His scent. It felt dangerous in a way, but he couldn't pull himself away.

Garron's head tilted back to rest on Mouse's shoulder. "I'm sorry," he said.

"For what?" Mouse replied, deliberately obtuse.

"I'm brooding."

"I hardly noticed," Mouse said.

Garron chuckled. "I'm only adjusting to the idea of being free again. It's a lot to take in." He was quiet a moment. Mouse tightened his grip around him and listened to his breathing. "Nothing's going to change, you know," Garron told him softly in his ear. "Nothing will alter what we planned."

The plan. When Mouse's contact arrived at the inn, Garron was to insist that Mouse be awarded his coin immediately. Once Mouse had the coin in hand, then Garron would announce that he was not returning to Har Dionante with the escort after all. The reward money would help them begin their new life together. Mouse and Lord Garron would disappear from the world. Simple.

We'll see, thought Mouse, but he kept his suspicions to himself. Instead he said, "I know."

They remained there a time, watching the fire as it danced and crackled. Fat from the hare continued to drip down onto the coals to sizzle and spit. Night sounds sang out around them in a gentle concerto.

Then Mouse caught a new sound. He stiffened instinctively and waited. Something out in the wood beyond their tiny clearing was out of place—a sound discordant from the rest. It was the snap of a dry twig.

"What is it?" Garron asked, his body stiffening in response to Mouse. His hand slid off of Mouse's arm.

"Not sure," he answered. Slowly, he released his hold around Garron and moved his hands to Garron's shoulders, ready to rise to his feet. He held his breath and reached out with his senses into the surrounding night for another indication that something was out there. His hearing worked to filter out the sounds he expected to hear and focus in on anything that didn't belong. It could have been just an animal of some form, drawn by the smell of the roasting meat. But bandits were always present in these parts. One always had to be vigilant when traveling the open roads. And there were other would-be dangers as well. His hand slipped from Garron's shoulder and crept to the dagger sheathed at his waist.

Garron saw where Mouse's hand was moving. He shrugged the blanket off his shoulders and reached for the scabbard that rested on the ground next to him.

Mouse looked to the horses, tied to a branch at the edge of the clearing. One was alert, ears perked up. He'd heard or sensed something as well, but whatever it was wasn't enough to spook the beast. Likely not a wolf or some other predator, then. Its scent on the wind would have caused more distress.

Mouse held his breath and waited.

He heard a soft click come from within the thick underbrush. It was mechanical—not natural. It was a distinctive sound he knew well.

Timing was everything. Heart thumping, he counted backward. Three. Two. One. Then he threw himself on Garron, knocking him to the side, just as he heard the louder click he waited for. The crossbow bolt whistled over their heads and struck a tree trunk behind them with a hard thud. Mouse rolled one way and leapt to his feet in one smooth motion while Garron rolled the other.

The attack came from all sides at once. Five men. They erupted from the surrounding brush, swords flashing in the firelight.

They were dressed in black leather and had their faces covered with black cloth. They moved in fast, silky and effortless. These were no ordinary thugs—some cheap blunt hammers sent into a tavern or market to take care of someone ordinary. These men were seasoned and skilled. And expensive.

Mouse armed himself with a dagger in each hand. His father's was in his left—his favored hand. He adjusted his fingers for just the right grip as he bent at the knees in a defensive position. The first attacker made a charging leap for him. He glided through the air impossibly high as if winged and landed like a dancer in front of Mouse, sword already in motion.

A bold attack meant to unnerve and drive Mouse back. But Mouse wasn't about to give up any ground this early. He pivoted on one foot to plant the other behind him to support himself from the impact, then caught the sword between the crossed blades of his daggers. Surprise registered in the eyes of the attacker—and provided Mouse just enough time to formulate a fitting response. He leaned in and brought the foot behind him forward in a swift kick. He struck solidly between the attacker's legs. A dirty move, but Mouse wasn't feeling particularly gentlemanly.

There was a grunt and sudden whoosh of air, and the attacker bent forward. Mouse thrust his knee up into his face, throwing his head back again. Mouse kicked again, only this time against the attacker's chest. The man tumbled backward into the fire.

Mouse picked up the same distinctive click he heard before and on instinct, threw one shoulder back to twist his torso. He felt more than saw the crossbow bolt whiz past him less than a hand's width distance. He was going to have to take care of that crossbowman. The bolt had come from the shadows still. There was a sixth man.

Behind him came the ring of steel as blades met. Garron had engaged one of the attackers. Mouse couldn't turn about to see, for another was bounding toward him. A wave of numbing anxiety flushed through him.

And it nearly cost him his life.

His fear for Garron dulled his reaction time. He only just avoided the next attacker's swipe at him. Mouse sprang backward, and the sword's tip passed close enough to his unprotected chest to snag on the tunic and rip it open.

Focus, damn you, he chastised himself.

The attacker recovered quickly. He pushed in closer and made a quick jab. Mouse caught the sword blade in the curved cross guard of his dagger and guided it to the side, twisting his opponent's torso to expose his flank. Mouse thrust out with his left hand. The Black Guard's blade sliced through the leather armor like parchment and dug deep into the man's side. It passed cleanly between his ribs at a steep upward angle.

The man stumbled backward, gasping. The stab must have punctured his lung. The sword in his hand was forgotten as he struggled to pull in a full breath. Mouse swung his leg behind the man's calf, throwing him off his balance. The man tumbled backward and hit the ground hard on his back—where he would remain, choking for air until he bled out of the wound.

One down.

Mouse turned about to assist Garron in his fight. But surprise halted him. Garron deftly controlled the sword, thwarting each attempt his attacker made to break his defenses. Garron appeared to toy with the man, but Mouse knew he was conserving energy and waiting for the right moment to make his own assault. Already the man was tiring and showing weakness.

Mouse wanted a moment to admire the shape of Garron's graceful form while he wore down his opponent—his shoulders and back that shown beneath the thin fabric of the tunic and the way his trousers clung to accentuate the cleavage of his perfectly formed buttocks. Garron moved with beauty and precision. He was well trained and undoubtedly skilled.

But two other men were jumping into the fray and closing in for an attack, forcing his attention. One barreled directly for him, while the other eyed Garron, edging around to his blind side to flank. The man Mouse had kicked into the fire had now rolled out and sprung to his feet. Seeming unfazed, he released the clasp at his throat and let the burning cloak fall from his shoulders.

And Mouse could hear the crossbowman arming a bolt. He made a quick mental note of how much time he had before the crossbowman would have a new bolt loaded and be able fire again.

Not long.

Mouse again took a defensive position as the next attacker charged, the man's sword arm already in motion in a wide backswing. He waited—his heart thumping madly as he calculated the timing. When the man was close enough, Mouse arched his back while shifting his center of gravity forward with his hips. The move dropped him onto his knees, his head leaning back. The sword traveled harmless over Mouse's head, and the attacker's momentum brought him nearly on top of him. Mouse sliced upward with his father's dagger across the man's sword arm. The edge cut deep into the flesh just below the elbow. It sliced through until it met with the resistance of the bone. Warm liquid sprayed down onto Mouse's face.

The man cried out in agony, high-pitched and animal-like. He stumbled to the side and doubled over, clutching the nearly severed arm to his chest.

Still on his knees, Mouse flipped the dagger in his right hand from hilt to tip. He pulled back his arm and let the dagger fly. The attacker that had climbed from the fire lifted his head up just in time to have the dagger impale him in the eye. Without a sound, his head whipped back, and he collapsed again to the ground and this time was still.

Mouse leapt back onto his feet in one smooth motion and took stock. Garron had run one man through, the body in a heap beside him, and was pressing the other hard.

All that remained was the crossbowman.

He sprinted out into wood.

WHEN MOUSE returned to the clearing, Garron stood over the fire with his arms folded across his breast. He stared blankly into the flames until he heard Mouse's approach and looked up with clear anxiety in his eyes. He breathed out, puffing out his cheeks, and cast his gaze downward again. "You're safe," he said softly.

"You're surprised?" Mouse replied, attempting a breezy tone, but it seemed out of place and tactless as soon as the words passed his lips. Now was not the time for bravado.

Garron looked to the clearing edge from where Mouse had emerged with tight lips. "Well?"

"He scampered off. No sign of him."

"More will come, then."

"Not tonight, I'd wager, but I agree it's best we not risk it. We should ride on."

Garron remained motionless and silent as he continued to stare down at the weak flames. Something in Garron's bearing made Mouse feel the chill in the night once again. "You're rather impressive with that." Mouse gestured with his head toward the sword he'd dropped to the ground.

"Just because I don't relish killing doesn't mean I'm a pacifist," Garron answered dourly. "I had adept trainers in my youth."

"Just glad you're on my side." Mouse looked around the carnage of their campsite. Garron had already dragged the bodies to the edge of the clearing, but the signs of the battle were still evident everywhere. The fire burned with less intensity than before, since the careful pile of logs had been knocked over. The spit Mouse had fashioned had been smashed apart, and the roasted hare was sitting in the dirt. "Bugger me!" Mouse said as he picked up the carcass. "Bastards ruined our dinner."

Garron's head tilted to the side when he looked up at Mouse, and then he was suddenly on the move. He crossed the distance between them in three steps. With a hand under Mouse's bicep, he gently turned him about to face the firelight. He scowled down at Mouse's shredded tunic.

"You're injured," he said, his face turning ashen.

"Not my blood," he replied, but even as Mouse said it, he knew he was wrong, for he became aware of the sting across his chest only at that moment.

Garron separated the gash in the fabric with his thumb and forefinger and looked closer. "Mouse—"

Mouse took Garron's hand and guided it away. "It's not deep." Still holding Garron's one hand, Mouse reached up with his other and put a palm to the side of his neck. "I'll be fine."

"Fine? Any deeper and it could have killed you."

"Not fucking likely. You should know by now I'm not that easy to be rid of."

Garron pulled away. He wiped the sweat from his brow with the sleeve of his tunic. "By all rights, we should have both been killed. They meant to ambush us while we slept."

"I know," Mouse answered. The ambush would have likely ended with both of their throats cut. But as the attackers closed in to lie in wait, someone mucked it up and made a noise. They could see that Mouse had heard it—so they had no choice but to attack. "I suppose we should have kept one of them alive. We might have learned if there are more of them out there. I'd like to know how they were able to track us all the way from Har Orentega."

Garron looked down at his feet. "They didn't. These were not Delgan's men."

Something about Garron's peculiar certainty sent a chill chasing down the length of Mouse's spine. Could he have questioned one of them already? What could he have learned in the short time Mouse was traipsing through the wood? "What are you saying, Garron?"

Garron looked down at his hand and seemed to only then notice the dark blotch staining his skin. He rubbed his palm on the thigh of his trousers. "I... I should have never put you in so much danger."

Mouse stepped closer. "Garron, what's going on?"

Garron seemed to struggle with the answer. "I looked beneath their armor," he said eventually. "Their tunics... they wear their livery."

Mouse understood immediately. They wore insignia to identify their house. "And you know them?"

"Know to whom they pledged their fealty anyway."

"Then you're certain. These were not Delgan's men."

Garron shook his head.

"Which then means you know who is behind this attack. And the plot to remove you."

This time Garron made a slow bob of his head. "I had suspected. Now...." His jaw tightened, and he didn't finish.

Mouse closed the gap between them. He grabbed the front of Garron's tunic with both hands, ignoring the stinging pain across his chest. He locked his eyes into Garron's. "Gods! Out with it! What is this about? If this is something that could get us killed, I should be privy to the details. Who wants you dead, Garron?"

Garron put his hands over the top of Mouse's. He held them there a moment, then gently removed them. He turned, strode away from the fire, and kept his back to Mouse as he spoke. "I suppose I haven't been entirely honest with you, Mouse."

Mouse felt his lips tighten. "Is that so?"

"I'm sorry. I cannot truthfully say why. To protect you, probably."

"Go on, then."

"In a way, this is about my brother. My older brother."

"The heir to the duchy."

"Yes. Tiamond. He has an aggressive disease. Tumors that riddle his entire body." Garron turned about and held Mouse's gaze. "Mages have been trying to heal the growths for years, but the sickness is outpacing their ability to combat the spread. They are losing ground."

Mouse suddenly understood. "So if he dies, the duchy passes to you."

Garron nodded.

"So, all of this," Mouse said as he gestured toward the ruined campsite and the heap of dead assassins. "This is to prevent you from becoming the heir?"

"Apparently."

Mouse's mind whirled about, grasping for understanding. Garron was honorable and decent; his moral character was unassailable. Who could possible object to Garron taking the seat of the duchy? "Is some type of rivalry behind this? Another family vying for power?"

"Something like that."

"Gods!" was all Mouse could say in response. He spun around, hand to his forehead. Not only had he bedded a nobleman—but the future fucking duke. "Hold a moment. You're telling me that you are walking away from the seat of the duchy? To run off with me?"

Garron glanced at Mouse. "Yes," he said in a tone that implied the question was idiotic, "Happily. And without a backward glance."

"So, who is going to inherit the seat now?"

"I have a younger brother as well. Dennithe. He would take up the mantle and rule Har Dionante as its duke."

Comprehension suddenly crashed in around Mouse. Of course, this had nothing to do with some rival family as Mouse had first thought. Garron's own brother was the one directly to gain from his disappearance. He was behind it all.

No wonder Garron had remained so reticent on the subject all along. He was being betrayed by his own brother. With Tiamond on the verge of death, the third-born son suddenly sees the duchy is within his reach. Of course, that was why Garron was also willing to just walk away. The thought made Mouse's heart twist. It had less to do with Garron wanting to live out his days with Mouse and more about avoiding a confrontation with a brother he might have once loved and trusted. Perhaps it was easier to disappear and abandon his claim than watch his brother hang for the crime of treason and attempted fratricide. Mouse was just a convenient way out.

"I know what you're thinking, Mouse," Garron said, then averted his eyes to the ground. Quickly. As if ashamed. "I would have loved our quiet life together."

"Would have?" Mouse felt everything around him crash to a halt. Here it comes, then. "And what has changed, Garron?" he asked in a quiet voice. His insides reeled in mad combat. Of course it wouldn't go as they planned. He had known this all along, though he didn't want to believe it. He was just waiting for the moment to arrive. The fight had just brought it on sooner.

But a part of him—a silly, childish, heartsick part of him—nonetheless believed in Garron's sweet vision of their future. He felt betrayed.

"You were almost killed tonight," Garron replied with hardened edge, as if annoyed he had to point out the obvious.

"A daily occurrence for me, really," Mouse mumbled.

"Don't joke, Mouse. How could I live with myself if something happened to you because of me?" Behind the flash of anger in Garron's eyes, Mouse discerned what truly kindled it. Pain and fear.

Mouse moved closer to embrace Garron but stopped himself. He wanted to wrap his arms around Garron's waist and put his head against his chest, but that felt like desperation, as if he was clinging to him to prevent him from leaving at that moment. So he stood there with hands at his side not knowing what to do. "Nothing's going to happen to me. Or you."

"You cannot guarantee that."

"Perhaps," Mouse conceded. "But I've gotten us this far. Have faith in me."

"This will not end." Garron let his head fall back. "I was such a fool, Mouse." He reached out and pushed his fingers through Mouse's dark hair. When the hand reached the back of Mouse's neck, Garron pulled him closer. Their lips met. The kiss was soft and tender but brief. "I honestly believed we could just leave," he said as he pulled away. "I hope you know that to be true. I honestly believed if I just disappeared the problem would resolve itself. But as long as I still breathe—"

"You remain the true and rightful heir," Mouse finished for him with a nod of comprehension. "And someone finds that particular condition unacceptable."

"Yes," Garron answered. "And it will not end until I'm dead. I realize that now."

"Garron, if that is what you truly want—if you want to abandon your claim, you still can. You can disappear, just like we planned—"

"And live in fear each day? Waiting for the time they find us again?" Garron shook his head. "I could not live like that, worrying each and every day that something might happen to you. That is no way to live."

"Garron, I can protect you."

"I know you believe that. And yes, if not for you I would not be here now. But tonight we were lucky. You know this to be true. Had you not heard something, we'd be dead before the morn." Garron moved one hand over Mouse's heart, over the wound that ran across his chest. "The breadth of a finger more, and you would be lost to me tonight. What if next time we are not so lucky?"

"Garron—"

"I must put an end to this, Mouse. Once and for all. I wanted to run away and put it behind me and live out my days quietly with you—but I realize now that was folly. I know now what I must do. I must confront this. I must return to Har Dionante."

Mouse took a step toward him. "No. *That* is true folly."

"I must. I have to try and end this. It's the only way."

"You'll be heading exactly where your enemies expect you to go. You'll be walking right into their hands."

"It won't be as easy as that. Out here, I would simply disappear, never to be heard from again. But there, within the walls of my father's keep? It would be much harder. You'll have to trust me on this."

Mouse looked into Garron's eyes and saw the resolve. He would not be able to persuade him away from this, though his entire being screamed at him from within to at least try. There must be some argument that could be made to sway him from this idiocy. But instead, he made a slow nod. "If you're determined," he said. "As I can see that you are. Then I am going with you. I'm not going to let you piss away all my hard work by getting yourself killed."

"Good," Garron replied. "I was hoping you'd say that."

CHAPTER 27

MOUSE DROPPED into a wide cushioned chair expecting a long sit. There was no telling how long they would have to wait. He lifted a book from the small table next to him and read the title along the spine. A silly romance. He had no interest in such drivel, but he opened the book anyway. But as he pulled back the leather cover to inspect the inside, he heard something coming from outside the chamber.

Voices.

They came from the corridor, muffled and distant at first, but they grew steadily louder. There was one speaker mainly, male, presumably, from the deep resonance of the tone. He spoke in a casual and unhurried cadence as if listing instructions, and the others with him made brief respectful replies. Mouse counted two others at least. Then, of course, there would be a guard contingent following as well, and perhaps a servant or scribe. A total of six. Seven, perhaps.

Mouse replaced the book on the table, leaned back and crossed his legs, and draped his arms over the padded arms. Ridiculously comfortable. Who knew such a chair existed? The opulence of the chamber was unequaled by anything Mouse had previously seen. It made Taurin's den feel like a village hovel in comparison. Every wall was paneled with warm wood, the ceiling richly painted, and the carpets felt like the forest floor beneath his feet. There was enough gold inlaid in the furnishing to provide him a rich existence until the end of a very long life.

He glanced over at Garron, who stood at the window frame with his arms folded in a tight nervous knot.

"How do I look?" Mouse asked him.

Garron shushed him, making a glance at the door. "Like a village drunk trying to pass himself off as a lord," he snarled at him.

Mouse made a face. "Rather harsh."

Garron turned back to the dark window, his expression hard. Mouse frowned. Every attempt to lessen Garron's mounting anxiety only managed to irritate him.

The voices were outside the door. In moments, it would all change anyway.

Garron stiffened and turned, unconsciously tugging on his surcoat. He very much cut the strapping lord in his finery, which Mouse had quietly pinched from his personal chambers earlier in the day. He was handsome and dauntless, like a valiant hero in a painting. Garron straightened his back, steeling himself for the confrontation to come. His countenance was a tight scowl.

The door opened.

A manservant entered first to swing the door fully open to make room for the others. He stood with his hand to the latch, ready to close the door again once everyone had come in. Focused on his task, he was not yet aware the room was already occupied.

Still in the middle of a lengthy diatribe, the man Mouse had heard from the hall entered next. He lumbered in like an ogre after a hunt, gruff and haggard. He was a sizeable man. He had the body of someone once strong and formidable but who had since been reshaped by age and languidness. The deep crags on his face were clearly the making of the persistent scowl he currently wore. He was dressed more as a military commander than nobleman at court, with a black leather jerkin and trousers and a fur-lined cloak draped over his shoulders, which he pulled off as soon as he crossed the threshold and tossed over the back of a chair. He was followed in by a few others—a young lord that Mouse recognized immediately, a middle-aged courtier, and a man with an armful of scrolls and ledgers and black-stained hands. The court scribe or perhaps a clerk of some kind. Three helmed guards marched into the room after that. Mouse pinned them as an honor guard by their elaborate attire and very shiny armor. They spread out across the room to stand at attention against the wall, hands clasped behind their backs.

The older man waited for the manservant to close the door, then scurry over to pull out a chair from a table. The man dropped down onto it as if the journey to the chamber had flagged the last of his energy and patience. He snapped his fingers. "Let's get this over with, then," he grumbled.

The scribe unloaded his burdens on the table and began to arrange them.

The younger lord, lingering off to the side with crossed arms, was the first to notice the room was already occupied. He glanced in Garron's direction and, spotting him, sucked in air and went rigid. The young lord's attire was quite different from the last time Mouse had seen him, back in the tavern where he first hired Mouse.

"Brother?" the lord whispered.

The hulking man at the table looked up at the younger lord, then turned his gaze to see where he was looking.

"Hello, Denn," Garron said quietly. He stepped away from the window and into the more direct light of the lantern on the table. He held his gaze squarely on the larger man. "Hello, Father."

The others in the room started, and as realization set in who stood before them, the room seemed to drown in a thick silence. No one spoke, but all eyes turned to the man at the table. Mouse could see the resemblance in the big man. Garron had his father's square jawline and the same intense eyes.

No one had noticed Mouse yet. He leaned forward, enjoying the reaction, as if this were some well-produced theater.

Duke Braddock lost what color he had in his already pallid face.

Of course, Mouse now knew that his earlier assumption that it was Garron's younger brother Lord Dennithe that had plotted against him was wrong. Garron had told him as much, insisting that Dennithe was above suspicion, but Mouse still had his doubts. But now, when he laid his eyes on him, he knew Garron was correct. It had, after all, been Dennithe who had met him in that tavern and hired him.

It was Duke Braddock's reaction that betrayed him. Mouse could see the calculations whirling in the man's eyes. He desperately struggled to keep his face unreadable while at the same time tried to reckon how Garron had gotten here and evaluate how much his son actually knew. Any remaining doubts that Mouse might have had, they were vanquished.

But the duke attempted to recover. "Garron, my son." He stood from the chair and forced a wide smile on his face that fell far short of anything convincing. "You... you escaped?" There was an awkward silence that followed as the duke struggled to mask his obvious distress and aggravation. "Why, that's wonderful."

Garron took a few steps closer but did not reply. His face was stiff and gave nothing away.

Duke Braddock laughed nervously. "You gave me quite a start, sneaking in like this." He put a meaty paw over his chest. "You could have sent word, you know."

"I wanted it to be a surprise," Garron said in a quiet voice.

"Well, you certainly accomplished that." He turned his big false smile to the others in the room looking for help. Garron's brother looked fearful while the others were still recovering from their shock. "What a happy occasion, indeed. However did you manage it, son? Last we all heard you were locked away in Delgan's tower."

"I had some help," Garron answered.

Mouse knew this was his cue. He pushed himself up from the chair with slow dramatic flourish. Again everyone started. The duke's face darkened as he glared at Mouse. He raked his eyes over him with disdain. Mouse held his gaze firmly on Braddock's, knowing such insolence would infuriate him.

"Guards, arrest that intruder!"

Two of guardsmen sprang at the command. They drew weapons and converged on Mouse, who on instinct reached for his dagger. Garron quickly held out his palm to Mouse and made a sharp shake of his head. Stand down, was the meaning. Reluctantly, Mouse pulled his hand from the dagger and allowed the guards to wrench his arms behind him. Garron certainly knew that Mouse wasn't in any real or immediate danger; if Mouse wanted to break their hold on him, he could at any time. One of the guards removed the dagger from its sheath at Mouse's belt. The third guard put himself between Duke Braddock and Mouse.

Duke Braddock's thin veil of happiness at seeing his son again faltered. He spun on Garron, his cheeks hot with sudden anger. He pounded a fist to the table. "How dare you bring this… this filthy guttersnipe into my presence."

Garron's voice was icy calm. "You don't wish to thank him personally for single-handedly saving me from the executioner's block?"

"I do not," Duke Braddock growled through his teeth. "I should throw him in irons for violating the sanctity of my chambers. His very nature is an offense to me. Remove him," he barked to the guards. Immediately, Mouse was dragged toward the door.

"Stop!" Garron's voice boomed out with sudden undeniable authority that rocked the room. Even the duke was taken aback by the force of it. His head jolted back with wide eyes, momentarily stunned that someone would dare speak to him so. Garron's voice dropped again, but it lost none of it potency. "He remains."

The guards froze, confused and afraid to contradict either of them. Mouse leaned close to one of the guardsmen's ears. "I'd listen to him," he whispered.

Duke Braddock's face turned purple with rage. All pretense of a joyous reunion had crumbled away. Before he could collect himself enough to respond, Garron pushed harder.

"Father, let's not pretend further." He paused as he moved a bit closer. "I'm curious, actually. What was I worth? Tell us all what you were willing to barter away of the duchy in order to have me eliminated."

The courtier gasped at the accusation. "Lord Garron! How dare you make such a heinous charge against your duke and loving father."

Garron raised a single brow. "Will you deny it, Father?"

The courtier looked to his sovereign and waited for him to voice a denial or show outrage. When none came, concern began to contort his features. "My lord duke? Tell him this outrageous allegation is truly false."

"He cannot, Lord Heldan," replied Garron's brother.

Duke Braddock swung his hot glare toward his youngest son. His face had turned so dark, Mouse wondered if something might rupture in the man's head. Then he looked to Lord Heldan. "Get out."

Lord Heldan looked as if he'd been struck. "But, my duke—"

Duke Braddock grabbed the front of the courtier's jerkin and gave him a harsh shove. "Get. Out."

Heldan made a hasty retreat from the chamber, taking one last look before he scrambled down the hall.

"You too, Denn," Braddock growled.

"No, Father. I believe I will remain."

Braddock looked at his son with wide unabashed surprise. "You dare say no to me?"

"I do. I will hear your answer."

Braddock could only stare back speechless.

"I can fill you in on the details if you like, Lord Dennithe," Mouse chimed in. His cheery tone seemed to grate against the tension in the chamber. "Your father signed away the lands to the east, the region that is in ongoing dispute with Har Orentega, an area I believe you call the Crimarc."

"The Crimarc?" Dennithe swung to face his father, his face crimson. It was a strange family resemblance, how their faces colored in the same manner and location. Mouse hoped to never see that on Garron's face. "You gave away some of our most fertile lands? *To the Orentegans?*"

"I did no such thing," the duke replied, but his voice held little conviction.

Dennithe was visibly incensed. "Those people have sworn fealty to our family for generations."

"I said I didn't, and that's the end of it. I'll hear no more about it."

"Well, we have documents that say otherwise," Mouse said. "You see, someone working for us inside Delgan's manor lifted some papers from his own chamber. Documents I'm sure you'll recognize. One of the more damning manuscripts is a drawn contract. With your name and your seal upon it."

Braddock's face dropped a fraction, exposing his sudden concern. "That's a bloody lie."

Mouse looked to the guard at his left. "Be a love and pull out the parchment I have tucked inside my jerkin."

When the guard moved to reach in, Braddock shouted, "Hold!" He stomped over to Mouse and roughly thrust his hand between the jerkin and tunic at Mouse's neckline. His prodding fingers found the parchment. He yanked it free and without looking at its contents tore into several pieces and tossed into the flames of the fireplace. "You'll not frame me so easily."

Mouse smiled at him. "Would I have been so foolish and naïve as to bring the actual document here?"

"They are in safe hands, Father," Garron added. "I assure you."

Dennithe glared at Braddock. "But your actions all but confirm the truth of what this man says."

"I'll not have you question me again, Denn." His voice was nearly a growl and thick with danger.

But Dennithe was unfazed by it. "Or what, Father? You will have me removed and imprisoned in some far-flung dungeon as well? I knew something was amiss in all this. I knew somehow you were behind it. You were too… lackadaisical about the charges against him by half. That was why I hired this man to find him. And free him."

"You? You brought this rampallian into this?"

"I did."

Duke Braddock picked up a glass chalice from the table and threw it against the wall. It shattered with a wild crash, sending shards in all directions and leaving a dark stain on the paneling. "You fool! Imbecile. You have always been the spineless mealworm that couldn't make the hard decisions."

Dennithe's face took on a steely hardness, but he did not reply.

"You stood to gain the entire duchy."

"At the cost of my brother? I would rather die, Father."

Still unnaturally calm, Garron stepped to the opposite side of the table from the duke and rested his knuckles on the surface. "Why, Father? Why did you do it?"

The point of denying it had long passed. Garron's father glared back at him with contempt. "You know why."

"I want to hear you say it."

Braddock hesitated, then seemed to come to some internal decision. "Fine. I did it because I would not have the likes of you taking the seat of the duchy when I'm gone. The family must come above all else. Even at the price of my one of my sons. The bloodline must be preserved."

"The bloodline?" asked Dennithe. "Garron, what is he talking about?"

"He's referring to my particular attractions, Denn."

"That's right," spat the duke. "He would rather get buggered by some man than lie with a woman."

Denn looked at Garron, then back at his father. "That's the reason?"

"Damn right it is!"

"But what does that matter, Father?"

"What does that matter?" Duke Braddock replied incredulously. "Gods, you're callow. You sound more and more like your fucking mother every passing hour."

Dennithe took a step closer, fists clenched. "Har Dionante has always been a province of tolerance for those—"

"Not for the bloody successor!" Braddock roared. "One does not produce an heir with a man's cock in the ass. Our family has ruled Har Dionante for fifteen generations. I will not have this faggot end that. If Tiamond dies, he stands to inherit the duchy and all its holding."

"But to have him killed?"

Garron remained silent and only stared back at his father with cold eyes. Mouse could not imagine what he was thinking.

"No, Denn." Braddock's voice was suddenly calm, as if trying to soothe a child from a nightmare. "Not killed. Just removed. They are trying to confuse you, fill your head with lies. Delgan was not to harm him, but just make him disappear."

"That is not the case, Lord Dennithe," Mouse said. "Garron was to be beheaded. We have the writ of execution to prove that as well."

"Shut your fucking mouth, cretin, before I cut out our tongue!" Braddock swung back to face Dennithe, immediately trying to curb his tone. "Do not listen to them. They are trying to turn you against me. You are the heir now, Denn. Think of that. It is you who will take my place as duke when I'm gone."

"No, Father, I won't." Denn put a gentle hand on Braddock's arm. "It's over. You cannot think to pursue this any further. If word of this scheme gets out to the public...." Dennithe shook his head. "Filicide is a clear violation of the king's law."

Duke Braddock whipped his arm about to remove Denn's hand from his arm and roughly shoved Denn away from him. "Should've known all along that you'd still be the fucking gutless worm that you've always been. Why can't you be like Tiamond? Either of you. He's a true heir. He's a fighter. But the gods are taking him away from me and leaving me with two worthless bags of shit." He leaned forward, knuckles planted firmly on the table and propping up his torso with two locked arms. He dropped his head and for a time was silent. "No," he said softly, more to himself to the room. "No, it is far from over." He pushed from the table and moved across the room at surprising speed for a man his size. In a heartbeat, he was standing directly in front of Mouse.

"I think you're bluffing, little man. I don't think those documents exist."

Mouse allowed the corner of his mouth lift in a knowing smirk but didn't answer.

"So, here's what the official word is going to be," Braddock continued as he took Mouse's dagger from the guard. He brought the point of it near Mouse's throat, leaned in, and spoke low. "After I managed to successfully free my son from the dungeons of Har Orentega and bring him home, an assassin snuck into my chambers and brutally murdered him right here in front of me. But I was able to bring the criminal to justice and killed him myself by stabbing him in the heart with the very same weapon he used to take my son from me."

The guards tightened their grip on Mouse as Braddock adjusted the dagger to prepare for the strike.

Out of the corner of his eye, Mouse saw Garron lunge, but the third guard moved to intervene, sword drawn.

Mouse was on his own. He had to act fast.

He pressed the small trigger on the side of his boot with the heel of the other and heard the small click as the blade sprang out from the back of the heel. He kicked backward. The blade impaled deep into the lower leg of one the guardsmen. The man cried out in sudden pain and flinched back, pulling his leg up. His grip on Mouse's arm loosened just enough.

Mouse made three lightning-fast movements. He twisted his body to break the injured man's weakened hold on him, kicked forward with his other boot, striking high on the shin of the duke's leg with his heel, and he punched underneath the helm of the second guard, striking the windpipe with his knuckles. The duke howled and stumbled backward. The second guard doubled over and collapsed to the ground while he gasped for breath.

The two guards were out of the fight, but Braddock was not that easily deterred. He limped once, then sprang forward as if suffering no injury at all—and surprisingly fast for a man of his size and age. He slashed Mouse's own blade at him in a powerful downward backswing.

The attack was intended to gut him, but Mouse arched his spine back, pulling in his stomach, and the tip whizzed past his midsection by a mere hand's width.

Braddock frowned down at the dagger. "Of course. A fucking bewitched blade." He threw the dagger to the ground in disgust as if it were diseased. "A coward's weapon to tip the fight in your favor." As Mouse stepped backward away from him, Braddock kicked one of the two men on the floor in the shoulder. The guard flopped over, allowing Braddock access to the sword sheathed at his belt. Braddock pulled the short sword free with a rough tug and faced Mouse again.

Mouse didn't dare take his eyes from Braddock—the man was quick and a wily fighter, but from the corner of his vision, Mouse could see Garron driving hard against the remaining guard. He'd drawn his own sword, and the two were already in heated combat. The duke's personal guard was well trained and matched Garron's assault swing for swing.

The duke adjusted his grip on the weapon and stepped closer. Mouse noted a slight favoring of the leg. He had injured him after all. Braddock's face split with a sinister smile. He believed Mouse was unarmed and this would be a quick fight.

Mouse let him think that.

"Even if you kill us, Braddock, your reign is over. The documents will be sent to King Harus."

"That is Lord Duke to you, gutter rat." Braddock made a thrust, which Mouse avoided easily.

"You are undeserving of that honor. You are about as noble as a boll weevil."

Braddock responded with another assault—a sweeping forward swing. This was less calculated, more impulsive, and fueled by anger. Mouse sprang left, and the blade smashed a vase on a side table.

"The truth will come out," Mouse continued to prod. "And the king has no patience for filicide. Especially among you nobles."

"I'll not fall for your lies, trickster. You have no documents in your possession. Why else are you here? If you had them, you'd have already used them to expose me."

"Garron's idea. He's a sentimentalist. Thought he might actually get you to see reason. I knew better."

Braddock feigned an attack, then sidestepped to the left. He grabbed a chalice off a table, splashing its red contents in all directions, and threw it. Mouse easily dodged the projectile, but Braddock was lunging for him again.

Mouse leapt backward again to stay out range from the sword but found he was nearly against the wall. Getting cornered by the big man would likely prove fatal. His eyes darted about for a possible exit.

Believing he had Mouse trapped, Braddock sneered as he pulled his arm up over his left shoulder for a broad backswing. As he leaned in to put his weight behind the swing, Mouse ducked and rolled. The sword whistled over Mouse's head as he tucked into the roll. As his shoulder and back hit the floor, Mouse's hand was already on the hilt of the dagger hidden in his boot. He wheeled back onto his feet, twisted, and drove the dagger into Braddock's hip.

Braddock threw back his head and howled like a bear, more in anger than in pain. Pulled by the inertia of his power swing, he swung about with impossible speed for a man of his size and flung his free hand at Mouse. Mouse lunged back, removing the dagger from the duke's flesh, but he wasn't quite fast enough. The fat fingers of Braddock's left hand nicked Mouse's tunic.

Tightening his grasp on Mouse's front, Braddock tried to adjust his stance and regain his balance. But as soon as he put his weigh on the injured hip, Braddock's leg gave out. He collapsed sideways, dragging Mouse down with him. Mouse attempted to break the man's hold and push himself free, but his own boot heel skidded on the stone floor, now slick with wine. His leg flew up, and he toppled backward.

His ass hit the floor—hard—and a heartbeat later, Braddock threw his heavy torso on top of Mouse's legs. He was pinned.

Braddock sneered up at him.

Garron, seeing Mouse's predicament, cried out in sudden alarm. Panic and desperation drove him in a sudden offensive and put strength to his assault. He broke through the guard's defenses, but instead of running him through, he shouldered him aside and raced to Mouse's aid.

Braddock kicked with his powerful legs and propelled his entire body forward. The force of the impact drove the air from Mouse's lungs. One massive hand crashed down on Mouse's upper arm and shoulder, holding it to the floor and preventing Mouse from lifting the dagger for an attack. The other arm, gripping the sword, lifted back. Braddock positioned the tip to be driven into Mouse's throat.

Garron used both hands to grapple the edge of his father's armor from behind the neck and the armor's arm hole. He heaved Braddock's body backward. The duke struggled, but Garron was stronger than his father. Braddock was pulled onto his side and off Mouse. Denied his kill, he roared in fury. He rolled onto his back and thrust his sword in blind retaliation.

The sword pierced Garron in the gut.

CHAPTER 28

TIME LURCHED to a halt, and a stunned silence flooded the room. No one spoke, or moved, or even breathed as Garron, eyes widened in pain and shock, stumbled backward and fell to the floor. The guards, Denn—they stared in horror and disbelief. Even Braddock was affected. For all his bold talk, having stabbed his own son left him ashen and silent. He dropped the sword and fell back onto his elbows.

But Mouse felt his entire world beneath him shake and crumble. His heart twisted in a brutal knot while the rest of his body went numb.

"No," he mouthed. "No, no, no." It wasn't supposed to end like this. Vision blackened around the periphery. All he saw was Garron and the look of fear and disbelief on his face.

Denn appeared at Garron's side, helping his brother to the floor.

Cold dread tightened around the agony of Mouse's chest. *It can't end like this. Not again. It can't.* He wouldn't allow it.

Then something inside him clicked. It happened in an instant. Dread changed to rage.

It swept through him like a deluge, from his head on down and seemed to stain him on the inside, and he felt he might never feel right again. It wasn't the hot fury he'd felt in the past, but instead a deep coldness. A calm stillness. A lifelessness. As if he too were feeling death's icy grip and nothing else mattered. It stretched through his limbs. His mind crystallized with intent.

Nothing else mattered. There was no longer any consequence that could match the pain he now endured and would endure for all time hence.

All that mattered was that Braddock pay.

In one fluid motion, he rolled to his side and plunged the dagger into Braddock's neck just above the collarbone. The blade sank deep—all the way to the guard and hilt. Braddock cried out and made a lurch forward as if to sit up but fell backward instead. Mouse pulled the blade free as he collapsed. Blood sprayed from the wound in a pulsating jet. Braddock gasped for breath and tried to lift himself, but his body only managed to twitch piteously. He stared contemptuously at Mouse the entire time.

In moments it was over. The spasms slowed, and the time between gasps increased. In one final convulsion, the body slumped to the floor and was still. Braddock's eyes remained open but unseeing.

Mouse discarded the bloody dagger and scrambled to Garron's side. Denn was already there, kneeling and holding Garron's hand, speaking softly. Mouse all but collapsed on top of him. There was blood everywhere now. It leaked from under his doublet in alarming measure. It spread across the floor in black rivulets and soaked into the rugs.

"No... no... no...," Mouse whispered. Tears stung his eyes and cascaded down his cheeks, but he barely noticed. He was only aware of how colorless Garron's skin was and the amount of blood. Gods, there was already so much. "Garron, stay with me."

But there was no response. Garron lay motionless on the floor. His eyes were closed and his breathing shallow. Mouse could see the life slipping from him.

"I will get help," Denn announced. He passed over Garron's hand to Mouse and sprang to his feet. Mouse took the hand in his own. It felt cold against his skin. Mouse looked haphazardly over his shoulder at Denn as he dashed from the room.

Help? Garron clung to life by a spider's silk. Was there help for him now? In moments the thread would break, and the last remnants of life would fade to nothingness.

"Damn you, Garron." He tightened his grip on Garron's still hand and put his face against his cheek, kissing him gently. He knew the guards were watching, but he didn't care.

Mouse felt his heart tear apart as if ravaged by mad dogs. How could he go on without him? It didn't seem possible. For the first time since he was a child, he had allowed himself to give his heart to another. He vowed never to love—but now once again he stood as witness as his love died. He would never recover, he knew. This would leave a hole so vast in his soul that he would likely never feel anything again other than grief. A grief so deep and dark, the light would forever be lost to him.

It all sounded so wonderful, their future life together. But Mouse should have known better. Someone like him just wasn't meant to live a quiet and happy life.

"You tried to save me," he whispered into his ear. "You tried. But the gods aren't finished toying with me, I suppose."

He choked down the sob rising up in his throat. But still the tears came. He could not stop the steady flow of them. They filled his eyes and blurred his vision and spilled down over his face in heavy streams.

He sat back and used the heel of his hand to wipe his eyes and cheeks. No. He couldn't do this again. He didn't have the strength. He could not sit here and watch Garron's last moments slip away, watch as the final fragments of life left his body. His heart simply wouldn't be able to take it. The pain was too great, and the wound would never heal. It would torment him for all time.

He had to leave.

As soon as the thought entered his mind, he knew it was what he had to do. He had to leave before death took him. He simply could not be a witness to Garron's beautiful face without all the warmth and light that spilled from him in life. He wanted to remember him as he was. He leaned forward again and pressed his lips against Garron's. He held them there long, telling himself that this is what he would remember. Not the blood, not the stillness, not the paleness of his face or the cold of his hand. He would lock the memory of the kiss in his mind—the soft feel of his lips, his smell, and the look of peace on his face. That was what he would hold onto. "Thank you for trying to save me," he told him. "I love you, you know. I didn't want to, but I do. And I think as long as I have the will to breathe, I will never be able to love another."

He placed Garron's hand on his chest and stood up weakly. In a numb fog, he stumbled over to where Braddock had thrown his dagger and retrieved it from the floor. After he sheathed it at his hip, he had to take a moment to steady himself on the back of a chair.

Then he did what he did best when faced with emotions he was not equipped to handle.

He ran away.

CHAPTER 29

MOUSE FOLDED the parchment in half twice and dropped it inside of the small wooden box atop the pile of coin at the bottom. With pursed lips, he stared at the contents a moment, then closed the lid with a definitive thud and gave the box a shove. It slid across the counter's surface and stopped in front of the barkeep who stood opposite with him.

Ludro gave Mouse a long, hard stare before he lifted the box. "They're not coming, Mouse."

Mouse held his face firm, expressionless. Of course, he feared Lu was right, but wasn't ready to admit it. Not yet. "They'll come for it," he replied coolly. And when they did, he would be able to track them. He'd paid good coin for a mage to pen the note in tracer ink. He didn't want to consider that he'd thrown good money after bad.

"They are what, six days late now?" Lu said. "They are never late to pick up your coin. Ever. Somehow they figured out that you know."

Mouse allowed a frown. "How?"

"How the fuck would I know? I just sling mugs of ale here, friend. You know me. I keep my nose out of the shit that goes on around here—"

"That's a load of horseshit if I ever heard it."

Ludro pounded his index finger on the counter. "But it's as clear as piss after five ales. They know. Can't say I'm sad about it, either. If I see any of them around again it'll be too soon. Those rat fuckers gave me the duck skin."

"Well, put the fucking box down there anyway." Mouse lifted his mug and took a long draught.

Ludro shook his head but did as he was told. "All right, all right. It'll be safe here at least until you give up on this nonsense."

Mouse almost spit out the ale he was about to swallow. "Nonsense? You know how much coin they bilked me for? I want it back, Lu."

"What would you have done with it anyway? Bought land and turned yourself into a lord? Not fucking likely. Let it go, Mouse."

Serafina leaned her hip against the bar next to Mouse. "So damn glad to have your cheery mug back here again, Mouse."

"Bugger off, Sera."

Sera rolled her eyes. "Isn't that your realm of expertise? Lu, how'd we get so lucky that he would choose this place over all the taverns in this city. Pour me two reds, would ya?"

Ludro turned to the kegs, grabbing two clean mugs from the shelf. "The gods must smile on us, I suppose." Holding both mugs by the handles, he pulled the lever on the keg with his free hand and allowed the ruddy liquid to spill inside.

Serafina gave him a level look. "Find yourself a client, darling," she said. "And get your ass out of this dung heap—"

"Hey, now," protested Ludro, depositing the two mugs on the counter. "Watch what you're calling my bread and butter."

"—and out onto the street where you belong." She straightened up and picked up the mugs. "I don't know what happened to you on that last job, but you've been one sour apple since you've slunk back. Not that you were ever a summer morning, mind you, but you're starting to even dull my sunny disposition."

Serafina swished away to deliver the ale.

Ludro wiped down the spills on the counter with a rag. "Dung heap," he grumbled. "Why I keep that ungrateful wench around is beyond me." He looked up and caught Mouse's eye. "But she's right, you know. About you. Not my tavern."

Mouse responded by taking another gulp of ale.

At his hip, Mouse began to feel the newly familiar sensation he described as a type of soundless hum. He reached down and placed his hand on the sheath that housed his dagger. His fingers tingled as they brushed the leather. The dagger seemed to swell with power and anticipation—like a faithful dog recognizing its master was approaching. "Well, if it isn't the triumphant return of the Black Guard," he said.

Ludro looked up past Mouse's shoulder and a smile lit his face. "Master Naevaro," he hailed with surprise. "Welcome back, good sir!"

Mouse waited for the footfalls to draw closer before he turned around on the stool, mug still in hand.

"Hello, Pa."

Naevaro tried to look cross, but Mouse knew better. "I never should have let you keep that weapon." He was larger than his son—Mouse was told he took more after his mother in that regard. Whereas Mouse was muscular but tightly framed, Naevaro had the broad shoulders and full chest of a man who'd labored hard his whole life. But he had Mouse's angular face and full black hair, only it was gray now at the temples, and his beard was more salt than pepper.

"I think it's taken more to me now, anyway."

"Then it's a traitor, and I should take it to the king and have it destroyed. How am I to ever make a surprise visit?" The corner of Naevaro's mouth lifted a fraction.

"I hate surprises. Lu, pour my father a dark ale, if you please."

"Please, huh?" Ludro exclaimed with a raised brow. "Well, ain't that something. Master Naevaro, you are welcome here always. Your very presence improves our friend's disposition one hundred fold." Naevaro could no longer sustain his scowl. His mouth broke a grin and he chuckled.

Ludro grabbed a mug, flipped it in his hand, and positioned it under the keg spout. With a foamy crown spilling down the side, he handed the mug off to Naevaro. "On me. If this reprobate isn't going to show you proper respect, I will. We all here are mighty grateful for the service you done for the throne."

Naevaro winced.

It didn't take Mouse long to learn that his father hated talking about his days back in the Black Guard. Hated even more that people knew that he was once counted among their ranks. In his mind, the incident that brought about the death of the old king and his queen was a failure that could never be forgiven. He couldn't absorb the fact that the general populace had now elevated the survivors of the massacre to legends. They'd saved the life of King Harus V, and in doing so, saved the entire realm. Their mysterious disappearance afterward had only added to the allure.

Usually, Mouse could give a shit if his father liked the attention or not. But for some reason, he was feeling generous and decided to let him off easy.

"Lay off, Lu. He's doesn't know any noble women to introduce you to."

Naevaro seemed to relax that no more would be said on the subject. He lifted the mug to Ludro in salute before he took a sip.

"What brings you back here so soon, Pa? Thought you hated the city."

"I was in the area. Can't a man make an effort to visit his son unannounced?"

Mouse frowned. Something wasn't right.

But before he could press him on it, Ludro dried his hands on a towel and leaned his elbows on the bar. "Funny you should happen in, Master Naevaro. We were just discussing you in a fashion. Perhaps you can talk some sense into your son."

Naevaro wiped foam from his beard with the back of his gloved hand. "As you can imagine, I've never had much luck on that score. But of what matter do you speak?"

"He's intent on finding the hoods that swindled him for all that gold. I keep telling him no good will come of it. All that matters is you're safe, Master Naevaro, and there is no warrant to take your son away in irons."

"I saw to that long ago," Naevaro replied, nodding. He took another drink from the mug.

Mouse clenched his teeth. They were all getting a good snigger over this, he could tell. The renowned and infamous master thief suckered out of his own coin, played at his own game.

"As if I could somehow know you paid for the pardon yourself," Mouse grumbled. "Or that you had that much coin in the first place." The coin remained a bit of a mystery, and Naevaro refused to elaborate on it. Mouse assumed it was a pension of sorts for his time in the Black Guard.

"If you had bothered to contact your old man once in the last twenty years," his father prodded teasingly, "I could have told you myself."

They'd been over this. His father knew that Mouse did not want to put him at further risk by contacting him. Mouse wasn't about to rehash all that again in front of a gleeful audience that would take far too much pleasure in it.

But the irony of it all hadn't escaped him. He had taken the job in the first place to finally put an end to the payoffs and to protect his father once and for all. If he had known his father was in no danger, he might not have taken the job and then would never have met Garron. He wasn't sure if that was the better option or not.

Naevaro's expression softened. "Let it go, Renneus."

"Don't call me that," Mouse grumbled under his breath.

Ludro's back suddenly straightened. "Renneus?"

"Yes," Naevaro answered with a decisive nod. "The name his loving mother gave him. A good name. I won't call him after some disgusting rodent. Ridiculous!"

Ludro threw back his head and laughed heartily.

"Lu, don't even think to call me—"

"Or what? You'll take your jolly business elsewhere? Don't threaten me with a good time! Master Naevaro, all the ale you can drink is on me tonight, sir. You have made my day, and half of tomorrow as well."

With a sigh, Mouse turned back to his father, who was chuckling away and winking at Ludro. "Pa, why are you here? Is this another attempt to lure me back home with you?"

"No, son, I know that tiny village is not for you."

"Then why? This isn't just some casual visit, Pa. Out with it."

Naevaro smiled, but this time it was a different smile. Not sad, exactly, but something close. "I brought you a client."

Mouse's head jerked back. That was unexpected. "A client?" He tilted his head in suspicion. "You hate the work I do."

"True enough. But this client could change everything for you." Naevaro turned toward the tavern entrance. "Perhaps then you can retire."

The man who stood at the doorway was dressed in a heavy cloak with the hood pulled up over his head. His face was shrouded in shadow.

He stood very still until Naevaro nodded to him once; then he stepped forward into the room.

Mouse felt a chill race over his shoulders and his heart quicken. He rose from his stool. "Father? What is going on?"

Naevaro said something to Ludro, but Mouse didn't hear the words. He was transfixed by the large figure stepping toward him. The man stopped about three paces away. Mouse thought he could hear him breathing. Then he pulled back the hood.

Mouse stumbled backward, knocking over his ale and the stool. He gripped the counter to stop him from falling to the ground.

"Master Ludro," Naevaro said softly, "be so kind as to clear your tavern for a time."

Mouse didn't hear Lu's response but was distantly aware of activity around him. Everything around the edges of his vision had gone black. He was only aware of the man who stood in front of him.

"Hello, Mouse," Garron said.

Mouse's heart leapt into his throat. He tried to inhale, but the air only drew into his lungs in quick staccato breaths. "Are… are you a specter? Have you come to haunt me for my crimes?"

Garron took a step forward. "No, Mouse. I'm real. It's me."

"That… that's not possible."

Garron held out his hand. "Take my hand. Feel me. It's me."

Tears were suddenly flooding his vision. He clamped his eyes closed and leaned heavily on the bar. "No, I saw you dying. You could not have lived. The wound was fatal."

"I did live. Denn went for help. Not two rooms over, mages were with my brother. They saved me, Mouse. They were able to save me."

Mouse's head spun. It was all too much. It was too much for him to accept. He was there. He saw the wounds. This couldn't be real. He wanted so desperately to believe, but his heart and his head would not allow it. His legs felt weak. He tried to take another step back, but something moved under his foot, and he started to fall.

Garron closed the distance between them in a heartbeat, caught Mouse by the jerkin, and pulled him back onto his feet. Garron's powerful arms surrounded him and tightened. "I'm here, Mouse. It's all right."

"Garron," Mouse said, choking on a sob. He pushed his face into Garron's chest. The feel of his arms around him, the smell of him, the warmth of his voice—it was all as he remembered it. This was Garron. This really was Garron. "Oh gods! What have I done?" Mouse looked up. "Garron, I'm so sorry. I'm so sorry." The words spilled from him in a torrent of heartache. "I should never have left you to die alone. Oh gods, I'm so sorry."

"You didn't know," he said softly in Mouse's ear. "You didn't know."

And he held Mouse against him, arms engulfing him. Mouse tightened his own arms around him and sobbed against his chest—something he had not done in a very long time. But the months of grief and guilt he'd locked away broke free all at once in an unstoppable surge. He was lost in it, swept away. He had no idea for how long.

At last, he pulled away. "You came for me," he said, wiping his eyes against Garron's cloak. It wasn't a question but more of a revelation. "You came back for me."

Garron's face scrunched. "Of course I did, you idiot." He rolled his eyes. "Took me a while to find you. Denn couldn't remember either the town or the tavern where he first hired you. He never did pay attention to such details. It's probably best he's not the duke. But in our time together, you had given me enough information about your father I was able to locate him. And as I hoped, he knew where to find you."

Mouse looked up at him. "Wait. You're the duke now!" he exclaimed with sudden realization.

"I am," he replied with a sheepish grin. "I haven't been officially recognized as of yet." A look of pain filled his eyes. "My brother still clings to life but is expected to pass soon. So, until then I am considered his regent. But for all intents and purposes, I am now Duke Garron. I will officially be granted the scepter of Har Dionante after my brother's funeral and I am deemed fully recovered."

"And all that has happened, Garron? Has that not changed everything?"

Garron shrugged. "With the help of my brother, neatly explained away. Our family was set upon by an assassin who remains at large. Your involvement and presence during the incident have been erased from any official records. You will not be held responsible for anything that transpired."

Mouse smiled weakly, not certain how to respond. He felt conflicted—torn—for it was he that killed Garron's father. Would Garron forever blame him for his death?

"Garron, what about Delgan?"

Garron's eyes narrowed. "Fuck him. What does he have to do with anything?"

"Other than he was involved in the whole plot to make you disappear?" Mouse ticked off the points on his fingers. "He lost out on a deal that would grant him the land his family coveted for generations. And lost his chamberlain too, who was the mastermind behind the power grab."

"Delgan doesn't worry me, Mouse."

"You aren't at all concerned he'll retaliate?"

"Not likely. Right now, I'm told his hands are rather full in his own duchy. Seems his tight-fisted control has unraveled of late. Deals inexplicably falling through. Political alliances severed. Merchant barges even refusing to moor at the docks. All this has led to open rioting in the streets, I hear." Garron attempted an innocent lift of his shoulder, but there was a devious glint in his eye. "All very strange. It's as if some surreptitious forces are at work there in Har Orentega."

Mouse's smile broadened. So, Taurin had taken his advice after all and put the Shadow Elite to work dismantling Delgan's power structure. Mouse straightened his spine and pushed back his shoulders. "Well, then, I suppose congratulations are in order, *Duke* Garron," he replied formally. "How should I address you henceforth?"

Garron placed his arms on Mouse's shoulders and ran them down the lengths of his arms. "Well, I'm glad you asked." He held a mysterious grin that Mouse couldn't quite qualify. "You see, as duke I am given license by the king to make laws as I see fit. So, I've made a few alterations to some of our official doctrine that has been in place for some time and was sorely in need of revision."

"Have you now?" Mouse replied cautiously.

"I have indeed. As one of my first acts, I decreed that the stipulations and limitations on marriage have been lifted. The citizens of Har Dionante are now free to marry whomever they wish." His eye had a sudden twinkle as he gazed down at Mouse. "And… to model that sentiment for the entire duchy, I wish to marry you."

Mouse could only stare back at Garron with his jaw hanging slack.

"Nothing to say?" Garron prodded.

Mouse felt like the room was spinning. "Garron, there's going to be pushback. People aren't go—"

"I'm the duke, remember? I make the rules." He smirked and rolled his eyes. "Mouse, Har Dionante has a long tradition of tolerance for those like us. I have only just made the convention official duchy policy."

"The people will see it as self-serving."

"They may. But I am prepared to face any backlash that may follow."

Mouse wasn't convinced. "What of the king—?"

"I have already spoken to him about it personally. Made a trip to the capital specially to address it with him face-to-face. He was rather taken aback, I'll admit, but he stands by his policy of letting the duchies stipulate their own laws. He will not interfere, Mouse. In fact, he plans to publicly offer us his blessing. Oh, and furthermore," he added, his grin widening, "I have taken the liberty to clear this with your father, as well. He has graciously granted me your hand." Garron took one of Mouse's hands in his own and slid his other behind Mouse's waist. "So, the decision is yours. What say you? Will you be Lord Mouse and rule by my side?"

Mouse's knees felt weak, threatening to drop him again. He thought a moment—more to compose himself than to really consider the answer—and scratched his jaw to stall for time. Then he said. "I will."

Everything else he planned on saying was lost and forgotten, for Garron's lips were pressed against his after that for a very long time.

MASON THOMAS began his writing journey at the age of thirteen when his personal hero, Isaac Asimov, took the time to respond to a letter he wrote him. He's been writing stories ever since. Today he is ecstatic and grateful that there is a place at the speculative table for stories with strong gay protagonists.

Mason, by all accounts, is still a nerdy teenager, although his hairline and waistline indicate otherwise. When his fingers are not pounding furiously at a keyboard, they can usually be found holding a video game controller, plucking away at an electric guitar, or shaking a twenty-sided die during a role-playing game. Mason will take any opportunity to play dress-up, whether through cosplay, Halloween, or a visit to a Renaissance Faire. He pays the bills by daring middle school students to actually like school and encouraging them to make a mess in his science classroom. He lives in Chicago with his endlessly patient husband, who has tolerated his geeky nonsense for eighteen years, and two unruly cats who graciously allow Mason and his husband to share the same space with them.

Facebook: www.facebook.com/MasonThomas999
Twitter: @MasonThomas999
E-mail: masonthomas999@gmail.com

Betrothed
A FAERY TALE
THERESE WOODSON

Also from Dreamspinner Press

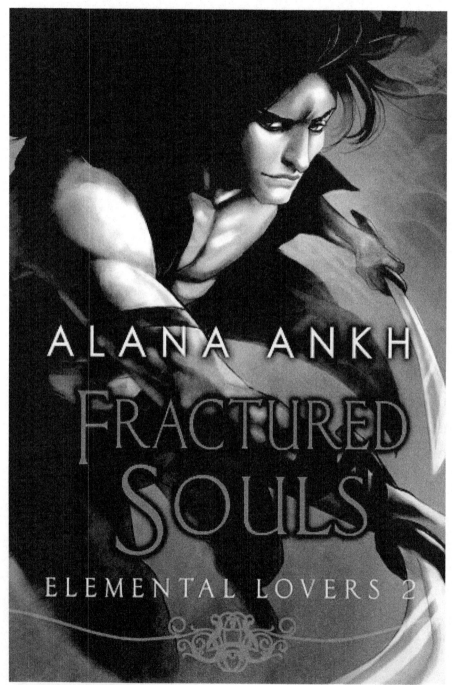

ALANA ANKH

FRACTURED
SOULS

ELEMENTAL LOVERS 2

www.dreamspinnerpress.com

Also from Dreamspinner Press

IMMORTAL

AMY LANE

Also from Dreamspinner Press

Cassie Sweet

Kiss of
Death

ALCHEMISTS AND ELEMENTALS BOOK THREE

www.dreamspinnerpress.com

Also from Dreamspinner Press

TJ Klune

THE
Lightning—Struck
HEART

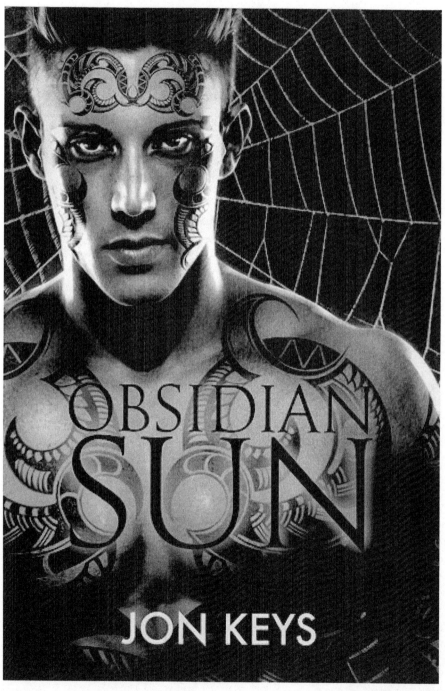

Also from Dreamspinner Press

JENNI MICHAELS

SONS
OF THE
COUNTRYSIDE

www.dreamspinnerpress.com

CPSIA information can be obtained
at www.ICGtesting.com
Printed in the USA
BVOW10s0751190217
476265BV00008B/214/P

9 781627 989947